at first sight

There are people in this world who are
Nobodies. No one sees them.
No one notices them.
They live their lives under the radar,
forgotten as soon as you turn away.

That's why they make perfect assassins.

The Institute finds these people when they're
young and takes them away for training.
But an untrained Nobody is a threat to their
organization. And threats must be eliminated.

Claire has been invisible her whole life,
missed by the Institute's monitoring.
But now they've ID'ed Claire and sent
seventeen-year-old Nix to remove her.

Yet the moment he lays eyes on her,
he can't make the hit . . .

D1100998

Also by Jennifer Lynn Barnes

Raised by Wolves
Trial by Fire
Taken by Storm

Every Other Day

The Naturals
The Naturals: Killer Instinct

at first sight

jennifer lynn barnes

Quercus

First published in 2013 by Egmont USA,
443 Park Avenue South, Suite 806
New York, NY 10016

This edition published in Great Britain in 2015 by

Quercus Editions Ltd
55 Baker Street
7th Floor, South Block
London
W1U 8EW

Copyright © Jennifer Lynn Barnes 2013

The moral right of Jennifer Lynn Barnes to be
identified as the author of this work has been
asserted in accordance with the Copyright,
Designs and Patents Act, 1988.

All rights reserved. No part of this publication
may be reproduced or transmitted in any form
or by any means, electronic or mechanical,
including photocopy, recording, or any
information storage and retrieval system,
without permission in writing from the publisher.

A CIP catalogue reference for this book is available
from the British Library

Paperback ISBN 978 1 78087 245 2
Ebook ISBN 978 1 78087 246 9

This book is a work of fiction. Names, characters,
businesses, organizations, places and events are
either the product of the author's imagination
or are used fictitiously. Any resemblance to
actual persons, living or dead, events or
locales is entirely coincidental.

10 9 8 7 6 5 4 3 2 1

Printed and bound in Great Britain by Clays Ltd, St Ives plc.

I'm nobody! Who are you?
Are you nobody too?

Emily Dickinson

Prologue
One week earlier . . .

Nine letters. Two words. He refused to think of them as a name. With detached objectivity, his steady hands set the thin white paper, with its evenly spaced black lettering, to the side.

He'd done this before.

One, Two, Three . . .

He'd do this again. More needles, more knives. More evenly spaced black letters that carved themselves, blood-red, into the recesses of his mind.

The only way you can make a difference in this world is to kill.

From the moment he'd opened the envelope and seen the name, the pictures; from the moment he'd committed those nine letters to memory, the outcome had been a foregone conclusion. His target had been marked. Death was coming.

So be it.

1

Have a great summer! Stay sweet! Have a great summer and stay sweet!

Claire Ryan had been reading permutations of those words in the pages of her yearbooks for almost as long as she could remember, but for some reason—either optimism or stupidity, she wasn't sure which—she'd thought that high school would be different. That *she* would be different. That by the end of freshman year, someone would have bothered to learn her name, invited her over after school, or at the very least asked to copy her geometry homework. But even the most egregious cheaters had remained as oblivious to Claire's existence as ever, and by the first day of her fifteenth summer, all she had to show for the year was a perfect attendance record and a yearbook filled with sugary, meaningless clichés.

Her classmates didn't like her. They didn't dislike her. They just didn't care.

It's not them. It's you.

Claire pushed the thought aside and sat down cross-legged on the floor. Sliding the offending yearbook very nearly out of reach, she tried to focus on something else. Her hands found their way to her cell phone, and before Claire knew it, her index finger was dialing a familiar number, just to hear the sound of the outgoing message.

She could almost pretend that "please leave a message, and I will get back to you as soon as possible" was Motherese for "I miss you, and your dad and I will be home soon."

Then came the beep.

"Hey, Mom. I wanted to let you know that the last day of school was—it was great. And things here are great. I'm . . ." Claire cursed herself, but couldn't stop the word from rolling off her tongue, ". . . great."

With the amount of time she spent reading and watching television, she really should have been a better liar, or at least a more creative one.

"Anyway, I hope you guys are having a good time. Don't worry about me. I'll be—"

Not again, Claire told herself sternly. *If you say* great *one more time, I swear to God, I'm never speaking to you again.*

4

"I'll be *fine*." Claire was spared the trouble of having to disown herself, but barely. She waited one beat, maybe two, and then she ended the Message That Kept Going and Going by clarifying one last point that might have somehow escaped her mother's notice. "Ummm . . . this is Claire. Love you. Bye."

The moment she hung up, her phone joined the yearbook on the floor, and she closed her eyes.

Have a great summer! Stay sweet! Please leave a message after the beep.

"Story of my life," Claire whispered, and the fact that the words came out quiet instead of hard was her first clue that the time for wallowing might be nigh. There couldn't be something wrong with everyone else in the world. Common sense said that there had to be something wrong with her. If she could just say the right things, do the right things, be a little more interesting . . .

It's never going to happen.

Claire Ryan was a ghost, a nothing, a nobody. *Invisible* would have been an upgrade. Oxygen was invisible, but it got breathed all the same. Sound waves were heard. Even clandestine farts had the distinction of being smelled.

Oh, God. I'm jealous of farts. Claire uncrossed her legs and fell backward, allowing her head to thunk viciously against her bedroom's wood floor. *I envy the noxious, gaseous excretions of the human backside. And my head hurts.*

It was a new low, even for Claire.

I should lie here. I should lie here forever and never, ever get up.

Claire pressed her lips together and kept a tight rein on that thought. After a long moment, she forced herself to open her eyes, sat up, and reached first for the phone and then for the yearbook. Two minutes of wallowing, once a year. That was all she got, the closest she could allow herself to the edge of the abyss without letting it devour her whole.

I'm better than this.

Claire's throat tightened, but she refused to let herself cry. Instead, she climbed to her feet and walked, one foot placed lightly in front of the other, to the bookshelf underneath her window. She'd made this trip many times before, to place other yearbooks on the bottom shelf and to pull old friends off more honored places near the middle and top.

A Tree Grows in Brooklyn. Ender's Game. The Secret Garden. I Capture the Castle.

Claire closed her eyes and ran her hand along the spines of the books on the outermost row of the top shelf. Like a blind man reading Braille, she let her fingertips explore the cracks and lines on the books' edges until she felt the zigging zag she was looking for, the near-velvet texture of a tome read so often that the paper on the cover had been worn to soft, threadbare nubs.

Anne.

Claire pulled the book gingerly from the shelf. She opened her eyes and took a ragged breath.

Anne of the overactive imagination. Anne, who took it as a personal insult when people spelled her name without the E.

Knowing she was too old for the book, but not really caring, Claire settled back down on the floor and opened it to the middle, confident that wherever she started, she'd know exactly where the story picked up.

An orphan girl, desperate for a family. A family who'd hoped for a boy. Dares and dramatics and the indignity of having red hair.

Claire actually felt her body let go of the harshness of reality. Her mouth curved upward. Her throat relaxed. And as she lost herself in *Anne of Green Gables,* she thought for maybe the thousandth time how lovely it would be to be the kind of girl who could smash a slate over the top of a boy's head in a fit of temper, how nice it would be to have someone misspell her name.

Clair or *Clare,* it wouldn't matter—so long as they said or wrote or thought it at all.

<hr />

Nix slipped in and out of the crowd, weaving his way down the street with imperceptible but deadly grace. His was the light touch of a warm breeze, the flow of a silent, colorless, odorless liquid. Water over the edge of a dam. A black adder ready to strike.

No one saw him. No one noticed. And if they had, moments later, his dark hair and light eyes, his scars and tattoos would have been forgotten. The small, arrow-shaped needle in his left hand would have disappeared from their minds, like a footprint from dry sand. The closeness of his body to his target's, the sleight of hand that allowed him to slip the poison straight into the senator's vein would never have registered to any passerby as more significant than an empty cup blowing haphazardly down the street.

"Eleven." Nix whispered the word into the air, knowing that the outside world would never hear or recognize the number for what it was.

Nix's sharp cheekbones and jet-black hair should have been striking. Nix should have been memorable. But he wasn't. He was nothing. He was Nobody.

And he never got caught.

<hr />

"Senator Evan Sykes was rushed to the hospital last night after suffering a major heart attack in his hometown of Des Moines. Doctors attempted a double bypass, but the junior senator from Iowa did not survive the procedure."

Claire's insides lurched as the newscaster's baritone segued from talking about Evan Sykes's untimely demise to his surviving family and potential successors, and then, just like that, the morning news was ending on a local interest story about a water park for dogs. Claire reached for the remote and turned off the television.

Death of a senator. Water park for dogs.

Watching the news was supposed to be Claire's way of staying grounded in reality, but she could feel the rest of the world slipping farther and farther away. If a senator ranked on par with dogs on slip 'n' slides, Claire didn't even want to think where she stood. For a moment, she was tempted to call her parents again. Sooner or later, they'd pick up—the laws of probability were on her side— but Claire could sense the need to wallow circling the walls of her mind, and she wasn't about to give it entry.

No.

She was going to have a great summer. She was going to be sweet. And sooner or later, she'd be sweet enough, independent enough, *something* enough that either someone else would notice, or she'd stop caring what other people thought (or, more accurately, didn't think) at all.

Determined, Claire put on a bathing suit. She pulled a pair of board shorts on over the bottoms. And, head held high, she and a copy of *The Hollow Kingdom* made their way to the community pool, ready to take on the world.

2

Nix's quarters at the institute were eggshell white and completely bare. The Society's scientist du jour believed that the less a Nobody was exposed to the outside world, the more potent his powers became. Deprive him of all contact with the energy that ran unseen through everyone and everything, and his ability to pass through the world unnoticed increased.

It was the latest in a string of theories that Nix detested.

He was nothing.

Nobody.

Putting something on his walls wasn't going to change that. It wasn't going to change him. Who he was. What he could do. Nobodies went through life unable to leave their marks on another person. Maximally unimportant. Metaphysically deficient.

That wasn't the kind of thing that scientists could understand.

At seventeen, Nix wasn't the kind of person who had any particular desire to be understood. Most days, he didn't feel like a person at all.

You're less than air. Less than shadow.

He put his back to the wall and stopped breathing. He'd learned this lesson so often that it was branded into his mind, the voice in his head a mixture of his trainers' lectures in stereo.

No matter what you do, no matter where you go, people will always look through you. They will affect you, but you will never affect them.

Nix's chest began to burn, and with silent, ritualized savagery, he slashed at himself, uneven fingernails carving jagged red lines into his stomach and arms. Beads of sweat rose on his bare skin.

If you let yourself, you could love but no one will ever love you. Even if they wanted to, they couldn't. That thing, that intangible thing that other people have that lets them form connections, that lets them matter—

You don't have it.

You are never going to have it.

Nix began to bleed. Darkness rimmed his line of vision. It wasn't enough.

It was never enough.

You're no one. You're nothing, and that is very, very special.

Sated and soothed by his outburst, Nix slid to the floor, sinking smoothly and effortlessly into lotus position. He sat his bloody, upturned hands on his knees and closed his eyes.

I am everything. I am nothing. I am powerful. I am forgotten.

His words, not The Society's. His handlers couldn't do what he did. They had never tasted his kind of power. The Society of Sensors had been studying metaphysics for thousands of years; its members had taught him what he was, what he would always be—but his trainers had never been *nothing* themselves.

I am shadow. I am air.

Forbidden thoughts. He breathed them in and out, and for the first time since returning from his mission, he spoke, his voice low and rough, but musical in the way of a gravel-voiced siren singing the blues. "I am Nobody." His lips curved upward, his breathing even. "I am Nix."

He was unchanging.

He was constant.

And whatever his next assignment held—back alleys, visiting dignitaries, monsters dressed as men—he was ready.

For number Twelve.

"Excuse me, could I get a towel, please?"

Claire signed in at the front desk, dotting the *i* in her name in a manner almost grand enough to pass for a circle. She could do this. Hot day, cool pool, good book. What more could a girl ask for?

"Could you please hand me a towel?" She spoke a little louder this time, determined to catch the attention of the boy working behind the sign-in desk. The boy in question ran his hands through his hair (blond and gelled and respectably thick) and stared straight past Claire with the kind of complete nonchalance only possible between the ages of fourteen and twenty.

"Ummm . . . excuse me?" Claire felt like she was shouting, but the boy didn't so much as blink. Brandishing *The Hollow Kingdom* like it was a flare, Claire stood on her tiptoes. Suddenly, the boy snapped out of it. Moved to grab a towel. Smiled. And handed it—

To the girl standing *behind* Claire.

I don't really need a towel. I can air-dry. That's what the sun's for, right?

Giving up, Claire turned to go into the pool area, but the towel thief turned at the exact same moment, and the two of them collided full force.

"Oh, I'm so sorry," Claire said, her apology reflex kicking into overdrive.

13

The girl she was apologizing to tossed red hair over one shoulder and tilted her head to the side. For a moment, she stood ramrod straight and so still that Claire thought she was broken. Then the girl brought one hand up and slowly ran it over the side of her own face. Claire watched, feeling like she was intruding on some kind of sacred ritual; the girl lifted her other hand up, palm first, and let it hover just over Claire's face, then her arms.

Maybe I really did break her, Claire thought.

"Are you okay? I'm so sorry. . . ."

The red-haired girl didn't register Claire's words. Her hands fluttered back down to her sides and in a completely impassive voice, she whispered a single, haunting word.

"Nothing."

Claire took a step back. The girl reached for her cell phone. And then she turned around and walked back toward the parking lot, the coveted towel still slung over her arm.

"Okay," Claire said, under her breath. "Now that was weird."

Determined to shake it off, Claire scanned the deck and found an open lounge chair angled between the baby pool and the diving board. It was, without question, the loudest, wettest, least desirable chair on the deck, but in her contrary moments, Claire liked liking things that went unappreciated by others.

Settling back into the chair, Claire offered her face up to the sun and closed her eyes. She breathed in and out, letting the din of the pool fade into the background, pushing the red-haired girl and her accusation—*Nothing*—out of her mind. The hum of Claire's brain waves settled into the requisite pattern for an old standby, perfect for sunbathing and guaranteed to keep overthinking at bay.

Situations, Claire thought, waiting for one to take hold, enjoying the feel of the sun on her face, her body, the length of her limbs.

Situation: What would it be like if you got hit by a car, and you desperately didn't want to go to the hospital, but the person who saw it happen—a total stranger—was dead set on seeing you checked out by a doctor? What if it were a mother, with several small children, who couldn't help but mother you, too, and pursed her lips when you said you didn't want to go? What if it were an undercover FBI agent, and you had somehow stumbled into an integral part of their case?

What if it were a boy, and he wouldn't let you stand up off the ground, because moving might upset your internal injuries? What if he kept his face close to yours and his hands on your shoulders? What if you wanted to fight him, even though you knew he was right?

For reasons she couldn't quite put her finger on, Claire quite liked that Situation. Flipping over onto her stomach, she felt the sun on the small of her back and gave into the lure of the image taking hold in her mind.

Car accident. Blood—not much, because then it would be stupid to refuse to go to the hospital, but a little on the back of her head, and a bruise on her side. The car that hit her peels off, not bothering to see if she's okay, and then the boy is there, beside her. He comes in a blur and bends over her, until he is all she can see.

His hair is dark.

"Are you okay?" he asks her.

No, that wasn't right. That was such a normal thing to ask. It would be a much more interesting Situation if her rescuer were a little abnormal. And if she didn't want to be rescued.

"What the hell were you doing?" he demands, his voice little more than a growl.

"I'm . . . who are you?" She tries to sit up. "Ouch."

"Lie still." He seems to expect that his words will be obeyed. Her eyes flash.

"Don't touch me. I'm fine. And if I want to get up, I'll—"

"You got hit by a car. You wandered into the street and got hit by a car. An ambulance is on its way."

"I don't want an ambulance."

He leans down closer toward her, his eyes narrowing, and for a second, she thinks he will kiss her. "Well, princess, that's too damn bad."

Princess? Princess?! Claire rears back, ready to tell

him what she thinks of his machismo BS, but he grips her
shoulders, holding her in place more by the power of his
touch than by force.

"Get your hands off me!"

"Be still." For a moment, the boy's voice is awful, but
then he softens. "You could be hurt. Humor me."

And then the ambulance came. End of Situation. Claire
opened her eyes and rolled back over, just in time for a
tsunami of water to body slam her like a professional
wrestler.

Curse you, cannonballs.

Claire sputtered and snorted and tried desperately not
to drown in her own chair. She blinked violently, and that
was the exact moment she heard the voice.

"You look like you're thinking deep thoughts, young
lady."

It took her a few seconds to locate the speaker: an
elderly man with a face creased like a worn leather sofa
and brown eyes so dark that she couldn't make out the
pupils. For a moment, Claire assumed that the man was
talking to someone else, in part because people, as a
general rule, didn't come up to Claire and start making
conversation, and in part because she was positive that
she looked more like a drowned rat than someone caught
in the throes of thought.

Say something. Respond. Be witty.

As Claire tried desperately to come up with the proper

response, the man leaned forward, the intensity of the gaze behind his centimeter-thick glasses swelling, his eyes fixated on a point directly over her left shoulder. Those pupil-less irises flicked left to right, then up and down with a concerted effort that reminded Claire of a squadron of soldiers searching a field in a grid.

"I was just sitting here," Claire said finally, but the words came out in a whisper.

"Have a way of going unnoticed, do you?" the man asked, his voice not unkind.

Claire nodded, but before she'd even finished the motion, the man glanced away, and something deep inside of Claire told her that he wasn't going to speak to her again. He'd seen what he needed to see, and now he was going to leave.

As Claire watched him disappear into the parking lot, she couldn't help but wonder what he'd been looking for, and she couldn't shake the single word her memory whispered over and over again in the red-haired girl's voice.

Nothing.

————◆✕◆————

White walls. White floor. White bed. Nothing to look at. Nothing to do.

Tired of the pretense that the door, locked from the outside, could keep him caged, Nix made the decision to fade. With expert precision and unnatural ease, he let go of his grip on the physical world.

He let go of his thoughts, his emotions, his body, his name.

He let go of the hard-earned whispers of pain from his newest cuts.

Less than shadow. Less than air. Nix let go of everything that mattered to him and became nothing—the kind of nothing that didn't have a right to anything in this world, because it was incapable of giving back.

The world was made of energy. Most people didn't even realize it was there—inside them, outside of them, everywhere. Except in Nix.

The world could touch him, but he had nothing to give in return.

At his worst, he wasn't even good enough for gravity.

Less than shadow. Less than air.

Nix faded. He was there, but the world couldn't see him. Couldn't feel him. Couldn't smell him.

Couldn't hold him down.

For all intents and purposes, he was invisible. Immaterial. Unimportant.

And as only someone completely nonexistent could, he walked straight through the thick wooden door and came out the other side. Keeping his thoughts still, Nix flowed through the halls and safeguards of one of the country's most secure buildings. This was his domain, the only home he'd ever known. From the outside, the institute looked like nothing so much as a sprawling country manor, but inside, it was state-of-the-art, immaculate, secure: a perfect match for The Society itself—ancient, secretive, a thing of legend, but on the cusp of modern science all the same.

Nix slipped into the shadows. He waited and watched. The Society was a machine with many moving parts, many members. Even those who came within a hair's breadth of him remained blissfully ignorant of his presence. They were Normal, and he was nothing.

Invisible.

Faded, Nix could see the way the light played off one man's eyes, a woman's fingertips, the odd nose.

Sensors.

To the average person, they would have looked just like anyone else, but faded, Nix got a visual reminder that Sensors were different, that of all of the Normals in the world, they were the only ones who stood a chance of recognizing him for what he was. Most people had no idea that there was an energy to life, an underlying, immaterial *something* that made them who and what they were. But Sensors were different: sensitive to the presence or absence of energy. They could smell it, taste it, feel it—the particular sense varied from person to person, but one constant remained. Sensors knew energy, recognized aberrations. And still, they walked by Nix, unaware of how easily he could have reached out and punched his immaterial hand through their bodies. They couldn't see him. Couldn't feel his presence in the pads of their fingertips or the buds of their tongues. Unless he was solid and they were looking for him—and why would they? Why would anyone?—his lack, his deficiency, his *presence* went unnoticed.

It was just as well that Nix was faded. Sensors and Nobodies didn't mix well.

"The old man is certain?"

From the conference room behind him, Ione's voice broke into Nix's thoughts, and he read in her tone and words that she'd found his next mark: another name to be slipped under his door, another life for his hands to snuff out.

Nine months. Six months. Two.

The time in between his assignments was shrinking.

Not weeks now, not months. Days.

"Cyrus confirmed the diagnosis that his sixteen-year-old apprentice made this morning. He's quite satisfied with this demonstration of Mariah's progress as a Sensor, but obviously upset with his own performance. To find this girl there, in his zone, lazing about a swimming pool, right under his nose—Cyrus was embarrassed to have missed something like this up until now."

"Well, these things do happen."

Nix processed Ione's words. *The Sensors must have found another Null.*

Nix's grip on absolute nothingness began to waver. He still blended. He was still unimportant. He was still deadly. But in mere moments, he'd lose his fade and be solid again. Real.

They always brought out this reaction in him. Not Ione, who'd been the director of the institute for as long as Nix could remember, or the Sensors, who'd been the backbone of The Society for thousands of years, but their topic of conversation. Nulls. Psychopaths. The ultimate somebodies. The terms were as meaningless as the scientists' theories as to how and why it happened that some people were born with an enhanced ability to leave their marks on others—and immune from being marked in return.

Nix didn't need to know *why*. He hated Nulls, hated that as little as he could affect anyone else, he could affect them less.

Soulless, broken monsters.

Master manipulators, devoid of human compassion.

Animals that had to be put down.

That was what Nulls were. That was why Nobodies existed—to hunt them. To protect the rest of the world. The Normals.

With his last moments at full power, Nix slipped into the conference room. Rematerializing fully, he walked forward. If he'd been a normal person, Ione and Richard, one of the oldest Sensors, would have felt his stare as a physical thing.

They didn't.

Instead, Nix was able to sidle up to them undetected. Standing eerily close, he leaned forward and whispered a single word into the backs of their necks. "Mine?" he asked, something like and unlike anticipation in his voice.

If he'd been anything or anyone else, his sudden appearance would have made them jump, but Nobodies couldn't inspire fear. Or hate.

Or any emotion, really, other than a vague discomfort.

"Oh, it's you." Ione turned to look at the area just over Nix's shoulder. She probably thought she was looking at him, but she was wrong. "You're not to leave your quarters on your own."

Nix shrugged. He knew every inch of this building, knew it better than they did. What were they going to do? To punish something, you had to see it. You had to care about it. You had to catch it.

The Society had other uses for him.

"My target?" Nix asked, nodding toward the folder and taking it as a foregone conclusion that he'd be the one assigned to the case. Normals like Ione—the kind who could give *and* take energy, affect other people and be affected by them, love and be loved—didn't stand a chance against this kind of psychopath, and a Sensor wouldn't fare any better.

To take down a Null, you needed a Nobody. And Nix was one of a kind.

Without another word, Ione passed him the file. With that single motion, the thing she'd ordered was as good as done.

The Null—whoever she was—was as good as dead.

I wonder what Ione and Richard see when they look at me, Nix thought. Not the tattoos, one line for each of his kills. Not the scars, the ones he'd given himself. Not danger. Not Nix.

He could have pulled a knife on them, and still, their adrenaline levels would have stayed exactly the same.

Nix dropped his eyes from their faces, and his fingers tightened around the file. So what if he was as good as invisible, even to the only people in the world who had genuine motivations to see him? That was exactly what made Nix so incredibly proficient at his job.

Nobodies were born assassins.

3

Claire's resolve to have fun and be sweet was wavering. It had been two days since her encounter with the old man at the pool, and she'd dutifully returned each day, sunbathing and reading and thinking her way through every variation of at least five different Situations. No one had spoken to her. No one had stared intently at a point just over her left shoulder. Her tan was progressing nicely.

And yet...

Claire was already counting down the days until school started, even though the logical half of her brain knew that three days into the school year, she'd probably start counting down the days until summer. It was, quite frankly, depressing—no, not *depressing*, she'd already had

25

her two minutes of wallowing this summer, so it couldn't be *depressing*—but it was certainly less than ideal.

With a light sigh, Claire slipped off her nightgown and began to put on her bathing suit. For lack of a better plan, she was going to stick with routine and she was going to be happy about it if it killed her. She slid into her bikini top, adjusting the straps on her shoulders. In a show of daring, she'd chosen white today instead of blue, but the clasp on her white suit was bent out of shape, and her fingers felt as thick as sausages as she reached back and clumsily tried to coerce the two straps together.

I will not be undone by a bikini.

The second the thought formed in her mind, it was replaced by an overwhelming sensation of pinpricks on the back of her neck. She froze, her fingers holding tight to the clasps of her suit, and the chills intensified, each individual pinprick sprouting legs and crawling like a spider down her spine.

Someone is looking at me.

Claire didn't move. She didn't turn around. She didn't finish clasping her suit. She just stood there, motionless, holding the top in place, very aware of the fact that she was alone in the house. That she was always alone in the house. That no one would notice if something bad happened to her.

That no one would know if she disappeared.

Claire felt goose bumps rising on her arms, like there was something inside her body fighting to get out. Slowly, she turned, her long brown hair brushing her shoulder as she did.

It feels like feathers on my shoulder. It feels like someone is about to grab me, but there's no one here.

She stopped breathing.

It feels like there's someone outside.

Claire forced herself to breathe. She crossed the room, raised her hand to the curtain beside her bookshelf. She closed her eyes.

I can do this.

She stood there, the curtain pulled, the morning light shining down onto her face for several seconds as she worked up the strength to open her eyes.

You are the dumbest person who has ever existed, she told herself. *Have I not taken you to eight million horror movies in the last five years? Stand there, with your bathing suit top unclasped in the back and your eyes closed, because you think someone is spying on you. Fabulous idea. Really. As your encore, are you going to run into a dark alley?*

And yet, she couldn't open her eyes. The chills turned to something hot and sharp on her skin, each one shattering like glass and crackling along the surface of her body. She could feel her hands shaking. She could feel someone staring at her, a phantom gaze carving its mark into her flesh. She could almost imagine a face on the other side of the window, but she couldn't open her eyes.

She just couldn't.

<hr />

His mark was, without question, the dumbest creature on the face of the earth. Like a deer caught in headlights, she stood there, frozen to the ground, the perfect target. He could see her heart beating beneath her caramel-colored skin, her entire torso jumping with each erratic pulse, as if it wanted him to know exactly where to put the bullet.

Nix wasn't normally one for leaving entry or exit wounds. He was a silent killer—poisons, asphyxiation, air bubbles straight to the heart. But for whatever reason, The Society had classified this girl Code Omega, a designation given to the most dangerous, most disgusting, most putrid Nulls.

Omega meant do not engage.

Omega meant kill from a distance.

More often than not, *Omega* meant making it bloody.

This in mind, Nix studied his prey dispassionately, wondering what twist of fate had brought her to the window. Did she sense the danger? Had she killed enough on her own to recognize the taste of death in the air? Did she know that after today, she'd never kill again?

The gun in Nix's hands was heavy and cold. His finger

slipped easily over the trigger—too easily, and he checked the silencer. It was an unnecessary precaution, but one he took nonetheless. He'd been watching her—this girl in the window—for too long. He'd allowed himself to become distracted by the shadow of her body.

I've never killed someone my age before. Not a girl.

It didn't matter. If this Null was Code Omega, she was a plague, and he was the only cure. Nulls were manipulative. They played with the emotions and hopes and dreams of others, without ever feeling any empathy or real emotions of their own. They were empty shells that mocked what it meant to be human. They were incapable of thinking of anyone or anything else, and sooner or later, they always killed.

Less than shadow. Less than air.

Nix held tight to the cover of his own invisibility. He couldn't think about this girl as a girl, and he couldn't think about her as a monster. He couldn't afford to think about anything, couldn't allow himself the luxury of personhood if he didn't want to get caught.

He needed to stay in the fade.

The world might never know how dangerous this girl was, but once the deed was done, they'd know that she was murdered. They'd wonder who would do such a horrible thing. They would never know why it had to be done.

They would never thank him.

You are nothing. You are nobody. You will never matter

to anyone, and the only way you can make a difference in this world is to kill.

A woman pranced past him, walking three dogs on two leashes. The third dog ran unleashed, and it was the one that paused, for an instant, in front of him. And then it shook its head, sneezed, and ran on. Nix lifted his arm. He aimed his gun just under the edge of his mark's white bathing suit, which lay lightly on her skin, held on by a hand behind her back.

He saw the suit as it would be—coated in blood.

Nix moved to squeeze, picturing the bullet entering her chest, the heart underneath her sun-kissed skin stilling.

The trigger pressed back against his finger.

Do it.

And then she opened her eyes. And instead of staring past him or around him or through him, Nix's target stared directly at him. She saw him. And she screamed.

<hr>

Claire felt, rather than heard, herself screaming. Now that her eyes were open, she couldn't close them. She couldn't look away—not from the gun pointed directly at her heart and not from the boy holding it.

His eyes were blue, so light that she wondered if they glowed in the dark. His hair was jet-black and long, and all up and down one arm, there were tattoos—black lines that slashed across his arm, each crossing the one before it in an uneven X.

There was a thin white line across his neck, and even from a distance, she could see a crescent scar on the left side of his jaw.

His cheekbones were sharp, his mouth soft.

He was the most beautiful boy she'd ever seen, and he was going to kill her.

I'm still screaming, Claire realized. *I'm not moving. I'm just screaming.*

None of this made sense—not the way she'd known he was there, not the gun he had trained on her chest, not the fact that he hadn't pulled the trigger, and not the disconcerting truth that she still hadn't jumped out of the way.

How can someone want me dead if no one knows I'm alive?

As far as questions went, it was a good one, though perhaps not the very most relevant at that exact moment.

I'm still screaming. I'm screaming, and there's no one to hear me. No Mom. No Dad. No Mrs. Milligan and her three little Yorkies. This boy is going to kill me, and she just walked right by.

Claire could almost understand her neighbor's not hearing her screams. She was inside, Mrs. Milligan was not. And she didn't expect the woman to turn back and look at the house, or to see her distress, or to even realize that a girl named Claire lived at number 116. But how could Mrs. Milligan not see her killer?

31

He was standing there, in broad daylight, with a gun. Danger rolled off his body in waves. Each muscle, each mark, each scar screamed for attention.

Claire couldn't take her eyes off him.

Her fascination couldn't have lasted longer than a second, or two at most, but to Claire, it felt like an eternity. A single unit of *forever* spent screaming and staring, staring and screaming.

And then, his finger bearing down on the trigger, the boy lifted his eyes from her chest to her chin. From her chin to her mouth. From her mouth to her nose, and then, finally, to her eyes.

If she'd felt his stare on her skin before, she felt it inside now. There was no metaphor to describe it, no natural disaster big enough to do justice to the unbearable pressure and tumultuous power crashing into and through and around her insides. This wasn't an earthquake. This wasn't a tsunami.

This was no hurricane.

It was *everything*—every single thing that had ever existed, every feeling she'd ever felt, every Situation, every wallow, every dream.

His gaze bathed her in warmth until she thought she would be sick from exposure, and—convinced it was the last thing she would ever do—she looked back at him. His eyes on hers. Hers on his.

The world exploded. And for a moment, a single

moment, as that deafening, all-encompassing roar filled her ears, Claire Ryan thought she'd been shot.

Situation: What if the only boy who'd ever really looked at you was dead set on seeing you . . . dead?

No blood. There's no blood. He shot me . . . I heard it. I heard something, and God knows I felt it.

With a start, Claire realized that there was no wound, no small, round hole through which everything she'd once been could leak out and onto the floor. Not believing what her body was telling her, Claire worked to pull her eyes away from his, and the moment she did, the spell was broken.

She fell to the floor and rolled as far away from the window as she could get. Her breath caught in her throat, and her hands—skeptical of what her brain was telling them—began to search her chest frantically for a wound that did not exist, from a bullet that had never been fired.

I felt it. I heard it. I . . .

"I have to call the police." Claire was not—contrary to what the past forty five seconds might have led someone to believe—entirely without common sense. She had to get out of the room. Away from the windows. She had to call the police.

Even if she didn't want to.

Even if they never caught him. Even if her would-be killer was already gone and never planned to come back. Even if the dumbest, most instinctual part of her wanted nothing more than to climb back to the window and look out.

To see if he was still there.

To look at him.

And to feel him, looking at her.

I'm sick in the head. I'm sick, I need help, and I am calling the police.

As she followed through with her promise, crawling toward the phone and dialing 911, Claire felt the last of the pinpricks, the fireworks, the *everything* leaving her body. For the first time since she'd walked to the window, she felt the safety of anonymity, the calm of being utterly and entirely alone. Of being Claire.

He's gone.

It made no sense, but she was certain. She knew what she'd felt when the boy was there, and she knew that it was utterly, entirely, unarguably gone.

She missed it.

Oh, God, Claire thought, as she stuttered out her name and address and emergency to the operator. *Someone just tried to kill me, and I'm sad that he left. He wants me dead, and I want to see him again.*

Need to see him again.

Okay, that's it. I'm officially crazy.

It was, without question, a new low—even for Claire.

It was an aberration. It was an error. It won't happen again.

That was what Nix told himself, over and over again, as he bided his time in the days after his failed attempt on the Null's life. He couldn't risk going back to the girl's house to finish the job—not immediately. Not with the police crawling all over the place that first day.

Not with the girl's parents at her beck and call, flanking her every move for the three days since. Why the Null had decided to use her unnatural charisma to lure her mother and father home, Nix wasn't entirely sure.

Maybe the threat of her own death was worth suffering the presence of the people who loved her.

Maybe she was planning on using them as human shields: living, breathing bulletproof vests that meant no more to her than the furniture.

Or maybe it just made her feel powerful to know that she could pull them back to her whenever she wanted, like puppets on a string, even though deep down, most parents knew that there was something wrong with their Null. Even as children, Nulls' hugs were empty. They were unmoved when Mommy accidentally sliced open her finger. Instead of reaching for the Band-Aids, they leaned forward to get a better look.

No compassion.

No empathy.

Defective. The ying to his twisted yang, a Nobody's polar opposite in every way. *I should have killed her.*

He was going to kill her. Only . . .

She'd seen him. She'd *noticed* him. And even after she'd started screaming, she hadn't pulled the attention of the woman with the dogs. She could have, if she'd wanted to. Nulls commanded attention—and adoration—as much as Nobodies repelled it. But this Null hadn't fought back.

She'd just stood there, staring at him. Not over his shoulder. Not through him. Directly at him.

And, God, it felt like someone had poured Icy Hot over his entire body. Like being hooked up to an electric chair.

It. Wasn't. Real.

Nix had always known that Nulls were dangerous. That

36

they could make you feel and do things that you didn't want to do. But until this particular Null had caught him, none of his marks had ever had the chance to use their powers on him.

None of them had ever seen him coming.

As potent as Nix's ability to fade was with Normals, it was ten times more powerful with Nulls. Nobodies walked through the world unnoticed, and Nulls saw only what they wanted to see. Nix couldn't affect anyone else, and this girl—this *Null*—couldn't be affected by the plights of others. He should have been able to walk up to her with a whirring chainsaw without meriting more than a second of her attention.

He should have killed her.

She should be dead. Nix found the thought unsettling. He'd never failed to carry out an assignment before, and he told himself that was why she kept him up at night. Why he hadn't faded completely since their eyes had met for the first time. Why he'd opened her file and read her name over and over again, even though she wouldn't have one for long.

Claire.

Claire Ryan.

The girl he was going to kill. *Number Twelve.* Today.

Nix picked up the gun and then set it back down. He was an excellent shot. He could hit targets. He could shoot marks. He could put bullets into hearts and keep them from pumping, and into skulls, just between the eyes.

But killing that way wasn't what he'd been trained for.

It wasn't what she deserved.

No, *Claire* deserved something a little more personal. She'd used her powers to make him feel like something, to make him feel worthy and noticeable, and then she'd taken it all away the moment he had realized that she was pretending. That if her life hadn't been at stake, she wouldn't have feigned noticing him at all. She'd used her unnatural aptitude for manipulation on him.

So he was going to use his abilities—all of them—on her.

She wouldn't see him coming. She wouldn't know what hit her, but when his needle pierced her arm, when she felt that tiny little prick and then *nothing*—then she'd know who and what he was.

She'd know that Nobody had killed her, and he'd leave her body on the sidewalk, for the police to puzzle over—*natural causes,* they'd say—and her parents to sob over with equal measures anguish and relief.

"Today, Claire," Nix said softly. He talked to himself so seldom that the sound of his voice had him looking over his shoulder to make sure that no one else had heard.

Not that anyone would pay it much attention if they had.

For the past three days, he'd stayed close, biding his time. He'd watched her. He'd waited. But now he couldn't wait anymore. The day before, he'd seen people near Claire's house. He wasn't close enough to get an ID on any of them, but he could tell from the way they moved, from the unmarked van they drove, that The Society had sent a cleanup team. Nix's superiors only had one Nobody, but they had many soldiers.

Sight. Smell. Taste. Sound. Feel.

When Sensors were too old or too young for active duty, they worked on their own, scouting for The Society in zones, looking for aberrations in the world's pattern. But when they were in their prime, Sensors worked in groups of five, one for each of the senses. Together, they were perceptive to the point of being prescient. They identified Nulls. They safeguarded The Society and its institute. They unraveled the mysteries of the universe, one data point at a time.

The Sensors were the ones who'd trained him.

The world has an energy to it. Everyone and everything—people, objects, animals, plants ... even rocks and dirt and molecules of air—they're all made up of energy. And when they interact with each other, they leave their marks on the world, and it is through that exchange of energy that all happenings happen. That love blossoms. That connections are made.

Do you know why we call you Nix, child?

He hadn't. Not at the age of three. But by four, he'd learned.

It's because you're nothing. You have no energy. You leave no trail. As far as the world is concerned, you don't exist. And you never will.

The Society had raised him.

The Society had trained him.

The Society had given him a purpose—or as much of one as a Nobody could have. When they told him to kill, he killed, and in the days, weeks, months in between, he molded himself into a better killer: quicker, faster, more untouchable. He let Society scientists poke and prod him so that his deficiencies might be fully understood, so that those working for the greater good might squeeze every last drop of data out of his flesh, his bones, the abilities he had that real people didn't.

And even though it did Nix no good, even though his emotions had and could have no effect on Ione or the Sensors or the many scientists who'd used him as a lab rat, he hated them for it.

Empty hatred, because he didn't count.

Claire is mine.

The thought was savage, feral in a way that usually had him tearing at his own flesh, desperate to feel something that mattered. Something he could count on. Something that wouldn't cease to exist, just because no one cared that it was there.

Claire was his.

These Sensors were out of their league. They thought

that because they knew about energy, because they could sense it, that made them less vulnerable to the kind of monsters The Society was created to combat. They thought that knowing *what* this girl was gave them the advantage.

But they were wrong.

If Claire had seen a Nobody coming, she'd catch the Sensors before any of them could lay so much as a finger on her. They could try to pick her off from a nearby roof, but unlike Nix, Sensors could be tracked, noticed, *seen*. If they killed her, they'd be caught. The Society was as ancient as the Knights Templar and twice as secretive. They didn't take the risk of exposure lightly.

Less than shadow. Less than air. That's what you have to be to kill my Claire.

Nix smiled at the rhyme in his mind. The Sensors couldn't kill this Null.

She was *his*.

So he'd take care of her.

———◆◆◆◆———

Claire watched the yolk slide out of the egg, broken and dripping. Trying not to burn herself, she bent over the skillet and began to pluck the bits of shell out of the sizzling mess on the stove.

This is why I don't normally cook.

That and the fact that normally she didn't have anyone to cook for. In the three days since the police had called her parents home, Claire had made breakfast every morning.

Eventually, they'd eat it. Sit down at the table across from her, say her name, and eat her eggs. Eventually, Claire and her mother and her father would have a real family breakfast, like countless TV families before them.

But not today.

Absentmindedly, Claire's mother brushed past her. Reached into the cabinet directly over Claire's head. Pulled out a box of cereal.

"I . . . ummm . . . I made eggs?" Claire didn't mean for the words to come out as a question, but they did.

"Hmmm?" Her mother's response wasn't a word so much as a sound, but it was something.

"I made eggs. For you. And Dad."

And me, Claire added silently, but she didn't get that far out loud.

"Oh." Her mother didn't put down the cereal box. "That's nice of you, but really, cereal is fine. And you should be out, doing things."

Out.

As in elsewhere. Bothering someone else. Claire's hand slipped and she burned its edge but didn't bother running it under cold water. Instead, she just sucked a breath in around clenched teeth and turned off the stove.

The eggs were only half cooked, but she wasn't really hungry anymore.

"Maybe I don't want to go out."

Claire's mother wrinkled her forehead in the manner of someone mulling over a crossword or trying to remember her exact relation to a second cousin twice removed.

"Claire?"

Claire perked up—slightly. Mouths were opening, words were being exchanged, and if she could think of the right thing to say, the absolute right thing, then maybe—

"Remember what the police officers said?"

The question stopped Claire's *maybe* dead in its tracks. Losing her developing smile, she poured the remainder of the egg mess down the drain and hit the garbage disposal, drowning out all other sounds.

Remember what the police officers said?

Claire remembered exactly what the police officers had said.

There was no one there. There was a witness on your street during this so-called attack, and she saw and heard nothing.

Are you sure you screamed?

Are you sure you're not just making this up?

And then later, to her parents, *Does your daughter have an overactive imagination?*

And that was all it had taken for her parents and the police to collectively decide that Claire spent too much time reading and not enough time around kids her own

43

age. They'd patted her on the head and spoken to each other and generally ignored everything she'd told them until it became perfectly clear that of all the people involved in this case, she mattered the least.

Her parents weren't pleased that they'd cut their vacation short, but they weren't angry with her. They didn't scold. They just held her hand and said "uh-huh" when she talked and then looked at their watches, as if time passed more slowly when Claire was involved.

They ate cereal for breakfast, while Claire's eggs died a slow, painful death in the drain.

Moving mechanically, Claire flipped the garbage disposal off before responding to her mother's question. "I remember what the police officers said, Mom. And I'm telling you—I didn't make it up."

"Of course not. No one is saying you did. Your father and I just think that you need to get back on the horse."

Her mother was a fan of empty metaphors.

"You know, get back out there, do the things you love."

Claire was tempted to point out that her mother had no idea what those things were, that if her parents had bothered to check in or—perish the thought—spend some actual time at home with their daughter, they might have seen the beautiful boy with the shining silver gun.

And, okay, maybe it did sound ridiculous, but they were her parents. They should have known her well enough to know that she wouldn't imagine something like this.

But they didn't know her. At all. And as much as she wanted to, Claire couldn't find it in herself to hate them for it, or to point out their shortcomings, because it wasn't as if they *tried* to ignore her. On the rare occasion her parents were home, they both actually tried quite hard to relate to her.

She just wasn't very relatable. Her eggs were subpar. And Maria and Jackson Ryan weren't the type who'd ever planned to have children. After fifteen years of Claire's presence, they were still simply very nice people who had a great deal of trouble actively remembering that once upon a time, her mother had given birth.

"You have to get back out there, Claire."

Claire heard something in her mother's voice that went beyond the words. "You're leaving again, aren't you?" she asked.

"No. Of course not. We've probably been gone too much."

Rationally, her mother knew this.

Emotionally, though, Claire had deep and abiding suspicions that her parents couldn't quite put their finger on why it was they were supposed to stay.

And no matter how this conversation ended, no matter what she said, Claire knew that she wouldn't be able to give them a reason.

"I guess I'll go swimming."

If her mother noticed the low and broken tone in

Claire's voice, she certainly didn't give any verbal indication of it. "I think that's a very good idea."

This is probably the closest I'll ever come to making her happy, Claire thought. *And nearly getting myself killed by what she's sure is my imaginary boyfriend actually made her frown.*

Sometimes, trying to make people see her felt like attempting to dent solid steel by kicking it with her bare foot. At the end of the day, the steel was steel, and her toes were broken or bruised. Flushed down the drain, like unwanted eggs.

"I'll go put on my bathing suit."

And just like that, Claire was back to routine. The house may as well have been empty. She may as well have been alone. And if she got picked off on the way to the pool, if she wasn't crazy, and the police and her parents and everyone who counted were wrong about everything . . .

What did it really matter?

Situation: What would happen if an assassin came to kill you—and you *let* him?

Claire picked up her bathing suit—the white one that she'd left on the floor for the past three days, a constant reminder of what had happened—and walked to the bathroom with it crushed in one hand.

I guess my routine has *changed,* she thought. Before, she'd always gotten dressed in her room.

Tears sprang to Claire's eyes, and she fought them.

Given her current situation—her parents, the police, the boy who wanted to kill her—it was ridiculous to break down just because she was changing clothes in the bathroom.

She squeezed her eyelids tightly together, but it didn't help. Tears trickled out the sides, and she bit down on the inside of her lips, trying to keep the rest of the downpour in.

Someone tried to kill me, and I'm going swimming. I'm going swimming, because it doesn't matter. I'm going swimming, because I don't matter. I'm going swimming, because that's what Claires do. We swim and we daydream and we read and we wait for someone to care, and they never, ever, ever do.

Her teeth lost their grip on her lips, and once freed, her lips trembled. Bathing suit still in hand, Claire slammed her fist onto the bathroom counter. And then she slammed it down again. And again.

She tried so hard not to get upset. She tried so hard to find the fun, to be happy, to be sweet. To not ask for things. To not make a nuisance of herself. She tried so hard to build her own little world and love it and not mind so much that the rest of the world left hers alone.

Does your daughter have an overactive imagination?

Claire glared at the mirror, the policeman's question echoing in her mind. "Yes. Yes, she does. She has to. Don't you understand that? She has—*I* have to!"

This was why Claire didn't wallow for more than two

minutes a year. It was so much lonelier this way. So much harder to believe that it would ever change.

Somewhere out there, there's a boy. He looked at me. He saw me. And sooner or later, he's going to kill me.

Mechanically, Claire began undressing, her body still shaking with the whirlwind of emotions she spent her life holding back.

She put on her swimsuit.

She reached down and did the clasp.

And then, tears still streaming down her face, she put on her oversized sunglasses, layered a worn yellow sundress over her swimsuit, and walked down the hallway and out the front door without telling either of her parents good-bye.

She's coming out her front door. She's closing it behind her. She's walking down the sidewalk. She's turning away from the unmarked van.

Nix catalogued Claire's movements in simple, mechanical terms, but even from nearly a block away, he couldn't take his eyes off her. The way she moved, her weight on the tips of her toes, like she was continually trying to make herself just a little bit taller. The slight slouch in her shoulders that rendered that effort useless. The rhythm of her steps, the color of her skin.

Even knowing that an entire team of Sensors was in the vicinity, Nix couldn't bring himself to look at anything else. He told himself that it was vigilance, that he was a fox and she was a rabbit, and like any good hunter, he was tracking her every move.

But the truth was, she was breathtaking.

He could almost understand why the universe had chosen her to be the type of person who could command love with a snap of her fingers.

She's walking toward me. Her footsteps are erratic, like she can't decide whether to walk or run. I wonder if she knows I'm here. I wonder if she knows I'm watching.

I wonder if she knows she's dead.

He decided not to wait for her to come to him. Slipping out of the bushes, Nix faded and walked toward her. She was wearing sunglasses, hiding her soulless eyes from the world, but he could still see them.

He could see everything, all of her, and he drank it in like a drug.

His heart began beating faster—

Less than shadow, less than air. That's what you have to be to kill my Claire.

He flicked his wrist, and the needle appeared in his hand. His was a specially made poison—untraceable, invisible, unreal.

Just. Like. Him.

She was within ten steps of him now. He picked up his

pace, his arm ready, his fingers shaking with anticipation.

And then she did it again. She whipped her head up like she'd been electrocuted, and she looked directly at him. Her mouth dropped open in a little O, her body trembled, and then she did the most amazing thing.

She picked up *her* pace.

And then they were running at each other, closing the distance between their bodies in a heartbeat. But his arm, the one holding the needle, wouldn't move, so he did the only thing he could think of to do.

Instead of slipping poison into her veins when she came within range, he ducked his head and just kept on running—straight toward her. Faded, he should have been able to pass through her body as easily as the door to his room, but he knew that he wouldn't.

Couldn't.

You have no energy. You can't affect anyone. Faded, you can't even touch them.

In a fit of impossibility, their bodies collided. Nix's target went flying through the air and onto the grass, her sunglasses falling from her face. In an instant, he was on top of her.

So much for his plan to take her by surprise.

Down the street, the unmarked van started its engine, and Nix knew that he had to move fast. The Sensors probably couldn't see him through the fade, but chances were good that they had a lock on her. And if they were moving, that meant that they were coming to take her away.

"You're mine," Nix said fiercely. "I'm the one who kills you."

His skin hummed every place that their bodies touched, like a tuning fork, adjusting to the perfect pitch.

Null.

She was doing this to him on purpose. To make him weak. Because she could.

"Who are you? Why are you doing this?"

Her questions seemed so human, but he couldn't let himself forget, even for a second, that she was a monster.

A monster who said she wanted to know who he was.

"Nobody," Nix whispered. "I'm Nobody."

For the first time in his life, that felt like a lie. He only had one thing going for him, and she was taking it away.

"You're nobody," the girl beneath him repeated. "Yeah, right." And then she started laughing hysterically.

This wasn't how it was supposed to go. He was supposed to kill her. He was going to kill her, and she was laughing at him.

Nix raised his hand, his fury propelling the motion, and that was the exact moment that he noticed the redness of her face, the tear tracks on her cheeks. It should have made her ugly, and anything that took away from her lethal beauty should have made her easier to kill.

But it didn't. Didn't make her ugly. Didn't allow his needle arm to inch even slightly closer to her veins.

She'd been crying.

Before he'd caught her, before she'd known that she was as good as dead, she'd cried long and hard enough to leave marks.

But Nulls don't have feelings. Not like that. They only cry for show.

His hands were drawn away from hers to his own arms and his own scars, and she scrambled away from him and to her feet.

She's not going to trick me again, he thought, but he couldn't make himself give chase—not until he saw her stumble backward into the street.

Not until he saw the unmarked van accelerate.

"No!"

Claire jumped at the sound of his voice, back onto the sidewalk, and the van swerved to hit her. They must have been aiming for a clean hit, but they miscalculated, and instead, the van clipped her in the side and sent her flying.

Nix was by her side in an instant. Her eyes rolled back in her head, and he knelt next to her. The Sensors had lost control of the car after it hit her, but it wouldn't take them long to recover, and then they would be here. They would finish what they had started.

No.

He couldn't let them kill her. That was his job. They'd almost taken it from him, and it was his.

She was his.

And if he wanted to kill her, if he wanted to be the one who saw through the charade she presented to the world, tears and all—

—*looked so real, they looked so real. She's hurting. She's beautiful, and she's hurting*—

He had to get her out of here. He had to get her away from the Sensors. Because if he wanted to kill her—and he *did*, truly—he'd have to save her first.

Less than shadow, less than air. Worthless. Empty. Void.

Nix covered her body with his. He lifted her up and projected his own nothingness outward, a strange warmth filling his body as his fade covered her. And then, with the Null in his arms, he walked straight past the Sensors and disappeared.

5

Claire was about ninety percent sure that she was asleep. An abandoned road stretched out on all sides of her. She was walking, but the dirt and gravel didn't crunch under her bare feet. It felt like she was floating, walking just above the ground instead of on it.

She hurt.

Wasn't I wearing shoes before?

Before. Before. Before.

The word seemed to echo all around her, its song interweaving with the eerie silence in a way that made Claire shiver.

There's something I'm supposed to remember. From before.

But she couldn't make her brain leave the abandoned road. She couldn't remember how she'd gotten there. And she couldn't get rid of that disconcerting ten percent chance that this wasn't a dream.

I hurt. Things aren't supposed to hurt in dreams.

She looked down at her side, expecting to see bruises or blood, but all she saw was blackness. Empty space where her torso and legs should have been. This, Claire knew objectively, should have been upsetting. But it wasn't.

Before. Before. Before. I'm supposed to remember what happened before.

She could remember kindergarten. She could remember the lunch box she'd picked out at Walmart, the way she'd gotten lost in the store and looked and looked and looked for her mother, who'd been so overwhelmed with back-to-school shopping that she'd checked out and packed up the car and driven home without realizing that she was missing something.

Someone.

Claire could remember fifth grade. She could remember the class play, and how everyone was supposed to have a part, and how she'd hoped and hoped and hoped that she'd get to be the country girl who changed places with her cousin in the big city, and how, when the cast list had been posted, she wasn't on it at all. Not as either of the cousins, or any of their friends, or part of the chorus, or even as a tree.

I wouldn't mind being a tree, Claire thought, her mind muddled. *Am I a tree?*

With her lack of body, it certainly seemed possible. Before she could ponder the likelihood any further, she heard something: a rustling of leaves, a parting of mist behind her. She whirled around. Even once she stopped, the world kept spinning—but through fog and mist and her own dizziness, Claire saw him.

The boy.

His face was expressionless. His eyes, which tilted up on the ends, met hers.

"You look at me," Claire said, trying to remember what it was that had brought this boy to her, what she knew about him, what he knew about her.

The boy said nothing, and a memory rose to the surface of Claire's mind—a van. It had hit her. It had sent her flying. And then there had been a blur, and a boy.

"What the hell were you doing?" he had said. And he'd called her an ambulance, and they'd fought. His face next to hers. His voice a low growl, his hands on her shoulders.

That's not what happened.

It was, and it wasn't. Why couldn't she remember? What was she missing?

She looked for the answers in the boy's face. His eyes were blue—light, light blue—and shaped like almonds. His skin was pale, light in color, but rich in tone—like his heritage had sprinkled it with gold that had been stripped only partially away by a complete lack of sunlight. His jaw was strong, his cheekbones razor sharp, and there were markings on his arm that made him look like a warrior from another time. And yet . . .

He looks so sad, Claire thought. His features were mature, but his expression—hidden behind a mask that blocked it from the rest of the world—was a boy's.

"I want to help you," Claire said. "Can you help me?"

It was a simple statement, a simple question, but the words were lost under the heavy silence of the fog. Somewhere behind them, a car revved its engine.

Van. It's gonna hit me. It's gonna hurt me. Again.

This time, Claire felt panic. Her emotions surged, breaking through the seal that had been placed on them.

"We have to get out of here," she yelled at the boy. Determined to save him, she reached out, and he lifted one of his hands out to her. She smiled, imagining the tips of his fingers brushing her palm.

And that was when Claire saw a glint of silver, and she realized that the hand she was reaching for was holding a gun.

The boy had it aimed directly at her chest.

Again.

Nix had never brought another person into his fade before. Never realized it was possible to spread his *nothingness* over someone else like it was a blanket. He'd never wanted to share his sanctuary with another living person.

Not a person. She's a Null.

The thought challenged Nix's grip on the fade, and after a moment's resistance, he stopped fighting and let himself solidify. The distance he'd put between himself— *and Claire*—and the Sensors was sizable, but it wasn't enough, might never be enough. Nix knew, better than anyone, how long The Society's reach was, how merciless Ione and her Sensors were when it came to eradicating a threat.

That was when he saw the bus.

Nix walked toward it. The Null was dead weight in his arms, but so small. Her chest leapt with each beat of her heart, and Nix tried not to feel it, see it. He closed his eyes and pulled her closer, cradling her body against his.

I'm only saving her so I can kill her, he reminded himself. But that didn't stop him from walking unnoticed onto the bus. It didn't stop him from taking a seat, and it didn't stop him from holding her shivering form, letting the heat from his body warm hers.

Weak, he berated himself. *Stupid. Worthless.*

She was marked for death. He was the executioner. He should have taken the Null's blackened heart in his hand and crushed it.

But even miles into the wilderness, he didn't dare place his cargo into an empty seat. She was a Null, and by definition, Nulls were noticeable. If Nix didn't want The Society to follow wherever he ran, he'd have to keep her close and hope that his nothingness would negate the beacon of her presence.

No choice.

He had to carry her. Hold her. Marvel at the curve of her cheekbones. Count the ways for her to die.

One, for poison.

She was so still. Soft.

Two, for knives.

Her wheat-colored hair, plastered with sweat to her forehead, called to the edges of his fingers. He wanted to touch it. To kill the Sensors for the steady trickle of blood at her temple.

She was beautiful, this Null.

Manipulative. No conscience. No soul. He forced himself to remember what she was, what it meant to be born a Null. His fourth kill, a psychopath who had a thing for carving up little boys, had looked as innocent as Claire did now. Nix couldn't afford to let himself forget that the bundle in his hands—no matter how sweet, no matter how small—had been on The Society's kill list for a reason.

Sensors located Nulls. The Society eliminated them. That was the purpose for which it had been founded, the mandate it had followed for thousands of years.

This girl was a monster. She had to die.

Is she warm? She feels warm. . . .

Claire shivered in Nix's arms, a high-pitched, keening sound caught in the back of her throat, halfway between a dog's whine and the wail of an ambulance. Her brow furrowed, and she jerked, trying to pull herself away from his grip. Away from whatever pain her body was fighting.

Nix tightened his hold on her frame, and without realizing it, he began rocking back and forth. His arm curved around her neck and he supported her head. Like she was a child. Like she was human. Like he'd have the right to care for her if she was.

Don't be hurt, Claire. Don't die.

The rocking motion seemed to calm her, and the awful sound emanating from her dreams subsided. Her cheeks flushed. She folded herself into him, and he felt her fever through his clothes.

I'm the one who kills you.

Nix glanced out the bus window: the trees were getting thicker, the grass wild. He couldn't say for sure how long they'd been on this bus, how much time he'd spent absorbed in the tiny details of his charge's body. If he wanted to hide her from the Sensors, they should get off the bus, trek deep into the forest to a place as forgotten as any Nobody.

Nix prepared himself to fade, closing his mind to their surroundings: to the mother and son to his left, who couldn't stop rolling their eyes at each other; to a sea of strangers sitting side by side, each ignoring the other without a thought.

Normals, Nix thought, the word bittersweet in his mind. Normals could love. They could be loved. They couldn't fathom what it would be like to be missing either half of the equation. And yet they walked through life with their heads down, not even bothering to look at each other, not knowing how precious each interaction, each glance, each dialogue was.

At least the unconscious girl in his arms had an excuse for her heartlessness. She *couldn't* feel, *couldn't* be touched by the plights of others. She was defective, fractured, incomplete—just like him.

Less than shadow, less than air—

Nix felt the change coming on, felt himself losing material form, and he pulled Claire close with every thought in his brain, every breath in his lungs, willing her to cross with him.

Nothing.

Immaterial, Nix and his quarry fell through the seat that had been holding them, through the back of the bus, and onto the pavement. Slipping out of his fade the moment they hit the ground, Nix landed in a crouch, protecting Claire's body with his own.

Mine.

She cried out. The sound ripped through Nix's flesh. It

wasn't fair that she could do this to him. It wasn't right, what he was doing—helping her. Saving her when he knew that for the greater good, she had to die.

And she will, Nix promised himself, as he began to walk into the woods, his inner navigational system set toward absolute isolation. *Just not today.*

If he walked far enough, looked hard enough, he'd eventually find a cabin that had been abandoned for the off-season. He'd tend to her wounds.

Inflict his own.

You can't die, he told the Null silently. *Not yet.*

If she did, her death would never be his.

As he walked, feeling her chest rise and fall with each hard-won breath, he thought of the long, thin scar that ringed his own neck and the fact that if he failed to kill Claire, technically speaking, it wouldn't be the first time he'd fallen short.

She'd be the second to escape him. And he'd hate her for it.

Almost as much as he hated himself.

———————◆◆✕◆◆———————

The blue-eyed boy had been aiming a gun at her for hours. For hours and hours and days and days, and every time the fog cleared enough for her to see the rest of the road, Claire tried to remember that she should run.

But she didn't.

He shot her, and he shot her, and he shot her, but she couldn't run. She had no body. No chest, no legs. Only a black, gaping hole where her body should have been.

His blue eyes never left her. They never glazed over. They never wandered far from her face.

Even when she averted her eyes, even when the pain and the fear and the certainty that she was going to die overwhelmed her—he didn't disappear. He shot her, and he shot her, and he shot her, but he was there. And for the first time in a long time, it didn't hurt.

Nothing hurt.

Claire could feel her body relaxing, could feel her mind losing its grip on this dreamlike place. As she began to drift into the kind of peaceful, inky darkness untouched by dreams, Claire saw the boy lean toward her, his face so close to hers that their lips very nearly touched.

"Maybe I won't die," Claire whispered. Her breath bounced off his lips and came back to touch hers.

She felt his response before she heard it. The words caressed her skin. "I'm the one who kills you."

Darkness washed over Claire. And just like that, she was gone.

6

Claire is smiling.

Nix leaned forward, his eyes locked on to his captive's face. Pink lips parted. Wrinkles—*three, two, one*—fell from her brow. It had been hours since he'd found this abandoned cabin and laid her gently on the couch. And still, he couldn't get enough of watching her, drinking in the tiny details of her *Claireness*. He memorized her features and catalogued her expression, running exploratory fingers over the edges of his own lips.

She was having good dreams, his Null. In the time he'd been watching her, that hadn't always been the case.

He'd already memorized the look, feel, and sound of her nightmares.

"For a girl whose days are numbered, you sleep a lot." Nix's voice was rough from lack of use, but he wanted to say something. To talk to her. "You have light brown hair. I think your eyes are green. Your veins are blue." He paused. "My hair is black. I'm not sure about my eyes. When I bleed, I bleed red."

Claire sighed, and he closed his eyes, savoring the sound, the look of her face, the haphazard spread of her hair. Her fingernails were uneven. Her wrists were small. She had six freckles on one shoulder and four on the other.

She smiled in her sleep.

Strapped to an exam table. Eyes closed. The memory came on suddenly, without mercy. *Nix is cold, but he doesn't want to wake up. He wants to stay in the dream, wants to—*

The table lurches. He's plunged downward into the tank. His eyes fly open. Water fills his nose, his mouth. If he was cold before, he's freezing now, but it doesn't matter—he can't breathe—can't move. He fights against the straps that hold him immobile, but it's no use. His lungs are tight. He's choking.

Drowning.

He can see familiar forms leaning over the dunk tank, their faces blurred, their expressions impassive. Ione. Ryland. They're not going to help him. They're going to watch him die, unless—

Less than shadow. Less than air. *He forces himself to stop fighting. Stop thinking. Stop existing—and he fades.*

Nix came out of the flashback to see Claire's lips still curved up in a gentle smile. Like she hadn't a care in the world. Like it wasn't *her* fault he'd been raised the way he had. So he could protect the rest of the world from Nulls.

Still gasping for breath, Nix slammed a door on the memory and concentrated on the present. "I shouldn't have brought you here," he told the sleeping girl in front of him. "I should have let you die."

But he hadn't. He'd propped her up and forced her to drink water. He'd taped her ribs. He'd covered her with blankets and put them back when she kicked them off.

"If you think I'm weak, you're wrong. If you think I care, you're wrong." Nobodies weren't allowed to care. They weren't allowed to ask questions. All they were allowed to do was kill.

Kill. Claire.

Beautiful, sleeping, breathing, dreaming Claire.

She's shifting onto her other side. Her hair is falling into her eyes. Her legs are stretching out. The muscles in her throat are moving.

As he documented Claire's movements, Nix felt his own throat clench. This was the most she'd moved since they'd been here, and there were sounds in her mouth, trying to get out. Not cries. Not whimpers.

Words.

"Where am I?"

It figured that one of the first words out of her mouth was *I*. Nulls existed at the centers of their own universes, puppeteers to hundreds of others. No one else mattered to them.

"I wish you'd stayed asleep," Nix said, each word as sharp as broken glass. While she'd slept, he'd crooned to her. Soothed her. Said things he shouldn't have even thought. But now she'd ruined it. Ruined everything.

"Asleep? How long have I been asleep?" Claire scrambled to a sitting position.

Claire is scared. I am scaring Claire.

Nix's target looked frantically down at her own body. Like she'd never seen it before. Like she didn't know how perfect it was.

Liar.

"What's wrong with me?" she asked, her voice hoarse.

"You're defective. You're a monster. You got hit by a van."

Her face went through a flurry of changes, so quickly that he could not keep up with them all: she sucked a breath in, and her entire face—*eyes, cheekbones, lips*—threatened to cave in on itself. Crumble.

This Null didn't like being told she was defective.

Eventually, her lips stopped trembling and settled into a thin and desperate line, and Nix wondered how many facial expressions a single person could have. He had never wanted to touch another person's face more.

She's doing this to you. She's making *you think about her. She's* making *you want—*

"Do. Not. Move." Nix's voice strained against his vocal cords, like an animal caged. "Don't try anything. Don't think you can use your abilities to escape. I'm immune."

If only that were true.

"My abilities? What abilities?" Her lips and eyes rearranged themselves once more, this time into an expression of pure bafflement—a testament to her abilities as an actress, the ultimate master of the art of deception. "I don't have abilities. I'm not good at anything."

Simple words, but they seemed hard-won. Like it hurt her to lower herself and pretend that she was nothing special.

"I'm not who you think I am," she said. "I'm really not." Only a Null could use that voice. Make herself sound as if part of her wished that she was the one he was looking for.

His.

Strapped to an exam table. Eyes closed. Nix forced the memory to the surface of his mind, like a man jamming his fingers down his throat to hurl.

"You can drop the act," he said, loathing and longing battling for supremacy in his tone. "No one will ever find you here, and there's no one within range for you to use."

"Use? What are you talking about? Use how?"

Don't, he told her silently. *Don't pretend you don't know.*

Don't act the innocent, unaware of the effect you have on everyone and everything.

Don't pretend you don't know what you're doing to me.

"Why are you looking at me like that?" Her voice was a whisper—tentative, scared—but the expression on her face didn't match. Her nose was scrunched, her head tilted.

Claire is . . . Claire is . . . puzzled, Nix realized, giving name to the expression, which he hadn't seen on the canvas of her face before. *Claire finds me puzzling. I am puzzling Claire.*

He rolled the thought over in his mind, letting her question go unanswered until the ugly, sordid truth—*I am nothing—she's pretending—so stupid to think that—*clawed its way back into his brain, digging in deep and holding on.

His whole life had been a nightmare, and she was playing with his emotions like a cat batting at a piece of string.

"Stop. Talking."

If she didn't talk, she couldn't lie—not with her mouth. Just with her body and her eyes—

"I won't stop talking."

There were question marks in her voice, and hesitations, and she didn't have a right to either of them. He wanted to rip the mask off her lying face.

He wanted to touch it.

"I . . . I . . . won't stop talking until you . . . until you tell me what's going on. Who are you?"

"Stop. Talking."

She matched his emphasis with her own. "Who. Are. You."

Tell me, tell me, tell me, her eyes seemed to say.

He cursed. He cursed her, and he cursed himself, and she pretended to flinch at the profanity that streamed from his mouth.

Nulls don't flinch.

To flinch, you had to feel fear. To be afraid of someone, your energy had to be marked by theirs. This Null was playing him. Again.

He needed weapons.

He needed her dead.

He'd left his knives and needles and poisons in the kitchen, out of sight. He had to stop her, before she pretended to flinch again.

Hands. Just my hands.

That was the way to kill this Null. His hands had bathed her temple. His hands had fed her. And in doing so, he'd committed a great evil—risked all the good he'd ever done, just because a Null had deigned to look him in the eye. To ask him for his name. To react to his presence—*puzzled, flinching*—as if he was the kind of person who could have an impact on anyone, ever.

Like he could affect a girl like her.

"I. Am. Nobody." The words came, not in answer to her question, but in answer to the ones he was asking himself

Who do you think you are, to look at her that way? You're nothing. She's everything. Kill her. Now.

"You're . . . you're . . . someone," Claire said. "You're the one who brought me here. You're the boy from my dream." She went very pale, the blue of her veins standing out like a pattern on porcelain. "You're the one who kills me."

He took one step toward her and then another. She sucked in a breath and watched him move. And then, without warning, the girl he'd held and helped and saved dove back under the covers.

Like she could hide from him.

Like she could escape him.

Lies.

<hr />

I'm hiding under a blanket. Claire's heart beat viciously against her rib cage. *I'm who knows where with who knows who, I just reminded the boy who brought me here that he intends to kill me, and now he's coming toward me, murder in his eyes, and I AM HIDING UNDER A STUPID BLANKET.*

I am a deficient human being in every way that matters.

Claire wished that she could blame it on the fact that

she'd been hit by a van, but in reality, she deeply suspected that she had always been deficient. Never said the right thing. Never made friends. Couldn't even get someone to hand her a towel.

Really, given the sum total of her life as evidence, it shouldn't have been that much of a surprise that she sucked at being kidnapped, too.

He's looking at me. He's going to kill me. I'm going to die.

Claire couldn't move. She couldn't run. She couldn't think of anything but the boy stalking toward her. Claire didn't *want* to think about him. Didn't want to anticipate the killer's touch, her own last breath, but there was a tiny part of her—the *Romeo and Juliet* part, the Heathcliff and Catherine—that thought for the briefest second that maybe this moment was what she'd always been meant for.

Maybe she'd been born to die by this boy's hands.

Situation: What would it be like to have an out-of-body experience? To watch someone kill you? When she was dead, would he put flowers on her grave? Would she haunt him, now and always?

"The game ends now."

The words brought Claire back to the present. To the terror. To the chilling understanding that death was never romantic; there was a difference between being stalked and being wooed.

Do something.

He was closer now, close enough that she could feel

the heat of his body on the other side of the blanket. Her heart beat faster. Her side ached like someone was splitting the bones with an ice pick.

You need a weapon. A way out. Something. Anything.

Slowly, her killer peeled the blanket away from her face. His features—each severe in its own right—came together to form an expression that was somehow gentle, full of longing. It made him look like someone who wanted something, wanted it as badly as Claire had wanted just one person to scrawl a private joke on the pages of her yearbook.

Me. He wants me.

Claire had read about this kind of knowledge—the kind you felt in your bones, from the tips of your toes to the top of your skull.

She'd read about it, and she'd believed in it, and she'd imagined it. But she hadn't spent even a second wanting it herself, because she'd been too busy trying not to long for simpler things—smiles from strangers, someone to eat lunch with, parents who took her picture on the first day of school.

He's going to hurt me. I'm going to die.

Claire couldn't hear herself think over the sound of her body's terror—the certainty that be it kiss or kill, there would be no escaping the predator stalking her now.

I can't stop it. Nothing I do will stop it. Can't think. Can't speak. Can't move.

Claire could feel hysteria bubbling up in her stomach and traveling like an air bubble through her throat. When it burst out of her mouth, she thought for a moment that she might have thrown up, but then she realized that she was giggling.

Like a lunatic.

And God must have had an awfully twisted sense of humor, because a second later, so was the boy.

Nix could not remember laughing. Ever. He'd tried once. Practiced. But with no one to listen, it was a horrible sound, and it hadn't brought him half the feeling of a single cut—long and thin—in one palm.

But now he was doing it. He was laughing. At Claire, clutching that blanket, giggling like a fiend. For a second, he thought that it would be enough, that this one moment would be enough to keep him and hold him and warm him for an eternity. He could kill her now.

Cut himself off, before this addiction went too far.

He dropped silently to his knees beside the sofa, bringing himself to her level. He cleared his mind, pushing away all thoughts of her—*her expressions, the sound of her laughter, the feel of her skin*—and concentrating on a single word.

Null.

She deserved this. For the life he'd been forced to live, for making him wonder and long for things best left unwondered and unlonged for, she deserved it.

He rose from his knees into a crouch. He closed his eyes and breathed in her soft, sweet scent—sunscreen and cinnamon—and then he reached down and placed his hands on either side of her neck.

Make it quick.

7

Claire had, not surprisingly, imagined what death would be like. In fact, close to one-sixth of her Situations had ended with her own untimely demise. She'd run into flaming buildings and jumped in front of bullets meant for those she loved, and she'd died of leukemia and gotten hit by cars—loads of them, as ironic as that was.

But she'd just never imagined going out like this. More whimper than bang. Desperate. Hypnotized. Her assailant's fingers brushing lightly against her throat.

I don't want to die. He's going to kill me, and I don't want to die.

His hands encircled her neck. She froze, paralyzed. She couldn't move. Couldn't breathe. And then, suddenly, it was over. He dropped his hands instead of tightening his grip.

She wasn't dead.

It's not death I want. The thought came unbidden, a side effect of her relief. *I want him. I want the boy.*

Okay, that was it. That was absolutely it! This sick, twisted *psycho* was playing with her. He'd attacked her, he'd kidnapped her, he'd sworn he was going to kill her, and now he was playing with her. Cat and mouse. And pathetically— *pathetically*—she was falling for it.

And that, Claire found, somewhat startled at the revelation, *pissed her off.* She was *pissed.* It was bad enough that people stared straight through her. Ignored her questions. Refused to give her towels and made her pour her best attempt at eggs down the sink. It was bad enough that this boy was trying to kill her, but *damn it,* he didn't have to touch her. He didn't have to make her feel like the world's biggest nothing because the alien sensation of contact with another human being was enough to keep her from fighting back.

He didn't have to look at her like she was something more.

Maybe I am. To him. Maybe I matter.

"Shut up," Claire told herself. Things like that, thoughts like that—those were the kinds of maybes that hurt you. That got your hopes up. That talked you into doing nothing while a killer tracked your every move.

Not happening. Not this time! Not with this Claire. She'd read the books. She'd seen the movies. She knew what Stockholm syndrome was, and she wasn't having any of that "forming emotional attachments to your kidnapper" nonsense.

Not anymore.

Logically, Claire knew that attacking her assailant wasn't much smarter than playing peekaboo beneath a blanket, but she wasn't about to sit around and wait for him to kill her and think pathetic thoughts about having his fingers wrapped around her throat.

"Don't touch me!" The words exploded out of Claire. She couldn't stay in her own head a second longer. She couldn't risk feeling sad or intrigued or any of the thirteen synonyms she knew for the word *incomplete*. She had to stay mad.

"You don't get to touch me. You don't get to ... to ... do that! You don't get to make me feel like—never mind. Never freaking mind, because it doesn't matter. You don't matter."

Lies, lies, lies.

He mattered. He mattered the way oxygen mattered. The way carbon monoxide did if you breathed in too much of it. But she didn't have to let him know that. She didn't have to make him feel powerful.

She didn't have to play his game.

Taken off guard by her vehemence—*yeah, buddy, that's right, I said it*—her would-be killer's laughter cut off, like someone had slashed his vocal cords. Claire scanned her surroundings for an escape.

Escape to what? She pushed down the question, because there wasn't an answer—not a good one.

Life is worth fighting for, she told herself. *I am worth fighting for.*

Even if she always said the wrong thing and sucked at making other people care, she could get better. Things could get better. Luckily, when given proper motivation, Claire could summon up beliefs on cue. It was a gift, a by-product of living so much of her life in imaginary worlds.

I'm worth saving, just a little.

She flew to her feet and stepped sideways. The killer stepped sideways as well, his face unreadable, his hands spread out on either side of his body. It felt like being circled by a panther, walking on its hind legs.

This boy wasn't quite human.

He wasn't quite real.

"I won't let you kill me." Claire was determined not to let herself fall under his spell again. "I'll fight you. I'll hurt you. You don't know what I'm capable of."

There. That sounded like a good bluff.

"I know exactly what you're capable of." The boy's voice had no inflection. None whatsoever. "You walk through this world like no one else matters. Maybe you want to feel things, maybe you don't, but you can't. Not the way Normals can."

I don't feel things the way normal people do. Claire took a step backward. One step away from him. One step closer to the door. *I don't feel things the way normal people do, because I feel them more.*

"People are things to you. They're scenery. Furniture. Disposable. You can see what they want, and you give it to them."

All I've ever wanted is to be able to give someone else what they want.

"You're a manipulator. An egotist. A mockery of humanity that thinks she's better than everyone else."

This boy was insane.

It was bad enough that he'd held her at gunpoint. And kidnapped her. And apparently nursed her back to health as part of some kinky obsession he had with being the one to kill her. It was bad enough that he'd almost strangled her and was now clearly in possession of what she'd heard a man on Animal Planet once describe as "the crazy eyes."

But this? Telling her that the world bent over backward to clear the way for her? That she didn't care about people? That she excelled in making them care about her?

Lunacy. Sheer, utter lunacy.

The boy rushed her. She rushed away. He feinted left. She went right. He paused. She paused.

It was a strange waltz they were dancing. A strange, strange, lethal waltz.

"You're not a very good killer," Claire found herself saying. Why was she baiting him? She wasn't sure. Except that maybe, she hoped that he would tell her something. Something that might help her find a way out of this alive.

"I'm *the* killer. I am death to all I seek. I am Nobody."

Nobody.

He said it like he meant it. Like he believed it. Like it was the reason for the shadows in his eyes and the scar across his neck.

Like this boy—this beautiful, insane, gun-toting boy—could possibly understand what it felt like to be truly invisible. To not matter. To anyone. *Ever.*

The boy in question closed his eyes again and then sank to the floor, moving forward at a crouch. She dodged, and then scuttled backward, into the kitchen.

Away from the door.

"How do you do that?" the boy hissed, following her.

Do what? Run? Considering the amount of time she'd spent staring at him instead of doing so, it was probably a fair question. Taking advantage of his distraction, she lashed out with one leg, trying to kick him off balance. He caught her foot and trapped it in a viselike hold. Then he stepped forward, working his way up the leg toward her, with detached precision.

His face an inch away from hers, he spoke. "You shouldn't be able to see me."

This close, there was no escape. There was no room to

maneuver. There was no hope and no chance. She didn't lean away from him. She didn't struggle. All she did was give in to the inevitable, with a shudder. "Of course I can see you. I'm not blind."

Not blind. Not blind*?*

How was she doing this? How was this girl, this *perfect-beautiful-cruel* girl looking at him?

Seeing him.

Acting like a person would have to be blind to stare through him.

His left hand held her leg immobile. He moved his right hand to brush the back of her neck. One motion. One movement. One jerk of his wrist, and she was dead.

"You will tell me how you're doing this," he ordered. "You will stop it."

"Stop *what*? Tell you how I'm doing *what*?" The words burst out of her mouth. She seemed ... agitated.

You shouldn't be able to see me, Claire. I shouldn't be able to agitate you.

He did not say the words out loud. The gleaming sheen of tears in her eyes stopped him from speaking. This wasn't possible. It just wasn't.

Claire filled the void of his silence. "I'm not doing *anything*. I can't do anything. Every time I try, it's like ... you stop me. God, you tried to shoot me, and I'm so pathetic that when I looked out the window and you weren't there anymore, I thought I was going to die because you were gone. And thirty seconds ago, I finally thought I had a chance to make it out of this, but now you're touching me, and you're looking at me, and you won't let go. I know you won't."

A single tear broke from the surface of her eye and slid down her cheek. Her face turned red and puffy. She wasn't a graceful crier, Claire. And she was right: he would never let go of her. *Never.*

"And you want to know why I'm looking at you!" she accused.

Like that was so ridiculous. Like it wasn't a legitimate question. Like she wasn't deliberately withholding the answer.

Nix watched as another tear slid down Claire's face. And then another. She looked down, but then lifted her head back up defiantly and stared him straight in the eye.

Nix was sure that no one had ever been looked at quite the way that Claire was looking at him. No Normal had ever been broken in half by a stare so pure. Ione and the Sensors, the rest of the world—they'd never have what Claire was giving him now.

Kill her.

Instead of snapping her neck, he tightened his hold on her leg, just slightly. And then, conceding defeat, he stepped backward, his hand trailing down her thigh, past her knee, and to her ankle before he gave her back that long, perfect limb.

I can't kill her.

He'd made her cry. Here, now, far away from the rest of her life or any other outside forces, she'd started crying.

Because of him.

And he didn't care if she was acting. He didn't care that it wasn't real. It didn't matter if he was just another stupid boy, falling for the charms of another heartless girl.

I made her cry.

Nobodies couldn't make people cry.

Nulls couldn't be made to do so.

She was the best damn actress in the world, and he couldn't hold it against her. He couldn't lift a hand against her, couldn't so much as leave a mark on her perfect skin.

"You won," he said.

"Won what?"

"You can drop the act," he told her. He opened one of the kitchen drawers. He took out a dagger, a gun, and a syringe. He laid them on the counter, one by one. And then he turned and looked at her.

Waiting.

She took a step backward.

Claire's eyes are opened wide. Her lips are turned downward. She's not breathing. She's holding her breath.

He wondered what her angle was. Hadn't he said that the game was over? Wouldn't the victor want to revel in her spoils?

"Please don't kill me," she whispered.

Nix stared at her, not comprehending her words. Hadn't he just exposed his weapons? Conceded defeat? Given her *exactly* what she'd wanted?

Years ago, he'd tried to kill himself. He'd failed.

Three times now, he'd tried to kill Claire, and he'd failed. He hadn't been able to bring himself to harm her in any way. He'd *saved* her. It seemed right, somehow, that she should kill him.

"Go ahead, Claire. I won't fight you."

"You're not going to kill me?"

She was going to make him say it. She wouldn't settle for less than absolute defeat. She wanted to break him.

"I'm not going to kill you, Claire," he said, savoring the taste and feel of her name on his lips one more time, as he played along with her game. "You're going to kill me."

For as long as she'd known him, this dark-haired, blue-eyed boy had wanted her dead. And now he wasn't going to kill her.

I can't take this. I really can't. Up and down and in and out, seesawing back and forth. First he was going to kill her, then he saved her, then he tried to kill her again. And now—

"You want me to *what*?"

The kitchen lights grew very bright. Claire's tongue swelled inside her mouth. Her mouth went dry. Tiny, iridescent spots dotted her peripheral vision. Her body felt very cold.

This must be what it feels like to go into shock.

The boy didn't move, not a muscle. She should have taken advantage of the moment. At the very least, she should have grabbed the weapons in case he changed his mind. But even in shock, Claire was stupidly certain that he wouldn't hurt her.

I'm not going to kill you, Claire. You're going to kill me.

Maybe she should want to. After what he'd almost done to her, maybe a normal girl would. But she wasn't normal. She knew that now, more than ever.

"What's your name?" she asked, her throat dry, her body anticipating the answer.

"I don't have a name. I'm Nobody."

"My name's Claire."

He obviously already knew that, but in faerie stories, it mattered, sometimes, if that knowledge was freely given.

"My name is Claire. What's yours?"

"Nix." His pupils flared. "Now you have it. You have everything. Kill me."

His tone was feral. There was no other word.

"Do it!" he screamed. His body twisted, as if he was in pain. "Pick up a weapon." The boy—*Nix, Nix, Nix*—hurled the words at her, each carrying the weight of a punch and the threat of something much, much worse.

He's going to kill me. If I don't kill him, he's going to kill me.

She took a step toward the weapons he'd laid out on the counter, trying not to look at them.

"Keep moving, Claire."

The closer she got, the more she averted her gaze. From him. From the sharp edge of the dagger, the glint of the gun. With each step, her body thawed.

So this is what coming out of shock feels like.

"Pick up the gun." Nix's orders were curt and clear. He hadn't moved, but she knew he would if she didn't do exactly what he said. *"Pick it up!"*

She picked up the gun.

I won't kill him. I won't.

"Aim it at me."

"No."

"You won, Claire. You won. This is what you want. This is what you've always wanted." He spoke the words like they were sacred. Like he was delivering his own eulogy, and somehow, it was all about her. "You're everything, and I'm nothing, and I. Can't. Kill. You."

Everything?

Everything wouldn't have been the most anonymous

girl in her ninth-grade class. Everything wouldn't have to nearly die to get her parents' attention. Everything wouldn't want a boy who wanted her dead.

"Aim the gun at me, Claire. Do it now." He stalked toward her, grace incarnate. "Point it at me. Pull the trigger. It's easy, Claire. So easy."

He was getting closer.

And closer.

"It wouldn't be the first time, would it? What, are you too good to kill me? Am I not your type?"

"No." She threw the gun down in a fit of rebellion. The second she did, he dove at her. Contact. His body. Hers.

Touching.

For a moment, Claire flew. Weightless. Entangled. And then he twisted, cushioning her landing, then moving to cover her body with his own.

He's afraid the gun is going to go off, she realized. She struggled against the shield his body was offering for hers. She was the one who'd thrown the gun. She was the one who'd put them in danger. Why was he protecting her?

The gun clattered to the floor, the safety still on. Silence filled the room, and Nix jerked his body away from hers, the ghost of his touch lingering on her skin.

"You threw the gun," he said, voice rough, eyes wide. "You threw it away."

"I didn't think about it going off. I just wanted it gone." Claire tried very hard to look as determined as she felt.

To choose the words to get her point across. "I won't hurt you. You shouldn't try to make me, because I won't."

For a moment, Nix resembled a shepherd who'd seen the messiah. Awe colored his every feature. Even his tattoos seemed to glow with some kind of inner joy. And then, as quickly as it had come, the expression disappeared, and Nix blanched.

No words.

Just a choking sound, like the air was suffocating him.

And then he leapt to his feet, and before Claire could stop him, her would-be killer was gone.

8

Nix's feet pounded against the ground. Limbs reached out to scratch him. The summer air, heavy and hot, stung his lungs with every breath. He had to get away—from the girl, from what had just happened, from the feelings threatening to suck him into a black hole of *asking* and *wanting* and *doubt*.

She'd thrown down his gun. People who trafficked in death didn't do that. True killers anticipated death—their own. Others'. They saw it everywhere. An active Null, one who'd given in to the impulse to play God, might have bucked at Nix's offer. She might have wanted to kill him with her own weapons, on her own time.

But she wouldn't have thrown the gun.

Claire has never killed anyone. Of that much, Nix was sure. And yet . . .

The Sensors had identified Claire as a Null. Ione had designated her Code Omega—too dangerous to approach, even for Nix. The last Omega Nix had killed—number Nine—had the bodies of fourteen women buried in his backyard. In pieces.

Nulls were evil. Those designated Do Not Approach were worse.

Nix stopped running. He backed himself into a tree and forced himself to breathe. To think. Not about Claire—*what if—what if—what if*—but about the fact that The Society had misclassified her.

Claire wasn't dangerous. At least, not yet. So why had The Society told him she was? Why had Ione ordered him to kill her from afar?

Why had she sent a backup team to finish the job?

It was almost as if The Society knew that she'd have this effect on him. As if they doubted that he would kill her. As if they'd feared he would figure out—*No*.

Nix couldn't breathe. His chest tightened, and he felt the urge to cut himself to slow the panic that was creeping up his spine.

Claire cried. She laughed. She got upset when he told her to kill him, and she was puzzled when there were things that she didn't understand.

Claire had never killed anyone.

Now that he had started his mind down this path, there was no stopping it. The facts bombarded him, one by one. Claire hadn't commanded her neighbor's attention the first day they'd met. The police had come to her house, but they'd left and never come back, which meant that either Claire had intentionally thrown away the protection they might have provided, or else, she hadn't had the power to make them stay.

Claire had dreams. Claire had nightmares. Everything she felt went directly to her face, and she felt everything.

She even felt him. His presence.

What if it wasn't an act?

What if Claire really was what she appeared to be? What if she was just a sweet girl? A sweet, Normal girl who couldn't even kill someone who'd come very, very close to killing her?

No. Nix was on his knees. He didn't know how he'd gotten there. The rocks in the soil pressed into his knee-caps, and a roll of nausea spread through his body.

"The Society protects Normals from the Nulls."

Without warning, Nix is nine years old again. His trainer's name is Ryland.

Ryland has a knife.

"For thousands of years, men with the ability to sense evil in others have banded together to hunt the monsters in their midst." Ryland twirls the knife around his finger-tips, and Nix wonders what the lesson will be this time.

A Nobody knows better than to hope that the knife is for show.

"You are the right hand of The Society. You are a weapon. You are a tool." Ryland brings the knife to skid lightly over the surface of Nix's skin. It takes the Sensor one try, two to figure out where Nix is standing—but he doesn't cut him. Not this time. Instead, he spins the blade, offering Nix the hilt.

Then they bring in the corpse. For practice.

Nix came out of it on all fours on the forest floor. Eliminating Nulls was his purpose in life, the altar on which his blood and tears and sweat had been shed. On The Society's orders, Nix had killed—One, Two, Three, Four. Nulls who valued the average human life no more than that of an ant. Five, Six, Seven—again and again and again, Nix had put them out of their misery and saved the lives they otherwise would have taken—Eight, Nine, Ten.

Eleven was the senator.

And now Claire. When Ione had given him her name, Nix had assumed that she was a monster. When Claire's file was designated Do Not Approach, he'd known that she was the worst of the worst.

But he'd known wrong. The truth was unfathomable, but impossible to deny. Claire didn't act like any Null he'd ever seen, *because she wasn't a Null.*

Nix lurched forward on his knees, his stomach emptying itself on the forest floor. Everything made sense now.

Claire wasn't the world's best actress. He was the world's biggest fool. The Society's lapdog. Their pet. Go, fetch, they told him, and he did. Go, kill.

But why Claire? What had she done to incur The Society's wrath? If she wasn't a Null, why would they want her dead? Nix wanted to go back to the institute. Wanted to beat the answer out of the people who'd sent him here. To surprise them in their beds and make them pay for what he'd almost done to Claire.

She's just a girl.

Nix sank back onto his heels, tears stinging his eyes. Claire wasn't a Null. She wasn't a heartless wretch. She wasn't a killer. If either of them were a monster, it was him.

Nix couldn't go back to the cabin. He couldn't face Claire, but he couldn't just leave her there either. Alone. Scared. Confused. He had to explain, and he had to ask—

Why could she see him? Why didn't she seem to notice that he was less?

That's why they did it. That's why they want her dead. Because when they told me no one would ever see me, they lied. When they told me I could never affect anyone, they lied.

The next thought—*when they told me no one would ever love me*—was too much, too fast. And even if it had been possible, once upon a time, it wasn't now.

The Society had made sure of that.

He'd kidnapped her. He'd almost killed her. She was the first person he'd ever been able to affect in any way, and he'd made her cry.

Claire. Claire. Claire.

Nix stood up, her image pushing out all other thoughts in his mind. He had to go back to her. To help her. To explain.

And then he had to go back to the institute.

For answers.

<hr />

He left me. He left me. He really, really did.

The longer Claire was alone, the more fully the memory of Nix's touch evaporated from her skin. It was over. He was gone. She tried to approach the situation rationally, to be glad that he'd given her the perfect opportunity to escape, but she couldn't shake the knowledge that she'd been *left*. Discarded. Probably already forgotten.

Again.

Situation: You've been kidnapped and abandoned at an empty cabin in the woods. No one knows you're here. They probably don't even know you're missing.

Claire could have daydreamed her way out of this cabin eight times over. She tried to pretend that was all this was: another Situation, a problem to be solved. She searched the cabin (unsuccessfully) for a phone. She gathered her assailant's weapons one by one and hid the guns and needles and knives under the front porch, in case he came back.

He won't.

Claire tried not to think those words. She tried not to think about waking up to his eyes on hers. But most of all, she tried not to acknowledge the fact that this wasn't a Situation—because in her Situations, she was never, ever alone.

Claire left the cabin. She ran out into the woods, but stopped. *I don't know where I am. I don't know where I'm going.* A thick tendril of panic began to slide its way up her spine. Too many horror movies. Too much Stephen King.

All alone in the woods. Because he left. Because I—

Claire's head throbbed. Panic rose inside of her. She was five years old again, alone at Walmart. In the park. In the back of her parents' car, locked in.

McDonald's.

Every place she'd ever been forgotten.

Claire bent her head forward, fighting back the panic, and then she felt a breeze on the back of her neck, saw a shadow on the forest floor. Slowly, she turned.

Nix.

"I'm not going to hurt you," he said. "I promise. And I'm not going to ask you to hurt me. Just listen."

Claire stumbled backward, but she couldn't help the words that came out of her mouth. "You came back."

People didn't come back. Not for her.

Claire scanned his face, but the lines of his expression held no answer. His lips were set into a narrow grimace, and there was a tension in his jawline that she couldn't quite diagnose.

He was either angry or desperate. Happy to see her, or shattered from the inside out.

"Claire, we need to talk."

There was a night and day difference between his tone now and the terse orders and accusations he'd thrown at her before. This was Nix being gentle.

This was the stuff of Situations.

Claire swallowed, and for the first time, she wished that she didn't have such an overactive imagination. She wished that things were black-and-white and simple and real. That he'd never tried to kill her, and that she didn't believe, deep down, that she might not have been his first.

"I'm not like other people, Claire." The assassin said those words easily—too easily, like they didn't matter. Like he'd said them so many times that they may as well have been the tattoos on his skin. "I'm not like other people, because I was born wrong. It's hard to explain, and it's probably going to sound crazy, but you just have to listen to me."

"I'll listen." She took a step toward him, and he jumped back.

"You can't do that. You can't come so close. You can't . . . touch me." He choked on the words. "I can't be near you."

He didn't want her. Of course he didn't.

He just wants to tell you something. He doesn't want to touch you. Why would anyone want to—

"You don't want to touch me, Claire. You really don't." The symmetry of his words and her thoughts stopped the onslaught in Claire's head. Nix looked down at the ground, then back up at her. He kept his distance. "Everything in the world has an energy. Most people can't see it, they can't smell it, they can't feel it. They don't even know it's there. But a small percentage of humans can sense it. They're called Sensors, and for thousands of years, they've been studying the pattern. They know how energy works. They know what it does. And just by looking at you—smelling you, listening to you, whatever—they can tell when something's wrong."

The back of Claire's neck tingled. A montage of images played in her mind: the red-haired girl at the pool holding the palm of her hand up to Claire's face; the old man scanning her body in a pattern that seemed more military than not.

"There's something wrong with *me*, isn't there?" Claire didn't wait for him to answer. "That's why you tried to kill me."

Nix closed the space between them in the span of a single heartbeat. He placed his hands on either side of her face, forcing her to look at him.

"There's nothing wrong with you, Claire. You're perfect."

She closed her eyes and leaned into his hands. She wanted to believe what he was saying. And for a half of a half of a second, she did.

———◆◆◆———

Nix knew he shouldn't touch her. He didn't deserve to. He'd almost killed her. And even if he hadn't, she deserved to know the truth—that he was nothing. That he wasn't worth even a moment of her time.

But his hands were hot. Her face was soft. And when she leaned into him, the pressure cascaded over his entire body. It only lasted for a fraction of a second, but Nix imagined it lasting longer, becoming something more.

No.

He jerked his hands away, fisted them by his side. He couldn't. Couldn't look at her. Couldn't touch her. He was a killer, and she was perfect. He was Nobody, and she was everything.

"I work for an organization. They call themselves The Society. And they did send me here to kill you, Claire." Nix paused, letting her absorb his words. "They made me think that you were something you weren't. A Null."

He could tell by the look on her face that he was getting ahead of himself, confusing her, so he forced himself to take a step back, to explain the things he'd been taught from the cradle, the things she'd never known.

"The kind of energy The Society studies isn't like gravity or electricity or heat. It's a substance, a *glow*, maybe even a person's soul. But sometimes people are born wrong. They have too much energy, or not enough, and either way, it's *wrong*." Nix struggled to keep his tone neutral, to fight back the flashes that wanted to come—of lessons learned and words spoken, of bodies and blood. "Under normal circumstances, when two people interact, they trade energy. Not all of it, just a little. And then they're connected. They mark each other. Sometimes, the mark fades after a while, if they don't see each other again. But sometimes it grows. And then you get stuff like love."

"Stuff like love," Claire repeated.

Nix hated himself then. Everyone else's indifference he'd been given. But her revulsion, the way she'd look at him once she knew what he was and what he'd taken her for—that, he'd earned.

"Normals—that's what The Society calls people who are born right—they can give their energy to people, and they can take energy from others. They can love, and they can be loved."

"But some people are born wrong," Claire whispered,

repeating his words, her tone laced with understanding—and horror. "They can't be loved."

The part of Nix's brain that had gotten used to seeing her as the villain wondered if she'd guessed what he was, and was twisting the knife on purpose.

"Some people are born wrong, but most of them aren't unlovable. They're worse. They can give their energy to other people. In fact, they're really good at it. They can mark someone just by thinking about them, and their marks take a really long time to fade. People think they're great. They think they're nice and normal. But underneath it all, they're empty, because nothing anyone else says or does can ever have a real effect on them."

"That's awful." Claire's reaction was so genuine—and so much of an understatement—that Nix almost smiled.

Almost.

"They don't care about anyone else. Sometimes they kill animals just to watch them die. Sometimes, they graduate to people. Some of them don't really mean to do anything wrong, but they just can't wrap their minds around the fact that other people matter, too. They're dead inside."

"So you kill them." Claire made the leap of logic herself, but she couldn't keep a horrified look from taking over her face, and when he met her eyes, she jerked her gaze away from him.

Backing away, like he knew she would.

Like she should.

"These people are called Nulls, and they're the enemy. The Society tracks them down, and once they get a lock on a Null's location, they hand the file over to me. Because I'm not right either, Claire. I'm not a Null, but I'm not right."

She opened her mouth, but he didn't let her speak. "I can slip in and out of any building. I can stand screaming in the middle of a street without anyone noticing or caring. I'm forgettable. I can kill without ever arousing fear."

Claire looked up. Looked at him. Into him.

"You're the other kind of wrong," she said, each word another twist of the knife. "And so am I."

9

It was one thing to think, during your worst moments, that you were unlovable. That it wasn't your parents' fault that they couldn't be bothered to stick around. That the kids at school would always stare straight through you. It was one thing to feel completely inconsequential.

It was another thing to find out that you were right.

Some people are born wrong.

It explained everything. No matter how hard she tried, or how sweet she was, or how often she went to the same places and did the same things, hoping that someone would eventually notice, no one ever did. And if what Nix was telling her was true, then no one ever would. She was constitutionally incapable of mattering, all because of some invisible birth defect she couldn't control.

It really is just me, and nothing I do will ever change it.

The death of a dream was an eclipsing thing, and the hope that someday things would be better had been Claire's mainstay for as long as she could remember. She wanted to fight to hold on to that sliver of *maybe*, but she couldn't bring herself to doubt what she was hearing, because it explained so much.

"You're not a Nobody, Claire." Nix was adamant, and his words managed to pierce the thoughts gumming up her head. "I'd know if you were."

"A Nobody?" Claire repeated dully. "Is that what we're called?"

It's what he'd told her over and over again when she asked him who he was—*Nobody*. He'd said it like it was a name, an identity, and a curse, all rolled into one.

"*Nobody* is the word for someone who can't give their energy to anyone else, yes. It's what I am. It's why I make the perfect assassin. People don't notice me. They look straight through me. They forget me."

"I didn't." In the days since she'd first seen him, staring down the barrel of his gun, Nix's face had never been far from her mind. She'd thought it was because there was something wrong with her, something that drew her—perversely—to her killer.

In a way, Claire supposed that she'd been right.

"You're special, Claire. No one else has ever been able to really see me, and no matter what I do, I can't shake you. Even when I fade, you find me."

"Fade? Is that what you're doing when you close your eyes?" Claire asked, her mind working through the logic of his words like a calculator crunching numbers.

"Fading is something Nobodies can do. Even if I wanted to be noticed, most people would look straight past me, but if I concentrate, if I push all of the thoughts out of my mind and stop trying to be worth something, then I fade. People can't see me at all. And because objects have energy, too, when I fade, as far as the world is concerned, I don't exist. The laws of physics don't apply to me. I can walk through walls. I can shake off gravity. I can disappear."

Claire wrapped her arms around her chest. What Nix was describing—it was beautiful. She wanted to disappear. She wanted to walk on water.

She wanted to fly.

But more than anything, Claire wanted the courage to take one step forward. One step closer to Nix, who didn't believe she was a Nobody for the same reason she hadn't been able to imagine anyone capable of walking past him without wanting to fall into the blue of his eyes.

"I see you," she told him softly, afraid that she would lose the words if she didn't let them loose. "Faded or not, Nobody or not, I see you. I see you when I close my eyes. I see you when you're not even there."

Nix took a step back, like she'd hit him. "That's why you're special, Claire. That's why The Society wants you dead. Normals aren't supposed to notice Nobodies. You must be some kind of outlier."

"I'm not special, Nix. I'm wrong."

"No. You're not. You're—"

"I'm just like you. Don't you get it? The reason I can see you is because we're the same."

"It doesn't work that way."

"How do you know?" Claire pressed. "Have you ever met another Nobody?"

Nix paused.

"You haven't, have you?"

Nix refused to shake his head, but Claire saw the answer in the set of his jaw.

"Think about it, Nix. You talked about energy, right? And everybody has it? And people exchange it, but for whatever reason, Nobodies can't give their energy to anyone else. Maybe it's because we're weak. Maybe everyone else's energy is like a laser beam, and ours is a cloud of smoke. So when you put us with someone whose energy is normal, we're practically invisible. But when you put us together . . ."

She'd *felt* his stare that first day. Before she'd seen him, before she'd had any reason whatsoever to believe that somebody was there, she'd known. Because she wasn't used to being looked at, and he'd been staring.

She'd never met another person who felt so *right*.

"You're not a Nobody," he said—like he could falsify her claim just by denying it out loud.

"Yes, Nix, I am."

"No, you're not. Nobodies don't matter, Claire, and I've never met somebody who matters as much as you."

Claire wanted to jump on his words, to say *aha* and victoriously explain that it made sense to think that smoke could leave its mark on smoke, but she couldn't make the words come, because there were no words. No thoughts. Nothing but a tightening in her throat and a loosening of the muscles in her chest. She swallowed, hard, trying not to let the stinging sensation in her mouth spread to her eyes, but the effort was useless.

She mattered. Maybe. Almost. Kind of.

Not to her parents. Not to the endless string of people she'd tried to befriend. Not to the towel boy at the pool or any of the teachers who forgot her name on a regular basis. She didn't matter to any of them, and she never would, but she maybe almost kind of mattered to Nix.

It was funny. The resurrection of a dream was almost as hard as watching it die.

━━━━◆◆◆━━━━

Claire is crying.

Nix didn't know what he'd said to make her cry. Every

time he touched her, he hurt her. He didn't deserve her, and now that she knew that truth, she must hate him. She had to.

"I'll go." He said the words quietly, hoping to ease her distress.

"Don't leave." She sounded panicked. "Not again."

Claire swallowed, and his eyes traced the motion down her throat before flickering back up to her face.

"Please don't leave."

For a moment, Nix thought that she'd retreat or crumble. Instead, she stalked toward him, her tightly balled fist the only remaining cue to the anxiety he'd heard in her voice.

"You can't tell me I matter and then leave like I don't." She didn't stop until she was standing directly in front of him, and even though he knew he should take a step back—for her sake—he couldn't.

Claire, unaware of how close to the pit she trod, coaxed her fingers out of their fist. Put her hand on his chest and shoved—not hard enough to move him, but hard enough that he could feel the warmth of her hand through his shirt. She might as well have reached into his chest and ripped out his heart.

"If I matter, then you stay," she said, her voice low, her hand unmoving. "You don't leave something that matters. You don't throw that away."

"You shouldn't touch me, Claire."

"And you shouldn't say my name like that—like it matters. Like it's more than just a word that belongs to thousands of other girls."

It wasn't just a word. Not to Nix. It was *her*. She was Claire, the one and only.

"Don't you get it, Nix?"

He didn't. He didn't understand why she was still touching him. Why his heart was beating faster and faster under her palm. He didn't understand why the sound of his name on her lips made it difficult to stand.

"I've never been anybody, Nix. I've never mattered—not to anyone. My parents barely even remember I exist. When I was little, they were always leaving me places. At the mall. At the store. They'd take me to the park and then forget and go home without me, and I'd sit under a tree or on a swing and just wait for them to come back. They used to have this big note on the back door that said CLAIRE in all capital letters, so that if they came home without me, they'd remember to go back.

"I made up this game to pass the time while I waited for them. I'd think up different scenarios, things that could happen, and I played them out in my mind. It was like watching a movie, but I controlled it. And in that world, I mattered. People never forgot me. They cared."

He could see her as a little girl, sitting on a swing, pretending that she was somewhere else. He could see her talking to friends who weren't there and reacting with the entire gamut of emotions to the situations in her head.

"I still do it. I still pretend that I'm somewhere else, that I matter, but I don't, Nix. Nobody even sees me. I'm a ghost in my own house. Most of the time, my parents aren't even there. I didn't come home last night, and they probably aren't even looking for me. And my friends haven't noticed I'm gone, because I don't *have* any friends."

He didn't believe her. He couldn't imagine anyone forgetting Claire, couldn't imagine losing her and not moving mountains to get her back. If the Sensors had taken her from him that day, he would have destroyed everything and everyone that stood between them to get her back.

"Do you know what I thought when you tried to kill me? The first time? I thought, *How can somebody want me dead when no one even knows I'm alive?*" Claire's voice broke, and the sound of it broke him. "I thought, *He's the most beautiful boy I've ever seen.* I thought, *Is this what it's like to be looked at?* And then you left, and I was nothing again. The police, my parents, my neighbors—nobody even believed me about you. They sent me out into the world, even though I knew you'd be back."

Claire coming out of her house. Claire walking down the street. Claire's eyes snapping up as he slipped out of the bushes.

Claire running toward him.

It couldn't be true. He'd believed she was a Null because the effect she had on him wasn't natural. He'd believed she could manipulate people into loving her, because he couldn't stop himself from feeling that pull. He'd saved her from the Sensors, because he *couldn't* let them take her.

The Sensors.

Nix stiffened. The day that they'd tried to take Claire away from him, to kill her themselves, the Sensors had missed. They'd tried to run her over, and they'd clipped her in the side instead.

Claire was hard to kill—not because she had the powers of a Null, but because she escaped notice altogether. The Society had sent Nix to kill her, because even a team of Sensors couldn't quite pinpoint where she stood.

To find the girl there, in his zone, lazing about a swimming pool, right under his nose—Cyrus was embarrassed to have missed something like this up until now. Richard and Ione's conversation at the institute floated back into Nix's mind, slamming the door on all other possibilities. *Well, these things do happen.*

Why hadn't he listened more closely to what they were saying? Nulls *didn't* have a way of flying under the Sensors' radar. Ione wouldn't have shrugged off a Sensor living side by side with a Null for fifteen years and never recognizing her for what she was. Pure energy, unmarked by any human interaction, was a flaming beacon over a Null's head. Nulls weren't a challenge for a Sensor's ability.

Nobodies were.

"We're the same, Nix. You can't leave me, because if you do, I won't matter, and I can't leave you, because you matter too much."

Too much?

He was still overwhelmed by the idea that he could provoke a reaction in her. Make her mad or sad. But mattering?

The only way you can make a difference in this world is to kill.

Nix pushed the voices out of his head. He bit the inside of his cheek—roughly—and put his hand on Claire's chest, exactly where her hand lay on his. He felt her heart beat. He felt its steady rhythm loosening his teeth's grip and warming him from the inside out.

It was wrong. Impossible. It couldn't happen.

It can't not.

Nix became highly aware of his own body: skin and heat and the rush of blood. He couldn't stop his body from moving toward hers, the space between them closing inch by inch, heartbeat by heartbeat, until his lips brushed softly over hers.

<hr />

Nix. Nix. Nothing but Nix.

For Claire, there was nothing else, nothing but the warmth of his hand through the thin fabric of her worn yellow sundress. Nothing but the feel of his breath on her face. His lips touched hers, and if his hands hadn't found their way to the small of her back and the back of her neck, the contact would have sent her to her knees.

No one touches me. No one ever touches me.

She brought her hands to the sides of his face, needing to touch it, to assure herself that this moment was real. His skin was warm, but her palms felt hot, and slowly, tentatively, she lost herself to the kiss, falling deeper and deeper into it, into him. Her hands moved down his neck and shoulders, and she pulled him closer.

I don't know how to do this.

She tried to close her eyes, but couldn't. Tentatively, she caught his lip in between her teeth and then let go, and in the moment that their mouths met again, hesitation gave way to something sweet, something pure.

She stood on the tips of her toes, her hip bone digging into the flesh just below his. She didn't know what she was doing, hadn't ever realized that kissing was something you could feel with more than just your lips.

Nix.

All there was, was Nix. The way he smelled. The way he tasted. The way he pulled back, dragging his lips away from hers and lightly down her neck.

No one ever touches me.

Neither one of them said it, but Claire could see it in his eyes and wondered if he could see it in hers.

I'm touching you. You're touching me.

She ran the tip of her thumb over the scar on his throat, and then, feeling his sadness, his loneliness and hers, she bent her head to his neck and traced her lips along the line her thumb had taken, inch by inch across his scar. Slow kisses, careful kisses, soft and light and from the soul.

I'm touching you. You're touching me.

He sank to his knees, and she sank to hers. There was nothing before this moment and nothing after. No up, no down, no left, no right, no secrets.

Nix. Nix. Only Nix.

Together, they were somebody.

10

Nix woke the next morning with a weight on his chest. For a moment, he thought that he had been buried alive. They did that with Nobodies sometimes, to teach them the necessity of being able to fade. But a moment's observation revealed that the weight on his chest wasn't dirt.

Back arching—lips on fire—bodies touching.

It was Claire.

They'd fallen asleep on the ground, dirt and leaves and damp grass beneath them. Claire's head was on his chest. As he watched, it lolled gently to one side. And just like that—

Nix is fifteen. In a strange bedroom. Watching. Waiting.

His target gasps. Collapses. The Null's head lolls to one side. His fingers twitch. Eyes roll back in his head—

Nix kept himself from following the memory any further. That was Three. Warren Wyler. Eleven letters, another body in the morgue.

From her spot on Nix's chest, Claire murmured something in her sleep. She was small and warm and *his*—but Nix couldn't let this go any further.

Couldn't risk bleeding his darkness onto her.

He knew how to do one thing, only one thing—and when he'd told Claire to kill, she'd said no.

Wyler's head lolls to one side. His fingers twitch. Eyes roll back in his head, and a sickly sour smell fills the—

Eleven targets, and Nix had never said no. Eleven people he'd thought were Nulls, because The Society had said it was so. Claire could have been number Twelve—another line tattooed onto his arm, another job well done.

He couldn't do this. Couldn't look at her. Couldn't touch her. Couldn't breathe because he *wanted* to look at her and touch her and not think about—

A sickly sour smell fills the room. From the shadows, Nix watches. He watches the man stop breathing, watches the fingers stop twitching, watches—and smiles.

Nix was sweating and shaking, and Claire just burrowed farther into his side. He couldn't do this. *Couldn't.* He pulled his body away from hers. Laid her head gently on the ground. Stood up.

I've killed. I'm a killer. I will kill again.

That thought was dull in his mind. Maybe once, he could have been something else. But not now. Never now, never with her. Killing was easy. Walking away from Claire—that was hard. Nix made it a hundred yards before his fingernails began to dig into the skin of his palms.

Pain didn't help. He barely felt it. Felt her light touch on his scars instead.

Keep walking. Don't look back.

He and Claire couldn't happen again. Ever. Eventually, he'd hurt her. He'd sooner cut off his own hands.

Nix focused on that as he walked away from her. He wouldn't hurt her, and he wouldn't let anyone else harm a hair on her head. The Society wanted Claire dead. Nix knew them well enough to know that they wouldn't stop. Not unless someone stopped them.

That, he could do.

<hr />

Claire woke up with swollen lips, a crick in her neck, and a smile on her face. She felt older. Wiser.

Special.

Like the Claire she'd been before kissing Nix was another girl. Like that girl was the one who people talked over and bumped into and stared through. And then she turned over onto her side, her fingers fanning out, one by one, exploring the crevices of the forest floor. Stretching her hand toward the place Nix should have been.

Stretching farther.

Claire opened her eyes.

The dawn had come and gone. And so had—*no*. She wouldn't go there, couldn't think that. She scanned the woods around her. Nervous hands found each other, her fingers interlocking.

Trees. Leaves. Dirt. Sticks. Bugs. Birds.

No Nix.

Interlocked fingers pulled Claire's knees tight to her chest. The longer she sat there, the more her thoughts began working their way up to a deafening roar, white noise that threatened to start saying things—horrible things—about girls who touched boys and boys who lied to get exactly what they wanted from stupid, stupid girls.

You're here, and he left, and this time, he isn't coming back. You know he's not.

"Situation." Claire said the word out loud, and her teeth chattered, even though she wasn't cold. "Situation: What if—"

What if he's the only one? The only person physically capable of really looking at you, seeing you, caring about you, remembering you? What if you're the only two Nobodies in the whole world, and he'd rather be alone than spend one more hour with you?

"Situation." Claire couldn't think of one. The sole thing

she could think about was Nix. Touching her. Kissing her. Hands on either side of her face.

All she could think was that he'd left her lying on the ground. Leaves in her hair. Lips swollen. He'd *left* her. The cacophony of emotion in her head receded, leaving only one emotion, only one thought.

You don't get *to leave me.*

<hr>

The road leading up to the institute was long and straight. Gravel crunched under Nix's feet as he walked the familiar path.

There's a knife in his right hand. His left is coated with blood. His body feels heavy.

He can't fade. Not now. Not after—

Nix shook off the memory. Not Three this time. Seven. He could feel the images fighting to take hold of his mind. Darkness dotted his field of vision. He forced himself to keep walking. Closer to the institute. Closer to the people who'd sent him to kill Claire.

There's a knife in his right hand. His left is coated with blood. His body feels heavy. He can't fade. Not now. Not after what he's done. Not this time.

He should feel something. Triumph, nausea, fear— anything. But he doesn't. His arms hang listlessly by his sides. The blade in his right hand swings gently as he walks.

He's never used a knife on a living, breathing being before, but this time, his orders were different.

This time, The Society told him not to fade. No poison, no guns, no "accidental" drownings.

This time, his orders said to make it messy.

With hard-won, painful effort, Nix banished the memory of his seventh kill, the blood. He focused on one thing and one thing alone.

At the end of this road and past the gates, through twisted hallways and beyond the security checkpoints—that was where he'd find Ione. The Sensors. The scientists.

The people who'd sent him after Claire.

11

Situation: You wake up in the woods with no memory. No name. No idea how you got here. There's a white index card beside you on the ground, telling you that you have until nightfall to find your way to civilization—if you want to get out of this forest alive.

As far as Situations went, it was closer to a horror movie than a daydream, but that was nothing new. Claire had imagined her way out of worse. The only difference was that this time, it was real. Not the amnesia, or the index card, or the imminent threat of death—but the problem.

She was alone in the woods. She had no idea how Nix had brought her here, no idea which direction to walk to find the closest town—or how far she'd have to go. The day before, she'd stalled. She'd given up. She'd wallowed in the fact that he left her—but Claire was done with wallowing now.

Done with hoping things would get better.

Done with being sad that they weren't.

Now Claire was *angry*. She'd spent so long trying to be so sweet, trying not to make trouble, waiting for something to happen—but *something* was never going to happen. Anything she wanted out of life, she'd have to take.

Starting with fighting her way out of these woods. Slipping back into the Situation, she imagined *stalking back to the cabin. To the weapons stash under the porch. Her hand closes around the hilt of a knife. She would have preferred a bow and arrow, but beggars can't be choosers, and she only has until nightfall.*

Claire mimicked the actions in reality. Gone was the horror she'd felt at Nix's weapons the day before. *This* was survival. This was taking care of herself, because no one else was ever going to do it for her. This was Claire making life happen instead of waiting for it to come to her.

She wanted out of this forest.

She wanted to live.

And she wanted to forget that last night—*painfully, impossibly perfect*—had ever happened.

Less than shadow. Less than air.

Nix slipped past the security checkpoints. Past the metal detectors and the Sensors and every safeguard The Society had put in place to make the institute impenetrable to anyone who mattered.

Unfortunately for The Society, Nix *didn't* matter—and faded, nothing was *impenetrable* to him.

As Nix made his way farther and farther through the labyrinthine corridors, he was overcome with a sickening sense of déjà vu. How many times had he walked these hallways? How many times had he overheard the Sensors' conversations, used their words to figure out what it would be like to be Normal? To hear what they said when they were talking to each other and not to him.

The only way you can make a difference in this world is to kill.

Nix had told himself that he was coming back here to protect Claire, to find out why The Society wanted her dead. But now that he was here, the memories were too close to the surface: the training, the lessons, the *experiments*— and all he could think, over and over again, was a number.

Eleven.

The fissure of doubt that had started that morning— with number Three—spread through Nix's body, through the rest of his memories, the men and women he'd killed. He'd thought they were Nulls. He'd seen what true Nulls could do: seen the teenage girl that One kept chained in his basement; seen the cigarette burns on Six's child's arms. Nix had seen the bodies and the horrors, and he'd known that Nulls were monsters—but what if his targets hadn't all been Nulls?

Nix's grip on the fade wavered. After a split second, he came crashing back to the solid world. His body felt heavy—as heavy as he'd felt after killing Seven and making it messy. He took a deep breath and assessed his current situation. Even when Nix wasn't faded, the people who worked here rarely bothered to take note of his presence—but that wasn't a chance worth taking now that he'd gone rogue.

Nix stopped questioning, stopped thinking—and he shed his solid form like a snake wriggling out of its skin. He faded, and this time, he didn't let himself remember. He didn't think about why he was here or what he was doing. He just stepped through wall after wall, working his way to the center of the sprawling building.

To the lab.

The scientists and Sensors scurried around, from computer to computer, screen to screen. Nix didn't know what they were doing. Faded, he didn't care. He watched them like a child examining an ant farm. The man closest to him was young: a decade older than Nix, maybe less. There was sweat on his brow and scars on his arms: tiny, round pinpricks, up and down the flesh, from elbow to wrist.

"What's our status?"

Nix recognized Ione's voice. She rarely spoke to him directly, but her voice had always been the one in his head when he read a target's name. *She* made the decisions. *She* was in charge. *She* was the one who'd sent him after—

No. Nix couldn't let himself go there, couldn't let himself think about anything the real world had to offer, least of all the girl he'd left behind on the forest floor.

"We've got facial recognition programs running on all sectors within a two-hundred-mile radius of the Nobody's house," one of the ants replied, scurrying to do his queen's bidding. "Alarms are set to go off every three minutes, per protocol, to remind us what we're looking for."

What they were looking for. Not who. Never who.

"And our defense mechanism?"

At this, the ant bristled. Said something about *testing* and *phases* but all Nix could think was that Ione was looking for the *Nobody*. She was looking for *Claire*.

Nix felt his stomach turning itself inside out, and he knew he wouldn't be able to keep hold of his fade for long. Thinking about Claire: the way he'd left her; the things they had done; the feel of her skin; the taste of cherries on her lips—

In his last instant of nothingness, Nix crossed the room. He stepped through the wall and came out on the other side.

In Ione's office.

Flip-flops were not conducive to trekking one's way through the wilderness, but Claire didn't let that stop her. Her ankles and calves were splattered with mud. Welts rose on her arms, courtesy of branches and trees. She watched the sun travel across the sky. She marked her progress, notching trees in case she got turned around.

Her muscles were sore. Her feet were screaming, but Claire didn't listen. She couldn't listen, because she couldn't stop. She couldn't pause. She couldn't let herself think about anything but making it out of this forest alive.

She wasn't going to be the victim this time.

She wasn't going to cry.

She wasn't going to sit and wait. She was *done* waiting, because you could spend your whole life waiting for something to happen. Something big. You could wait and wait, and even if something big happened, even if it *finally happened*—it didn't change anything.

Even if it changed everything.

The sound of traffic broke Claire out of her thoughts. *Northwest, about a hundred yards out.* She ran, ran with the knife in one hand, her feet bleeding, her heart pumping faster and faster. She broke through the edge of the woods. She stepped out onto the road. Wind whipped through her hair. A car whizzed by, close enough that she felt its motion.

The driver didn't see her.

Claire stood there for five minutes, ten, watching the world pass her by. She was covered in mud, bleeding, holding a *knife*—and nobody noticed.

Claire felt something give inside of her. *No matter what you do, you will never matter. No one will ever see you. No one but—*

Claire walked across the highway. She walked and walked until she came to a town. She stepped onto a sidewalk, in front of a store. Someone bumped into her from behind. She dropped the knife, scrambled to pick it up, and from her spot on the ground, she realized something.

It didn't matter what she did—and that meant that she could do *anything*. This was a brave new world, because even if she was alone, even if she would *always* be alone, the world had given her permission to stop trying.

Trying to be sweet.

To be nice.

To be good.

As Claire stared at the shops and the people and the thrum of life all around her, she realized that for once in her life, it might be nice to be bad.

12

The décor in Ione's office was all metal and sharp corners, glass tabletops and see-through chairs. There was art on the walls, a splash of cool color: blue and silver against a palette of black and white.

Make it messy.

Ione had said those words to him here. He could still feel the knife in his palm, still hear the man's screams—

Not a man. He was a Null.

But standing in Ione's office, Claire's face still fresh in his mind, Nix wasn't so uncompromisingly sure. Everything he'd thought, everything he'd believed in—

He moved swiftly toward a filing cabinet behind Ione's desk. Locked—but not so hard to open, given proper motivation. He bypassed file after file, searching for something he recognized—*someone*. And then he found it.

One file after another after another. Eleven of them in total. Neatly labeled with serial numbers that didn't match up with the numbers in his mind.

One, Two, Three . . .

He slipped open the third file. Warren Wyler's lifeless face stared back at him, swollen and puffy, eyes clouded with milky white death. Autopsy reports, biographical details, pictures—

Nix stopped. He closed the file and took another. And another.

Four. Five. Six. Seven.

"Make it messy," Nix murmured. His fingers lingered on the file. He ran the tip of one gently along the edge, daring himself to open it.

The door to the office opened instead. Nix looked up from the file.

"Oh," a familiar voice said. "It's you."

Ione. She looked exactly as he remembered: blue eyes, blond hair, eyebrows dark enough to call that color into question. The director of the institute wasn't upset to see him. She wasn't glad. Objectively, she probably knew that she'd been looking for him, knew that he was an asset she didn't want to lose, but subjectively—

"You don't care." Nix wasn't sure why he was saying the words. Clearly, neither was she.

"No, I suppose I don't. It's for the best, really, that you've returned—"

Nix stood, and she saw the file in his hands. Saw the others spread out on the floor. *He* couldn't provoke emotion in her, but they could.

"And what, pray tell, do you hope to do with those?" Her tone—icy and controlled—matched the colors of the room exactly.

Make it messy.

Until that moment, Nix hadn't planned on doing anything with the files. Wordlessly, he gathered them from the floor. Ione took a step forward, but seemed to remember—belatedly—that even if she wasn't scared, she should be.

These were her files, after all. She'd seen what he could do.

Her hand slid slowly into her pocket—

"Stop." Nix's voice was low and cold, a match for hers. "I don't know what you're reaching for. I don't care. Keep your hands where I can see them."

I've killed. I'm a killer. I will kill again.

Ione couldn't hear the tone of warning in his voice. She wouldn't register the lethal set of his eyes. He didn't frighten her—but she couldn't afford to ignore him, no matter how hard it was not to. She stopped, freezing in place.

"Why?" Nix asked simply.

Nobodies didn't ask questions. Nix knew that—but the

knowledge was shallow, replaced by the time he'd spent watching and observing and *touching* Claire.

"Why did you send me to kill her?"

Ione shrugged, her eyes failing to find his, her demeanor poised—like he wasn't *this far* from snapping her neck just to hear the sound. "You've never asked why before."

Those words hit Nix hard. The files in his hand, his *kills*—he hadn't asked, and he hadn't said no. He'd done what they'd said, always.

"I should kill you." He said the words calmly. She didn't flinch. Her hand moved, ever so slightly, toward her pocket. He was on her in an instant, his free hand closing around her throat. He didn't slam her against the wall. He didn't make a single noise.

"Why?"

Why had she sent him to kill Claire? Why had the sight of the files triggered a response in her that he could not?

Ione opened her mouth. Nix loosened his grip on her throat, just enough so that she could speak, in a harsh whisper that cut through the room. "If you kill me, I'll only be replaced. Cut off one head, come up against seven more. You can't stop The Society. You can't hurt us. You're *nothing*, and we're more powerful than you've ever imagined."

Her hand disappeared into her pocket. He tightened his grip, cutting off all air.

"Don't," he said.

She stilled. He looked at her. She looked through him. He was killing her, and she wasn't even watching.

"Wait." She mouthed the word. For the second time, he relaxed his grip on her throat. If she had last words, he needed to know them.

"There's a panic button in my pocket. I've already pushed it. This room will be crawling with Sensors in an instant. You can't kill us all."

He thought of everything The Society had made him do. He thought of staring down the length of his gun at Claire. He thought of Claire's nightmares, Claire's pain—*their* fault.

"I can try."

Ione shrugged. "And while you're here, trying to kill us, we'll be out there, taking care of a problem."

It took him a moment to grasp her meaning. *We* as in The Society. *Problem* as in Claire. The computer program running in the other room, the scientists—what if they'd found her?

The door to Ione's study burst open. Shots were fired. One of them grazed Nix's shoulder. He didn't have time to think. He reacted.

He faded: instantaneously, a matter of reflex, the hard-won fruit of his trainer's methods—drowning him, burying him, cutting him. They'd made fading a survival skill—and he was a survivor.

Ione gasped for breath, her hands flying to her throat.

Nix had brought the files into the fade with him, but the second he'd faded, he lost the ability to choke the life out of her.

She'd lost her ability to see him, to feel him, to *hurt* him. Unless she could make him lose his fade, he was untouchable.

"Do you think this changes things? Do you really believe that the fact that there are two of you changes anything?" Ione spoke loudly, unaware of how close to her he was standing. "She'll never love you, you know. Never care for you. You are what you are. A killer. She'll never understand that. How could she?"

Nix closed himself off to Ione's words. She was trying to hurt him, to weigh down his mind, to bring him out of the fade. She was trying to stop him from leaving with the files—and saving Claire.

<hr/>

Claire walked out of the store, clothed in pilfered goods. A security alarm sounded, but no one stopped her. The salesclerks didn't notice that she'd helped herself to a pair of barely-there jean shorts and a sinfully soft cotton tee. Just like they didn't notice that she was mud splattered, scratched, and bloody.

There was a power to being able to walk through the world unnoticed.

After everything she'd lost in the past twenty-four hours—the hopes and the dreams and the *maybes*—Claire figured that fresh clothing was the least of what she was owed. She pushed down the familiar stab of guilt and kept walking. Her fingers tightened around the hilt of her knife.

She'd spent years berating herself for every little thing. Every imagined faux pas, every failure to matter. But none of that had been her fault. In the past twenty-four hours, she'd been kidnapped, abandoned, forced to fight her way out of the woods—she wasn't going to feel *guilty* about stealing clothes.

Anger was easier than guilt. Still, Claire looked back over her shoulder, half expecting to be caught. As she turned, something flashed in the corner of her eye. The hairs rose up on the back of her neck, and she remembered—suddenly and with an eerie sense of premonition—that Nix wasn't the only one who'd wanted her dead.

She whirled back around. Nothing. Nothing but her own imagination. And still, she couldn't shake the feeling that something was coming, that the knife in her hand wasn't enough.

"Claire."

She heard her name and whirled again. *Nix.* Her body recognized him before her mind did. Reflexively, she took a step backward, even as her hand reached out to him.

No.

She wasn't doing this. He didn't get to leave her and then show up. He didn't get to look at her and stop her heart. He didn't get to make it beat harder, faster—

"Are you okay?" The whispered words exited his mouth with the power of a gunshot.

"I'm fine," she spat, but she couldn't shake the feeling that something was wrong, something more than just the fact that he was here.

"I thought they found you." His words were low. He reached forward to take her arm, but caught himself and aborted the motion halfway through. "We need to go."

Claire didn't move.

"Now," Nix said, his voice rough, every muscle in his body tensed as his eyes scanned the crowd.

Claire wanted to fight him, to keep herself from getting sucked back under the force of this thing between them. He was a Nobody. She was a Nobody. That didn't have to mean anything. It *didn't* mean anything—but for the first time, she took in his appearance, the look in his eyes.

If there was one thing Claire knew like the back of her own hand, it was the edge of the abyss, and Nix was wearing darkness like sunscreen. SPF 70, slathered thick. He held a stack of folders in one hand, his knuckles white with the force of his grip.

He was bleeding.

She lifted her left hand to his shoulder. Unlike him,

she didn't pull back. And once her skin touched his—she didn't want to.

Either Ione had been bluffing and The Society didn't know where Claire was, or Nix had beat them here. Her fingertips grazed the wound on his shoulder. He sucked in a breath.

"You're hurt," Claire said.

"So are you."

There were scratches on her arms and legs, and she held a knife in a death grip in her right hand.

"We need to get out of here," Nix said. He turned to leave, walking away from her touch. She didn't follow.

Ione's words echoed in his mind. *She'll never love you. You are what you are.*

"I'm not going anywhere with you." Claire's voice shook, but she may as well have carved the words into his chest with her knife.

"They're looking for you," he said, lowly. "They'll *hurt* you."

"They won't find me," Claire countered. "Isn't that what you said? We're unnoticeable? Two Nobodies can have a fight on a street in a strange town, and people will just brush on by."

Nix had forgotten that they weren't alone, that there

was anyone else on this sidewalk but her. His gaze darted from one person to the next: assessing them, looking for a tell that any of them were more than what they seemed.

"Claire—"

She took a step forward, until the two of them were dangerously close. "You *left* me."

"I had to go back."

Nix hadn't meant to tell her where he'd gone. He didn't want to explain the files in his hands, didn't want her to see firsthand evidence of the things that he'd done.

You are what you are. A killer.

"Back to The Society?" The anger drained out of Claire's voice. Her face softened, and silently, Nix begged her not to look at him that way. Like she could *fix* him.

She'll never understand. How could she?

"I went to the institute," he said. "The building where I—"

Nix couldn't say *grew up*, and he couldn't say *lived*. He'd never felt as inhuman as he did in that moment, trying to explain his life to Claire.

"—where they *kept* me." Nix could feel the memories hovering at the edge of his mind, and he prayed they'd stay there. He didn't want Claire to see him like that. He didn't want to risk the chance that, caught up in the throes of a flashback, he might lose control and hurt her.

"The institute is The Society's headquarters." Nix concentrated on facts over feelings, keeping the past at bay.

"From the outside, it looks like a mansion, but the inside is state-of-the-art. There are laboratories dedicated to studying energy and metaphysical abnormalities. Libraries for keeping The Society's histories. Training facilities for Sensors, so the ones who've been inducted into The Society can learn to use their powers."

Training centers for Nobodies, so they can learn to kill.

"And you went back." Claire was stuck on that one point, and Nix wondered where she'd *thought* he'd gone when she woke up that morning and he wasn't there. "Why would you go back there?"

Nix's gaze went involuntarily to the folders in his hand.

"What are those?" Claire asked.

Nix wasn't used to masking his thoughts. Clearly, he needed to be more careful around her.

"I mean, obviously, those are folders, but what's in them?"

You are what you are.

You're a killer.

"It's none of your business, Claire." Nix gritted his teeth, his words sharp as fangs. "It doesn't matter why I went back. It doesn't matter what's in these folders. All that matters is that The Society is still looking for you. You need to go back to the cabin."

"I already told you that I'm not going anywhere with you. Not until you explain."

Nix reached for her, and this time, he allowed himself

to complete the action. His hand closed lightly over her arm. "I can't protect you here."

"Maybe I don't want to be protected." Her voice was softer now. He had to lean forward to hear it.

Shouldn't lean forward.

"I need," he said, the words sticking in his throat. "I need you to be safe. It's not safe here. Please, Claire."

"Tell me what's in the folders, and I'll go with you."

She asked for the one thing he didn't want to give her. He let go of her arm.

"You want to know what's in these folders?" It was either tell her or touch her—and he couldn't let himself travel back down that road. "I stole the files from Ione, the current head of The Society. They detail the people I killed. The Nulls."

A week ago, he wouldn't have referred to Nulls as people. But now—

"Do I have a folder?" Claire's question cut off that train of thought.

"Ione gave me a dossier before she sent me after you, but it didn't say anything about why The Society wants you dead. It just said that you were dangerous."

Claire's gaze traveled back down to the folders in his hand. "But you think there might be answers in there."

She read him too easily, too well.

"I'm the one they want to kill," Claire said. "I have a right to know."

Nix wanted to argue, but he couldn't. She had a right to know—what he was capable of, what he *was*.

"We could check." Claire's voice was soft and steady. "We could research your . . . targets. That might tell us what The Society is up to. Why they want to hurt me."

They want you dead because they don't want me to have you.

Nix knew, logically, that there might be another answer. That it could be about her as easily as about him.

"They shouldn't care about either of us, either way." He said the words before he'd fully processed the thought. To want to kill them, The Society would have to care. There would have to be something at stake.

Something bigger than two people who didn't matter at all.

"I'll look into my previous targets," he told her, his words carrying the weight of a promise. "See if there are any anomalies. Figure out who's involved and how to deal with them."

Claire's chin jutted out. "I'm helping."

"You can't—"

She cut him off, her eyes ablaze. "Don't tell me what I *can't* do. I'm tired of just letting things happen and then hoping for the best. If you just let things go on and on and on, the best doesn't happen."

Nix couldn't keep himself from thinking that she was beautiful when she was angry.

She'll never love you. How could she?

His fingers curled into fists at his sides.

"If you want me to come with you to the cabin, you're going to let me help, Nix. If you try to leave again, I'll follow. I'm not just going to sit around and wait for something bad to happen, because nothing good ever does."

Nix realized then that she wasn't bluffing. If he left her and she followed, she'd get hurt. But if he stayed, eventually, he'd hurt her. He destroyed everything he touched. He was only good for one thing.

You are what you are.

"Fine," he said.

"Fine?" Claire asked suspiciously.

"If you come back with me to the cabin, if you let me protect you, if you do *exactly* as I tell you, I'll let you help me investigate The Society."

Before Claire could respond, Nix held up a hand.

"I have two conditions. One: what happened before can't happen again."

Lips on lips, bodies melding together. His hands— soaked with blood—*touching her. His mouth—killer's mouth—kissing hers.*

"Last night can't happen again, Claire," he repeated. "Ever."

She stopped breathing. He paused, waiting for her to start again, missing the sound.

"And two: when I say you're done, you're done. You

want to know why The Society wants you dead. You want to protect yourself. Fine. But when it comes down to it, I'm the one who's going in, and you're going to hide."

"Fine," she said, matching him tone for tone. "I have a condition, too."

Nix raised an eyebrow, waiting.

"You have to teach me to . . ." He could see her searching for the right word, one she'd heard him speak once before. ". . . *fade*."

The word made him want to close the space between them. Run his hands through her hair. Teach her the only thing in the world that had ever been really, truly, exclusively his.

He met her eyes. "It's a deal."

13

"Less than shadow. Less than air."

Claire let Nix's voice wash over her body, ignoring the way the grass stuck to her legs in the summer heat and concentrating on the sound and shape of each individual word.

Nicer words than *don't touch me*. Nicer than anything he'd said to her since they'd returned to the cabin. Since she'd dressed his wound. Since she'd realized what was inside those folders—and why he'd left.

"Less than shadow. Less than air," she repeated. She expected her voice to sound older, lower—but it didn't. She sounded like herself. Like a little kid, playing make-believe.

Like someone who couldn't handle what those folders held.

"You have to concentrate." Nix sounded peaceful, fluid, almost drunk. Completely unlike the boy draped in darkness, who'd come for her in town. "Let everything leak out. Every thought, every desire, every hope. You have no future, and no past. You have no name. You are nothing."

Claire realized, suddenly, that he wasn't talking to her. He was talking to himself. Telling himself that he was nothing. Believing it. A jolt of electricity ran up her spine. She could still see Nix, but she wondered what someone else would see, observing them from the edge of the woods.

Was Nix invisible?

In answer to her silent question, he stood. His feet barely touched the forest floor, like gravity was having difficulty getting a firm grasp on his long, lean frame. He reached out, and his hand passed straight through the closest tree.

Claire shivered. "Less than shadow," she whispered. "Less than air."

"Worthless. Empty. Nothing."

Nix's words came at her from every side, as if spoken by the forest itself. Becoming nothing, becoming everything—it was all the same.

It was beautiful.

His face looked almost incandescent, like the film of a bubble floating on the surface of water. He had no worries. No hopes. He wasn't the Nix who'd left her. The one who'd come back bleeding.

He wasn't anything, and Claire desperately wanted to be nothing, too.

"Why isn't it working?" she asked. "What's wrong with me?"

It figured that she'd be a bad Nobody. It took a special kind of lame to fail as much at being unimportant as the reverse.

"It's starting," Nix's voice said from all sides of her body. "Whatever you're thinking, keep thinking it."

Less than shadow. Less than air. That wasn't her mantra. That was his. She had her own ghosts, her own doubts.

I'm jealous of farts. As far as mantras went, it didn't have a very enticing rhythm. It didn't sound dangerous. It didn't make her feel powerful. It made her feel like less. But maybe, to be more, you had to give up trying to be anything at all.

I'm not Claire.

I'm nothing.

I'm nobody.

I'm the pages in my yearbook. Meaningless. Forgettable. Generic. I'm the girl who's never invited. Never noticed. When I'm drowning, no one saves me. When I speak, nobody listens.

I'm a Post-it note on my parents' back door.

I'm the messages I leave on their cells.

I'm the middle of the middle. I'm Nobody.

The thoughts in her mind stilled until she wasn't Claire. She didn't have a name. She didn't have a family. She had nothing.

And, God, it felt good.

Claire stood, surprised by how little effort it took. She walked on the balls of her feet, barely contacting the ground.

This was what it felt like to let go. To stop trying. Stop wanting.

Claire strode forward. Toward the trees. They were firm, solid, old. They'd been here for hundreds of years and would be here for years to come.

They couldn't touch her.

Nothing could.

So she walked straight through them, and a song began to hum through her body. She belonged here.

"Claire? Can you hear me?"

That wasn't her name. She wasn't Claire. Not anymore. She was nothing. But still, she turned toward Nix. He was the one who had brought her here, to this wonderful alternate world where she could walk through trees and dance and never hurt again.

"Let's stay this way," she said, forgetting about The Society. About the body she was supposed to have and the people who wanted it dead. About Nix's *conditions* and his secrets. "Let's stay this way forever."

Nix had never seen anything quite like Claire faded. If anything, she became brighter. More noticeable—to him, at least. The physical world seemed to disagree. She danced through the trees like some kind of pixie, a sprite taking impossible joy in a world that mere humans couldn't see.

Everything Nix had been taught told him that to fade, you had to let go of emotion. You had to feel nothing. The second he met Claire's eyes, he should have lost his grip on nothingness. The moment he heard her voice, coming from everywhere and nowhere at once, he should have started gritting his teeth, trying not to care.

Seeing her should have stripped him of his powers. But it didn't, because right now she was nothing, too. He was faded. She was faded. It was *easy* to think of nothing but Claire, to let her presence in the fade ground his.

In the real world, he resisted touching her, didn't *deserve* to touch her, but here, now he didn't have to hold back.

No such thing.

Faded, Nix should have been able to pass straight through her.

Faded, their fingertips shouldn't have been able to touch.

Faded, he shouldn't have been able to feel that touch all the way to the ends of his toes.

But he could, and the second they connected, everything

changed. The rest of the world faded to gray, its sounds to silence. The wind stopped blowing; the leaves froze at the angles to which they'd been pushed. A bee paused just above a flower. Nix looked farther, harder at the rest of the world. Ants on logs. Birds midflight.

They were frozen.

Fading meant leaving the physical world behind. It meant being weightless and transparent, insubstantial, empty. But this—his fingers interwoven with hers, her fade connecting with his—they hadn't just slipped out of the physical world.

They'd fallen out of time.

<hr />

Claire noticed the world slowing down around her, but she shrugged it off. That world didn't matter. She'd lived there long enough. It didn't understand her—or Nix.

They were *more*. He was touching her, and she couldn't remember a time when he wasn't. Couldn't quite grasp the fact that back in town, he hadn't wanted to. Couldn't get a grip on anything that had happened in the fifteen years leading up to this moment.

"Let's run." Claire had always hated running, but she couldn't just stand there, not when every barrier between her and things that lay just out of reach had been removed. She dropped her counterpart's hand, knowing instinctively that *this* Nix would touch her again, that he would touch her, follow her, *chase* her.

The moment their fingers parted, the world shifted, a phantom wind blowing through Claire's body as time sped up around them. She broke into a sprint, amazed at how easy it was to run when the world didn't fight to slow you down. There were no obstacles. Her feet barely touched the ground before they left it again, and her lungs breathed a different kind of air.

Nothing. Nothing. Nothing.

Her feet stopped touching the ground. They stopped touching it at all. She was floating, flying, blurring. And everywhere, there was Nix. Through the trees. Through the woods. Out the other side.

A road, abandoned, stretched out before them. Faster, farther, higher, more.

If my parents could see me now—

The thought came from an older part of her brain. A part that didn't belong here, in the sky, with Nix and the glorious nothing.

Cruelly, abruptly, Claire's body solidified and she lost her grip on the thing that she had become.

I'm Nobody.

Nothing.

I don't care what my parents think.

They don't matter.

She thought those things, frantically, but the power

and everything that came with it hovered out of reach, and Claire fell.

Faster.

Farther.

Lower.

And right before she hit the ground—the solid, ugly, unforgiving ground—Nix caught her. And the second after that, he lost his fade, too, and they both took entirely ungraceful nosedives into the dirt of the road.

"Ouch."

"Are you okay? Are you hurt?" He was above her in an instant, running his fingers over her ribs, her side, up and down her legs, checking for injuries.

"I'm fine. Just sore."

"Lie still, Claire. Something could be broken."

"We both fell, Nix." She struggled to sit up, but he wouldn't let her. His hands moved to her arms, and she wondered if he realized that he was touching more of her now than he had the night before.

"You fell from higher. I shouldn't have let you try it. I shouldn't have let you go so high. I should have warned you—"

"That I had to let go of this world to stay in that one? It's not rocket science."

"It takes practice. Discipline. Are you sure you're not hurt?"

"You caught me."

Her words reminded him that he was touching her, and immediately, he stopped. Jumped to his feet. Backed away from her. "Two conditions, Claire, and the first one is that we can't—" The words tore their way out of his mouth like something was clawing out his insides. "When you touch me . . ."

When I touch you, she thought, the words an echo of his. She stood up.

"We touched before," she said, "when we were nothing."

Nix shrugged off her words. "That was different."

It wasn't. Not to Claire. But she wasn't about to say that, wasn't about to set herself up for the inevitable rejection.

"When we touched in the fade," she offered instead, "something happened."

"Time stopped." Nix said. "My hand touched yours, and everything else . . . just . . . stopped. That's never happened before. It's not even possible."

Claire gave him a look. "You walk through walls, Nix. When we fade, we can fly. *Impossible* lost most of its credibility a while back."

Claire wanted impossible. She wanted to let go. She wanted to bring Nix back to her in a world where condition one did not exist. And for once in her life, what Claire Ryan wanted, she was darn well going to get.

Eyes on his, she sank back to the ground. "Let's do it again."

14

She's better at this than she should be. Nix couldn't shake the thought. It had taken him years to learn how to fade on cue—years of waking up underground or underwater or with a knife at his chin. Fading took power. It took concentration. But for Claire, it was easy.

With Claire, it was easy. Fading, stopping time whenever his faded hands touched hers—it was as natural to Nix as inhaling and pushing the air back out of his lungs. Before, when he'd thought Claire was a Null, he'd brought her into his fade—but now she didn't need him, and Nix was beginning to process the fact that there were things The Society hadn't taught him.

Things about what it meant to be a Nobody—and what happened when there was more than one.

"They never told you, did they?" Claire's voice sounded different in the material world now that the two of them had spent an afternoon flowing in and out of the fade. "The people you worked for never told you that there were other Nobodies. They never told you it would be like this."

This, as in the boost to his powers, the ease with which the two of them could fade when they were together? Or *this*, as in the way that looking at her made him feel? Like each cell in his body was electric and alive.

Like she was carving out his heart.

"I was fourteen the first time I killed." He said those words to push her away. To punish himself for letting her get as close as she was now. "Before that, there was another Nobody. I never met him. Never saw him. Didn't even know his name. So, no, Claire, The Society never told me that *this* would happen."

"What did they tell you?"

He swallowed, hard. He thought of the folders back in the cabin. The things he'd promised to show her.

"Come with me," he said. "And you'll see."

<hr />

The folders felt heavy in Claire's hands. Back in town, her demand had seemed so simple: if Nix was investigating the people who wanted her dead, she had a right to help. But an afternoon of fading had dulled her anger—at him, at the situation, at the things she'd discovered about herself. What Nix had taught her how to do—it was beautiful. It filled the lonely, hollow places inside of her—and now she was holding Nix's past, his secrets, his dark and twisted, empty places in her hand.

"Open it," he told her.

She didn't want to, but she did. She sat on the floor of the cabin and set the folders in front of her. She opened the file on the top, and dull eyes stared back at her: a man, in his early twenties. He was handsome enough, but there was something chilling about the way he stared at the camera. Claire fumbled with the pages in the folder and flipped to the next one.

Another picture of the same man. He was naked, lying in a bathtub. His skin was charred.

"One," Nix said. "My first. Richard—one of the Sensors—he drove me there, dropped me off three blocks away. He told me that I was a killer, that no matter what I did, someone was going to die that night, and the only choice I had was whether it was the monster or the girl."

Claire didn't want to ask—but she did. "What girl?"

Nix closed his eyes. "The girl he had chained in the basement. She was wearing a metal collar, and she was so dirty, you couldn't see her skin." Nix's eyes jumped beneath their lids. Claire opened her mouth to tell him that he didn't have to do this, but it was too late.

There was no stopping him now.

"I went upstairs, and the man who was keeping her in that filthy cage like some kind of animal—he was in the bathtub, listening to the radio. Classical music. He was clean, and he was smiling. He never heard me coming." Nix opened his eyes. "I dropped the radio into the tub."

Claire's gaze was drawn back to the picture: the welts on the man's skin, his empty eyes. After a long moment, she set the folder aside and opened the next one.

"Two," Nix preempted. "Shot through the temple. I would have gone with poison, but she'd set up a cult of sorts, and her followers were worshipping her like she was a god. If she'd had any idea she was going to die, she would have taken them with her, children and all."

Claire thought back to what he'd told her in the forest. He was fourteen when this started. Younger than she was now. She glanced up at him. His entire body was tense, like a rubber band stretched too tight.

"Tell me about the fade." Claire knew instinctually that this was the one thing she could ask to diffuse the tension. Things were different in the fade.

"Fading isn't magic, Claire. It's not some fairy tale. It's just a physical expression of a metaphysical deficiency."

"No," Claire said firmly. "It's not. Whatever The Society told you, whatever they taught you—how would they

155

know? How could they ever understand what fading is like?"

For a second, Nix looked like he might agree with her—but he didn't.

"The Society studies energy, Claire. Once upon a time, they called it alchemy. Now they just call it science. The Sensors, the scientists, the people who trained me—they never sat down and explained fading to me. They beat it into my head." Nix paused. "Every action has an equal and opposite reaction."

Without warning, he strode toward the far end of the cabin. He stopped near the wall and held his hand an inch from its surface. "I'm not touching the wall, and it's not touching me," he said, and then he moved his hand forward, pressing it gently to the wall. "Now I am touching the wall, and it's touching me."

Nix leaned against the wall, putting all of his weight behind the motion. The muscles in his arm tensed, and Claire could see him—dumping a radio into a monster's tub, setting his sights on a cult leader and pulling the trigger.

"The harder I push, the harder the wall pushes back, but when I stop"—he righted his body—"the wall stops pushing back. The wall is static—it doesn't move. Unless I push on it, it can't push on me. When I push against it, it pushes back against me with exactly as much force as I applied. If I push lightly, it pushes lightly. If I push harder, it pushes harder."

Claire thought suddenly that, in another lifetime, the two of them could have been having this exchange over a physics textbook while they studied for the big test. Normal girl. Normal boy. Happily ever after.

"When Nobodies fade, we can't touch anything. We can't affect it. We can't push. And when we can't push—"

"The wall can't push back," Claire finished for him. If she'd meant to distract him, she'd achieved her goal—but he didn't stay distracted for long.

"There are nine more folders."

Claire picked up the next folder. She'd forced him to deal her in. She'd said she could do this. And now she had to—for him.

"Number Three," she said, opening the third file. This time, Nix didn't say a word. He let her read the file for herself. The man's name was Warren Wyler. He'd been poisoned in his own bedroom in Washington, D.C. The file didn't enumerate Wyler's sins, but it did tell her his occupation.

"You killed a U.S. senator?" she asked.

Nix glanced down at the file. "No," he said. "I killed two U.S. senators. Three and Eleven. Nulls and the government are a bad mix. They can make people do things. Make them believe things. Give them genocide, call it ice cream."

Claire thought of Hitler. Of Stalin and Napoleon and atrocities committed across the world. If The Society's goal was to keep monsters from power, it didn't exactly have a history of doing a bang-up job.

Four. Five. Six.

Claire went through the next three files without comment. When she opened the seventh, she was completely unprepared. "Jacob Madsen," she said, but that was as far as she got, because The Society had stocked this file with crime scene photos.

Unlike many of the others, there was no question that Madsen had been murdered. Sliced and stabbed and skinned like an animal.

At her silence, Nix came to stand behind her. He caught sight of the picture. And then he snapped.

———◆•◆•×•◆•◆———

Nix can't see anything but the blood. Can't smell anything but the blood. It's on the walls and the floor and his hands.

Oh, God.

He has to get out of here. Has to fade. The part of his brain that's screaming has to be cut off, silenced. He lets himself go numb. He stops caring, stops thinking, stops remembering—

The feel of the knife in his hand.

The icy blue tones of Ione's office.

Make it messy, she'd said.

Make it messy.

So he had.

Nix came out of it, his hand gripping the back of the futon so tightly that the wood had cracked. There were blisters on his fingertips. He sank to the floor. Within seconds, he remembered that he wasn't alone. Claire was there, beside him. She didn't reach for him, didn't touch him.

He didn't want her to.

He didn't have the strength to fight her.

"Shhh. Shhh." She shushed him like he was a baby, and Nix realized he was making a broken, mewling sound. "You're okay. You're okay, Nix. I'm here. I'm right here."

She'd seen the pictures. Didn't she understand? What he was? What he'd done?

"Finish it," he whispered. Once she saw it all, once the truth sank in—Ione was right. For all that he and Claire had in common, there was a chasm between them filled with bodies and blood. She wouldn't understand. She *couldn't.*

"I don't need to see the rest to see what this so-called Society did to you."

"I want you to finish it," he said.

Slowly, reluctantly, she left him. She read through the rest of the files. And then she started sorting them into piles on the floor.

"What are you doing?"

She looked up from the floor. "I'm looking for a pattern.

I was supposed to be your next kill. You said that The Society has two purposes: studying energy and killing Nulls. But I'm not a Null, and they didn't try to study me."

When he'd grabbed the folders, he'd hoped there might be a pattern, but it made no sense that after seeing what was in those folders, Claire wasn't running for the door. He came closer to her, and she didn't flinch.

She'll never love you. You are what you are.

"This stack's political," Claire said. "This stack has mob connections. This one is media—and miscellaneous."

This wasn't what was supposed to happen. He was supposed to show her the files, and she was supposed to run.

"This isn't a story, Claire. This isn't a game."

Vulnerability flashed across her face, then disappeared under steely resolve. "I know that."

"You're not ready for this." What he really meant was something along the lines of *I don't want you to be ready for this, ever*—but the less she knew about what he wanted, the better.

"You shouldn't have to do this alone."

Her words undid him, but he couldn't crumble, couldn't let her follow him any farther down this path.

I kill. I'm a killer. I will kill again.

Even after everything she'd seen, she didn't believe that. It wasn't real to her, the way it was to him. The people in these folders were just names on paper, pictures printed with ink.

"Stand up," he said.

After a long moment, she obeyed. He had to do this. He had to show her. He had to make it real.

"Time to put what you learned about fading this afternoon into action," he said. "We're going on a little trip."

"Where are we going?"

Nix prepared to fade. "We're going to see number Eleven."

15

Middle of the middle. Generic. Nothing.

Sweet, sweet nothing.

Claire concentrated on that feeling—not what Nix had said before they faded. The cabin and the forest were long gone. The real world, already gray and muted in her eyes, fell away beneath her feet, small and unimportant. There was no wind to brush against her face, but her skin felt cool. It was like every flying dream she'd ever had, only better.

She didn't look down.

"Almost there." Nix's voice was strong, powerful, primal. Faded, Claire reveled in it, ignored the meaning behind his words. Beside her, Nix slowed, and though a part of Claire—the wild part, the hungry one—wanted to blur past him, she didn't. She let the real world, ugly and solid and unimportant as it was, come slowly into focus, enough to realize that they weren't in Kansas anymore.

How many miles had they traveled? How far had they come? She shook off the questions. The real world was waiting to pull her back, back to memories and words exchanged. Back to the memory of those folders and the people Nix had killed.

"Your pupils are dilated." Nix's voice was all around her. She shivered with the sound of it. Suddenly, the two of them were standing very close together. Faded, Claire could do things, say things, take what she wanted.

No rejection.

No fear.

The moment they touched, the fade exploded outward from their bodies, the world around them going instantly and unnaturally still.

"Oh." The sound Nix made as her skin met his was halfway between a hum and hallelujah. Gone was the darkness in his eyes. Gone was the way he kept pushing her—back, back, back. He brought his hands up, fanned his fingers out on either side of her face.

Nix and Claire and nothing.

That was when Claire realized they were standing

in a cemetery. It shouldn't have mattered. Nothing did, but the second she caught the name on the closest tombstone, Claire's brain switched back on.

Evan Sykes.

Eleven.

Even though Claire didn't care about the real world, even though she wasn't a part of it, even though the fade was her world now—

She couldn't help reading the words on the tombstone.

BELOVED HUSBAND. LOVING FATHER. CIVIL SERVANT.

Water park for dogs.

Ultimately, that was the thought that did it, because faded Claire didn't care about the gravestone or the words, but real Claire remembered seeing the news. She remembered thinking that the world moved on so fast, and then she thought of her parents, moving on without her. She wondered if they'd get her a tombstone if she never came back.

Wondered if they'd even noticed she was gone.

Reality was a crushing weight against Claire's chest. For a moment, when she lost her fade, she couldn't breathe.

"Claire?" Nix lost his fade on the heels of hers. Realizing that his hands were still on her face, he made a choking sound in the back of his throat and pried them away. His eyes went to the tombstone. Claire's stomach sank.

This was why Nix had brought her here.

Monster, an unnatural *knowing* said from the pit of her bowels. Nix wanted her to think he was a monster. Because by some definitions—most of them, probably—he was.

"Evan Sykes." Claire said the name out loud, like that would make the man less dead. Like it would change the fact that even if The Society had pulled the trigger, Nix had willingly played gun.

"Senator Evan Sykes," Nix echoed. "A man with an underage girlfriend, a serious drug problem, and the most melodic voice on the Senate floor." Nix paused, but Claire couldn't bring herself to say a word. "I saw her. The girl he was dating. She was younger than you. Completely in love with him, as was his wife. His own daughter spent most of her nights sleeping over at other people's houses. I try not to wonder why."

"He was a Null." Claire finally found her voice. Before she'd looked at Nix's files, the word hadn't meant anything to her. She'd never thought a person could be evil, really evil, deep down inside. But now she'd seen first-hand evidence of what some of Nix's targets had done. If Nulls really were soulless, if they didn't care about other people, if they were just born like that and couldn't help it—

"This is real, Claire." Nix said the words gently, but Claire felt her temper flare up. She was sick of him acting like she didn't know that.

"Maybe we should go someplace private to talk?" she suggested tersely. Nix arched an eyebrow at her, and she realized the obvious: even without fading, she and Nix were so very unnoticeable that they didn't have to worry about things like eavesdroppers, even when Nix was practically confessing to murder at a public figure's tombstone.

"It can't be a coincidence."

Nix eyed her warily. "What can't be a coincidence?"

"The fact that he's a senator." Claire had divided Nix's kills into piles—and Sykes hadn't been the only senator.

"I told you. Plenty of Nulls go into politics. They're good at it. Too good." Nix looked down, his dark hair falling to obscure his eyes from her view.

"But Evan Sykes was—" Claire checked the tombstone. "He was almost fifty. How long had he been in politics? And why did The Society decide he had to die now?"

"He must have slipped past our earlier screening measures."

Claire realized with a start that Nix had said *our*. This was the boy who The Society had raised. This was the killer who had bathed in Seven's blood—but he was also the boy who had saved her. Kissed her. Taught her to fade.

She couldn't just give up on him. She couldn't walk away.

"This is what I am, Claire. This is what I do. This is why when I say it's over, you run. You run, you hide, and you get the hell away from me."

Claire walked toward him and then past him. "Come on."

Nix hesitated, and for a moment, she thought he'd let her walk away without batting an eye. Like fingernails on a chalkboard, the rejection grated. But then, in an instant, he was beside her, his long stride easily overtaking hers.

"Where are we going?"

Claire met his gaze and stuck to short answers. "The library."

The library? He'd taken her to the good senator's grave to scare some sense into her, to force her to see what he and The Society were capable of doing, and now she wanted to go to the *library*?

For a few seconds there, Nix had actually thought that he'd succeeded. He'd seen it in the rings of her hazel eyes, the way her gaze lingered on the grave of the man he'd put down like a rabid dog.

And now they were going to the library.

"We're going to find out more about the senator. You see, there's this thing called the internet."

Sarcasm. Claire is being sarcastic.

"I know what the internet is," Nix replied tautly. "I've killed people who use it."

Ten had been an up-and-coming technology mogul who dabbled in human trafficking on the side.

"You mean you've never gone online yourself?" From the expression on Claire's face, you would have thought he'd announced that he never bathed.

"I live in an eight by eight room with no windows and a door that's padlocked for show. What do you think?" He didn't realize until he'd said the words out loud that she wouldn't have had any way of knowing that. He hadn't told her.

"You don't live there anymore." The quiet vehemence in Claire's voice knocked the breath from Nix's chest. "And out here in the real world, when you need answers, we have this wonderful thing called Google."

"And this Google lives in libraries?"

Nobodies don't ask questions.

He hadn't meant to. He'd trained himself—not to wonder. Not to think. To breathe in and out and let the entire world bleed out through his skin.

Nobodies don't ask questions.

But Nix had, and Claire answered it.

"Google's a search engine. Libraries have computers, and most of them have free internet. Sykes was a senator—there will be news articles."

Nix didn't reply. A Nobody's education tended more toward Mach 7s and arsenic than computer how-to's. They'd only taught him to read so that they wouldn't have to bother giving him his orders in person.

So they could slip them under his door.

Name. Date. Place.

"Do you even know where the closest library is?" he asked sharply, pushing away that thought, the memories.

Claire paused. Flushed. And then pink lips tilted upward in a bewitching, beseeching grin.

"No?"

He didn't either. The only thing he knew about this city was that Evan Sykes had died three streets over. Heart attack—or so they said.

"We'll have to ask someone." Claire scrunched her mouth into a skinny O. "I *hate* asking people."

Nobodies don't ask questions.

But Claire didn't know that. She'd probably asked hundreds. Maybe she'd even gotten some answers. Probably not a lot. That was probably why she hated it. But she'd asked them anyway.

Nobodies don't cry.

Nix wasn't sure why he wanted to. For Claire—asking and asking, again and again—or for himself. Because he couldn't. Couldn't go up to a stranger, the way she was doing now. Couldn't look them in the eye. Couldn't be around Normals without feeling like he should have tried harder the day he'd tried to slit his own throat.

"Excuse me, ma'am? Errr . . . sir? I'm sorry to bother you, but—" On the fourth try, Claire finally got someone to stop. Her voice went up at least a decibel or two in the process.

"Oh, you don't know? Okay, well ... excuse me? Could you maybe ..."

Five more tries. Six.

By the time she came stomping back toward him, Nix had gotten over his shock at watching her march up to total strangers. Ask them questions. Blush and bite her lips when they ignored her. Press on.

"I *hate* asking questions."

But she did it. Knowing that they'd probably ignore her. Feeling smaller and smaller each time. For him.

Brave. Claire is brave.

The realization surprised Nix. Claire was innocent. Claire was sweet. Claire was stubborn and funny and irresistible and Claire.

Brave was a problem.

"The closest library's a few miles away," she said, reporting back. "If I tell you where it is, can you get us there in the fade?" Even talking about fading changed Claire, brought something otherworldly to her eyes. "I can't think when I'm faded. I just ... I lose it, you know?"

"I know," Nix replied. To find something after you faded, your body had to want it. You had to be single-minded, because when the real world slipped away, conscious thoughts went with it. All that remained was the id: wants, needs, *desires*.

"We should just walk." He could have found the library from the fade. They could have slipped out of the here and now, been there in a heartbeat, no worse for the wear. But it didn't seem wise, because right now Nix's id wanted nothing more than to touch Claire.

To be with Claire.

Beautiful, brave, irresistible Claire.

"It'll be dark by the time we get there," she objected.

"Good." Nix glanced over his shoulder. Anonymity wasn't an excuse for sloppiness. The Society had found Claire once. All odds to the contrary, they could do it again. "We probably shouldn't have gone out during the day anyway."

Nix knew nothing about libraries, or the internet, or what it felt like to talk to strangers, but he knew this much: nighttime was Nobody time. The real monsters came out with the sun.

◆◆◆◆◆

By the time they got to the library, it was closed, and Claire felt a familiar pang of disappointment in the pit of her gut before she realized it didn't matter. The ice cream truck always left just before she got there. Play auditions closed while she was sitting there, waiting for her turn. Absentminded teachers were always losing the field-trip permission forms she'd painstakingly forged. But what did it matter if the library was closed? If the doors were locked?

This time, she didn't ask Nix if they should fade. He'd been quiet on the walk over, more so than usual, and Claire was getting tired of feeling his stare, not knowing what it meant.

I don't matter. Middle of the middle. Left behind. Nuisance.

Once upon a time, those words would have hurt.

No one notices. No one cares. When I ask questions, I have to beg for the answers.

She felt the real world rolling off her body, like water. No, oil. Thick and greasy, numbing, it slipped from her veins and her skin and her brain until all that was left was the deepest kind of ache.

Nothing.

She didn't wait to see if Nix would follow her. He might back away from her in the real world. He might look at her like she'd done something wrong, just because it had taken her ten minutes to get someone to point them toward the library. He might expect her to turn tail and run away when things got hard.

But down beneath skin and bones and the things they'd done and hadn't, the two of them were the same. Fading stripped off all the other layers, and like a beacon, she called to him.

I'm like you.

Reality broke around his body, crumbled, as his face began to glow. Claire felt the earth give the moment he crossed over.

The moment he took her hand.

There were people on the street. Not many, this late at night, but some, and as Claire's faded skin brushed Nix's, the world shuddered. The street and the people and the flickering streetlamps froze like a photo, snapped an instant too soon.

"Time stops for us." She said the words like they were music. "Let's run."

Nix shook his head. The movement hypnotized Claire, and it took her a moment to decode its meaning as something other than his dance to her song. He led. She followed—through locked doors, through walls, through shelves and shelves of books that another Claire would have loved to read.

I'm here for a reason.

Her brain was slow in catching up to her body, but somehow, that thought made its way to her like breath bubbling at the top of a pool.

Concentrate.

Thinking about the real world would have forced her to return to it. But thinking, in the abstract, about the kinds of things that she might have thought about if she were real—

Why? Why would I want to? Why are we here?

"Library," Nix reminded her.

It was one of those words. The real words. The heavy ones. The ones that made her think about things on the other side of the veil. Books. And people. And asking over and over again to find out where the closest library was.

No. I don't want to lose it. I don't want to let go. Can't.

But she could and she did, and when Nix joined her a moment later, she recognized a glint in his eye as something akin to laughter.

"You did that on purpose."

"If you want to stay faded, you can't think about anything else," he said. "And if you're going to use this so-called internet, you can't do it with hands that pass through solid objects."

Claire nodded—but she had to ask. "Didn't you want to stay there? Even just a little?"

Nix didn't miss a beat. "Every time."

One second, they were all-powerful, immaterial, and too good for the real world, and the next, they were two kids in the library after hours. Claire glanced out the window at the street below. People were moving. Lights were flickering.

"Internet?" Nix put the emphasis on the last syllable instead of the first, like it wasn't a word he was used to saying. Trying not to think about the life he'd lived—*eight by eight room, no windows, trained to kill*—Claire sat down in front of one of the computers and tested her fingers out against the keys. Solid, she could type.

Senator Evan Sykes

Within five minutes of hitting search, Claire had added three more terms to her search list.

Iowa. The good senator's home state.

Congressional Subcommittee on Domestic Defense. His most recent appointment.

Proposition 42. His claim to fame.

Nix read over her shoulder, looming like a shadow. But for once, Claire didn't find her counterpart's presence distracting. She was too entrenched in Evan Sykes's story, which was becoming clearer and clearer, the more she read.

Lucked his way into a state senate seat at the age of twenty-five. Never brought a single motion to the floor. Tried and failed three times to make the House of Representatives.

And then, almost overnight, the senator's luck had changed.

The previous junior senator from Iowa, dead of a heart attack.

The governor called upon to name a replacement.

Likelier candidates defamed. Scandals.

And suddenly, Evan Sykes was the golden boy. He'd inherited an almost full term. Claire couldn't make any sense of his voting patterns, couldn't see anything nefarious about his pet projects. He was bland. Uninteresting.

And on the Congressional Subcommittee on Domestic Defense, advising Homeland Security.

Exactly where someone wanted him.

"You're going too fast."

Claire barely heard Nix's complaint. If he'd been anyone else, his words would have been consumed by the

175

vortex of information bounding and rebounding around in her head. But since he was Nix, she heard him.

Barely.

"I'm what?"

"I. Can't. Read. That. Fast." The words cost him—enough that Claire thought to wonder how he'd learned to read at all, living in one room, raised by people who saw him only as a weapon.

"You know what? It doesn't matter. Just go ahead. Do whatever. It doesn't matter."

Claire was smart enough to know that the only time anyone said something didn't matter twice was when it really, really did. So she slowed down. Took a step back. And let him read.

Slowly.

Painstakingly.

And her mind kept going at thirty thousand miles an hour: making connections, drawing conclusions, and coming back to the same question, over and over again.

"He lost three elections." Nix said the words slowly, like saying them fast would make them less true. "He lost three elections?"

The second time, it was a question, and she answered it.

"Yes. And then he got lucky. He couldn't have engineered things better if he tried."

"That's because he didn't engineer it."

Claire took Nix's words as confirmation that he had

reached the same conclusion she had. *Sykes didn't engi-neer his appointment to the Senate. The Society did.*

"Sykes didn't make this happen. I did."

It took Claire a moment to realize what Nix was really saying, to look for the name of the junior senator whose heart attack had opened up a seat in the Senate for Sykes.

Warren Wyler.

Number Three.

Claire thought of the folders, the pictures. Nix hunched, his body shuddering. Claire tentatively ran her hand up his back, letting it come to rest on the nape of his neck.

He didn't tell her to stop.

She wasn't even sure he felt it.

"I thought Wyler was a Null. Ione said, the Sensors said—"

Nix cut off, and Claire couldn't think of a single thing that she could say that wouldn't make things worse. What were the chances that two Nulls had filled the exact same Senate seat? Not nearly as good as the chances that The Society had put Evan Sykes in the Senate—and two years later, taken him out.

Somebody had discredited all of Sykes's opponents. *Somebody* had seen to it that a seat had opened up in the Senate. *Somebody* was the special interest group that funded large portions of Sykes's campaign.

"But Sykes—he was a Null. I know he was. I saw him. I saw him, with the girls. And I heard him. I watched tapes, and when he talked, you had to listen. That's not natural. It's—" Nix broke off, and for the first time, Claire wondered how old he was.

Right now he looked heartbroken and twelve.

"Why would The Society have me kill Wyler to put a Null in the Senate? It doesn't make any sense. We protect the Normals from the Nulls. That's what The Society does. It's what *I* do."

"You didn't know." Claire brought her free hand up to his good shoulder, running it down and over his arm even as she kept the other cool and steady on the back of his neck. "It's okay, Nix."

That should have felt like a lie, but it didn't, because when Claire needed to, she could make herself believe anything. She could believe that things were going to get better. She could believe that if she just tried harder, people would notice. She could believe that Nix would be okay, because she wouldn't let him not.

"You shouldn't touch me." His words were soft, quiet, defeated.

She brought her head to rest against his back. "Yes, I should."

He said nothing in reply.

"You didn't know," she tried again.

Silence.

"They're the ones who did this. Not you."

"I'm the one who slipped the poison into his veins. Just

like I slipped the poison into Sykes's. Just like I almost put a bullet in your heart." He shuddered, one more time, and then pulled away from her. "Get away from me. You need to get away from me, Claire."

"Stop telling me what I need."

"I'll stop telling you what to do when you figure out life isn't fairy tales and forever. Condition two, Claire. I say when this is over. You run and hide."

She didn't let him finish that thought. "It's not over yet."

"We wanted to find out who was corrupt. I think this is pretty good evidence for The Society as a whole—or at least, all of the people in charge."

"You don't kill people based on pretty good evidence."

Nix snorted. "Apparently, I do. I killed Wyler because Ione told me to. I saw what my first two targets were like, I saw what they'd done, and so when they sent me after number Three, I assumed that he was a monster, too. They didn't tell me that his crime was standing in the way of their plans. I didn't even know they *had* plans. I did this. I killed him, and he wasn't a Null."

Claire balled her hand into a fist and smacked it into his side. "Senator Wyler wasn't your fault. Sykes wasn't your fault. You never even had a chance, Nix. But you have a chance now, and if you kill the people behind this—"

"Ione told me to kill you," Nix said simply. "She tried to kill me. She gave the order to kill Wyler. She gave the order to kill Sykes."

"Don't you want to know why?" Claire asked, stalling for time. She couldn't let him leave the library, not like this.

"I don't need to know why."

"The Society put Evan Sykes in the Senate. Don't you want to know what he was doing there?"

"No."

Claire wracked her mind for a question that would spark his interest. Hold him here. Keep him from running off. Getting himself killed. Killing somebody else.

"Don't you want to know . . ."

He opened his mouth to interrupt her, but she managed to squeeze the magic words out, just in time.

"Don't you want to know why Sykes lost his first three elections?"

The words took a moment to register. Nix was already denying interest when they sank in. When he realized the implications.

When the plot thickened.

Claire stepped toward him. He stepped back. She laid her ace on the table. "You asked why The Society would put a Null in the Senate. The real question is, if Sykes were a Null, if he had the kind of energy that made him unnaturally good at manipulating other people—why couldn't he get there himself?"

16

Nix tried to concentrate on Claire's question. On Evan Sykes. But his brain went somewhere else.

Nix is standing in the corner of his target's bedroom, an empty syringe in his hand. He was supposed to leave as soon as he made the injection, but he didn't. He stayed. Now he's watching from the fade. Waiting. Anticipating.

His target's name is Warren Wyler. Looking at him, you'd never know he was a Null. As Nix watches, Wyler calls his wife on the phone. He tells her he loves her. Nix wonders what this Null keeps chained up in his basement. How many people he's killed. What he does when he's not alone in his D.C. residence, flipping channels on the TV.

Finally, without warning, Wyler gasps. Collapses. His

head lolls to one side. His fingers twitch. Eyes roll back in his head. A sickly sour smell fills the room. From the shadows, Nix watches. He watches the man stop breathing, watches the fingers stop twitching, watches—and smiles.

The worst thing about the memory wasn't the fact that Nix could recognize, in retrospect, that Wyler—like Claire—hadn't been a Null. The worst part was the fact that he had stayed to watch. Nix had killed an innocent man, and he'd smiled.

Wyler wasn't a Null. He was just a politician.

Normals probably couldn't tell the difference, but Sensors could. And that meant they'd sent him after Wyler *knowing* he wasn't a Null. So that Sykes could inherit his seat in the Senate.

"Sykes was a Null. I could practically smell it on him." Nix paused. Why would The Society want a Null in the Senate? And more importantly, why would a Null need The Society's help?

Nulls were charismatic, magnetic, easy to like, and hard to forget. They were very good at getting what they wanted.

"Maybe he was a Null," Claire said slowly, "but he just wasn't very good at it."

Nix had to remind himself that she was new at this. That twenty-four hours earlier, she'd known nothing about energy or Nobodies or Nulls.

"Being a Null isn't the kind of thing you have to practice, Claire. People just care about you. They're the puppets. You're the puppeteer."

"You're teaching me how to be a good Nobody. If fading takes practice and concentration, why doesn't being a Null?"

Nix didn't want to think about Nulls. He couldn't think of anything but Senator Wyler lying dead on his bed. "So, what?" he asked tersely. "The Society taught Evan Sykes how to use his powers? Why would they do something like that?"

Claire's eyes flitted back to the computer screen. "I don't know, but I'm guessing it might have something to do with Proposition 42."

Proposition 42? Nix didn't want to ask her what that was. She'd read about it, obviously, and if he hadn't been so slow, he probably would have, too.

If he'd been quicker on the uptake, it wouldn't have taken meeting Claire to realize that something was very wrong inside the institute's walls. There were so many things he didn't know about The Society. So much they hadn't bothered to teach him. So much he hadn't asked.

He watches Senator Wyler stop breathing, watches his fingers stop twitching, watches—

"You know what? I've got this, Claire. I don't need your help. I don't need you. What I need is for you to get out of

183

the way and let me read all of that garbage you pulled up on the computer."

She jerked away from him and stumbled backward, doing a good impression of someone who'd taken a knife to the gut.

Claire asking and asking and hoping for answers, trying not to care when people walk right by.

He hadn't meant to make her look like that.

"Sorry." It wasn't a word he'd said before. Ever. But Claire had said it plenty, and Nix knew, in an abstract way, that it was supposed to make things better.

Didn't, though.

"Don't be."

"Fine."

"Fine." She wrapped her arms around her waist, nursing her wounds. "You can use the mouse to click from one window to another. If you want to know more about Proposition 42, type those words into that little box there." She nodded with her head, but since he couldn't bring himself to meet her eyes, he didn't follow.

"I'll just go . . . books."

And then she was gone, disappearing into the nearby stacks like a rabbit taking to its hole, and he was left with a computer he didn't know how to use, words he could barely read, and the knowledge that he wasn't just a killer.

Most of the time, he was a pretty poor excuse for a person, too.

Situation: What if you'd been raised from the crib to be an assassin? What if the people who'd trained you had brainwashed you into believing that everyone you killed deserved to die?

What if you found out they lied?

Claire knew, logically, that was the kind of thing that would mess with a person's head.

They told him he was killing monsters, and then they made him kill people. He thought it was just me who was different, and he didn't go through with killing me. He thought there was a chance that it wasn't too late. That everyone he'd killed really had been a dangerous Null. That he really was a hero, working in the shadows to make the world a better place for people who'd never even looked his way. That he wasn't just an unimportant little boy raised like an animal and let out of the cage only when The Society wanted someone dead.

He wanted to believe that, and he just found out he was wrong.

Claire could see this from Nix's perspective. Her heart broke for him, but no matter how deeply she imagined herself in his position, no matter how much she understood rationally that her imagination wasn't doing his torment justice, she couldn't shake the tiny voice in the back of her own brain.

He doesn't want me. He told me to go away.

Claire hated herself for thinking like that—like everything was about her. Like the fact that she felt crappy and small and like he'd thrown her away held even the tiniest candle to what he was going through. She knew rationally that he'd weathered a big blow, that he needed some time to himself.

She just wanted him to need *her.*

And that was stupid and selfish and idiotically idealistic. Almost as bad as the fact that when she'd seen him breaking, sensed the fault line running straight through his psyche shift with each revelation—part of her was relieved.

Because that meant Nix wasn't a monster.

He was scared. And lost. And lonely. And he hated himself.

Without meaning to, Claire headed straight for the children's section of the library. The building was dark. She could barely see without the light from the computer's screen, and she kept bumping into stuff, but kids' sections had a vibe about them, and she found it before the first tear splashed out of her eye and onto her cheek.

Then she went a little nuts.

It started with *Up a Road Slowly.* Then *The Westing Game. Number the Stars. Rilla of Ingleside* and *Rainbow Valley.* She picked up *Shiloh*, then put it back, because she couldn't take a book about a dead dog right now.

And *Black Beauty* and *Beauty*—she couldn't read those either.

She should have outgrown these books.

She should have been in the adult section, or at least up in teen.

But she wasn't.

Little Women. The Secret Garden. And, oh—*The Little Prince.*

Feeling like she really was just seven or eight, Claire sat down on the floor, books all around her, and she opened the last one she'd picked up. Even though it was dark, and even though her eyes couldn't see the words, she knew them.

Knew the little prince's story as well as her own.

She closed her eyes. She leaned her head forward against the book. And she sobbed.

———————✦✧✦———————

Proposition 42 was wordy and long and Nix was sure that Claire would have been able to find a shorter explanation of it. With the mouse. And the box she'd told him to type into. And Google, which sent chills of terror down his spine.

I'm out of my element. I'm not good at this.

Of course, thinking that led him to thinking about the things he was good at. His perfect aim. His ability to move quickly, quietly. To follow directions. To do whatever it was that had to be done, no matter the cost.

Murderer.

The real irony was that he'd hated Claire when he thought she was a Null, because he'd assumed that she didn't have a conscience. That she killed other people like they didn't even matter. And all along, he was the monster, no better than a dirty, rotten Null. Worse, maybe, because he hadn't been born without empathy.

He'd just taught himself not to feel it for the people The Society said had to die.

"Proposition 42." Nix tried to force himself to focus. He willed the letters to stop blending together. He sounded out the words. Slowly, painstakingly, he worked his way through the vast amounts of information on the screen. He tried to make sense of it.

And the entire time, all he could think about was the look on Claire's face. She knew he'd killed Wyler. She'd held him. Told him it wasn't his fault. Looked at him like they were the same, as if she were trying to think of a way to leach away some of his pain and feel it herself.

And he'd sent her away. Not for her own good. Not to protect her.

Because he couldn't take feeling evil and stupid, too.

Proposition 42. Nix concentrated and, bit by bit, he read. An hour later, he had answers. Questions, too.

"Proposition 42 was pitched as the common man's

protection from the Patriot Act." Nix summarized what he'd read, hoping it would make more sense out loud. "It gave a designated congressional subcommittee oversight of a variety of shadow organizations that would otherwise report only to higher-ups within the FBI and CIA. Sykes, not surprisingly, positioned himself as the head of that committee, and if he hadn't pushed to delay voting on the proposition, it probably would have passed."

After Sykes died, Proposition 42 had never even made it out of committee. Nix took that to mean that The Society must have *really* wanted Sykes dead, because they'd been willing to make sacrifices to see it done. Nix may have been ignorant. He may have been gullible and stupid and slow, but even he could see that Proposition 42 had never been about protecting the common man.

It had been about protecting The Society.

With its pet senator positioned at the head of the oversight subcommittee, The Society would have been in perfect position to derail any potential investigations into its activities. Maybe the higher-ups had a bigger plan—government funding for their research? World domination?—who knew?

Nix had never thought about it—the fact that The Society might have to work to stay secret, the fact that the people who called the shots might have something more to hide than killing Nulls. A week ago, Nix would have sworn that he knew every inch of the institute, every purpose The Society worked toward, every tragedy they hoped to avoid. But now Nix had to admit that he'd missed things. That Ione and her little foot soldiers had managed to keep their secrets, even when they hadn't known he was standing in the shadows, listening to them speak.

"Did you find out what you needed to know?" Claire's voice was tentative and hoarse. Nix wanted to go to her. He wanted to tell her that he'd never meant to take any of this out on her. He wanted to apologize again, but knew it wouldn't help.

"I found what I needed to know. You could have found it faster." The words were an admission that she wasn't just nicer than he was, or more moral, or right. She was smarter, too.

"You ready to go?" She didn't acknowledge his words. He didn't expect her to, but the puffiness around her eyes told him that they weren't enough.

He needed to make it up to her. Even if there were things he'd done that could never be made up. That meant he had to make up for the little things more.

So he told her everything he'd learned about Proposition 42. About the fact that when he'd died, Sykes had been in the process of stalling the vote—which still didn't explain why The Society wanted him dead, other than the fact that he wasn't getting the job done fast enough.

Nix watched Claire take in the information, waited for a spark of interest, and was rewarded when it flickered to life in the creases of her face. And then his eyes trailed downward, and he noticed the small mountain of books she held in her arms.

She followed his gaze, bit her bottom lip, and shrugged. "It's a library." She paused. "Books."

He moved forward to ease her load a little, but she just hugged her bounty harder. "I've got it," she said.

"You might not be ready to take objects with you to the fade," he said.

"I take my clothes with me."

That was a point he'd never considered. "We fade when we stop trying to be someone and embrace being nothing. You can take a physical object, like a shirt"—*Or a gun. Or a needle. Or knives*—"with you, if you consider that object an extension of yourself. It's easier with clothes."

He waited to see if she would surrender the books, but she didn't.

"I can imagine these books are part of my body. I can imagine anything. I'm good at that."

Nix heard the things she wasn't saying—about how she'd gotten so good at playing games in her mind, pretending the world was the way she wanted it to be instead of the way it was.

"We should go," he said, wishing she would let him help her, knowing she wouldn't. "It'll be dawn soon."

And if The Society wanted you dead before, he added silently, *I'm betting we're both pretty high on its hit list now.*

"Okay. Let's go." Claire closed her eyes. Nix listened as her breathing slowed. And then he followed her—and her fourteen pilfered library books—into the fade.

17

Faded, Claire flew. She didn't think. She didn't cast a single glance over her shoulder. She just let go and flew, back the way they'd came. Down streets. Past the cemetery. Over forest, over fields.

I am silence. I am power. I am more.

All she wanted was to go home and go to sleep.

Claire kept a muzzle on the thought, refusing to give it meaning and hanging tight to her fade.

I WANT TO GO—

She arrived back at the cabin just in time, and gave in to the rush of unspoken words in her head, letting the thought suck her body back into the physical world. The books in her arms—weightless a moment before—grew suddenly heavy, and Claire almost fell over sideways as their weight threw hers off center.

It wasn't until she'd regained her balance and crossed the threshold of the cabin door that she realized: even though her mind had been thinking *home*, her body had been thinking *here*. This cabin, the forest.

She'd lived in the same house her entire life, and after two days, this isolated cabin and the woods surrounding it felt like home. If Claire had let herself think about it, that probably would have been depressing. So she didn't think about it. Instead, she took her books and walked over to the far side of the cabin. Lined them up, just under the window. Tried to get them to stand up straight, but failed and ended up stacking them, one on top of another instead.

It wasn't the same as having a shelf, but it was better than letting them fling themselves out on the dusty cabin floor. Not wanting to turn and face Nix, she ran her fingers across the spines of the books.

Earlier that week, she'd done almost the exact same thing with other books. Except at that point, she hadn't known what she was or what it meant or why she never seemed to be good enough for anyone else. And now she knew.

Lot of good that does me.

This was why she needed to go to sleep. She wasn't doing anyone any good this way. Nix needed her. He was probably the only person in the entire world who really needed her, and she couldn't shake the sting of his sending her away.

Or maybe she just couldn't shake off the horrible feeling of helplessness that reared its head every time she looked at him.

I want to make this better for him, and he won't let me. I want to help and he doesn't want it.

She wanted to kiss him. To be with him. To take some measure of his pain into her own body. But some hurts were too big, and next to Nix's, she was nothing.

I'll sleep on it. I'll go to bed, and I'll wake up, and I'll be better.

Tomorrow, she'd know what to do. She'd come up with a plan. She'd figure out a way to convince him—

Convince him what? That it doesn't matter that The Society made him kill innocent people?

Of course it mattered. How could something like that not matter? How could anyone make something like that better?

And even if somebody could, in the abstract, how could Claire?

"I'm going to go to sleep." She forced herself to turn around and meet his eyes. "Tomorrow, we'll figure out a plan."

"A plan?"

She nodded and held his gaze. *You will let me be strong*

for you. She tried her hand at psychic persuasion, but couldn't even manage to convince herself.

Bed.

She needed to go to bed. But first, she had to say something.

"The Society wanted Proposition 42 passed. Sykes kept delaying the voting, but after they killed him, the bill went down in flames. So it stands to reason that they didn't kill him to make the bill pass."

"They killed him because he went against orders." The certainty in Nix's voice was chilling and absolute.

"They do that?"

Nix didn't answer. He didn't have to.

"Maybe that's why they wanted you to kill me."

"To test my loyalty?" Nix spat out the last word.

"I was thinking more along the lines of the fact that I couldn't take the kinds of orders they gave you."

It figured that Nix thought this was his fault and she thought it was hers. Claire guessed that maybe that was a Nobody's lot in life. She barely even noticed the tremor that passed through Nix's hands until it was too late.

He was upset about having killed people, and she'd just rubbed it in his face that when he'd told her to kill, she'd said no.

Go to bed. You'll feel better tomorrow. You'll do better tomorrow.

"I'm going to go to bed." Claire's voice was so tiny that

she could hardly hear it, but Nix didn't seem to have any trouble sorting out her words.

"I'm sorry."

He was still apologizing. For sending her away. For making her cry.

"It's okay," Claire said, willing him to believe it—and willing herself to believe it, too. "You . . . there was a lot going on today. You didn't mean it. Or maybe you did. It's okay. I'll be . . ."

I swear to God, if you say it one more time . . .

". . . okay."

He nodded, but Claire saw the indecision flicker across his face. Like he was thinking about saying something else.

"You can have the couch," she offered. The look he gave her in return was nothing short of incredulous—with a side of disgust.

"Or I could take the couch," she amended her previous statement. He nodded.

The last time they'd slept in close proximity to each other had been in the woods. On a bed of grass. Limbs so tangled that she almost couldn't tell where her body ended and his began.

"Good night, Claire."

She sighed and tried to manage a smile for him. "Good night, Nix."

Nix couldn't sleep. They'd gotten back to the cabin late. It was almost dawn now, and he still couldn't sleep.

Couldn't close his eyes without seeing a slideshow of everything he'd ever done. Every life he'd taken. Every syringe he'd emptied. Every hole he'd put in a stranger's chest.

Eleven. From the psychopath in the bathtub to Sykes, there'd been eleven.

And interspersed with every one of those images was one of Claire. Smiling in her sleep. Laughing. Crying because of things he'd said to her.

I made her cry.

In his mind, that sin bled into all of his others. She slept, and he kept watch. The way he had when he'd thought she was a Null.

Claire is curled into a ball. Claire is shifting onto one side. Claire is breathing out of her mouth.

She was sad. He'd made her sad. And maybe that was easier to think about than the other thing. The thing he'd almost done to her.

The thing he'd done to others.

Wyler.

Nix stood up. He had to move, to get away, but he couldn't leave Claire. He had to watch her. He had to keep her safe, because she was right. The Society probably hadn't put her life on the line in some kind of elaborate test of his loyalty. If they'd never sent him after her, he never would have questioned that each name they slipped under his door belonged to someone who deserved to die.

By giving him her name, they'd taken a risk. Why?

Maybe they weren't lying when they designated Code Omega. Maybe they do think she's dangerous.

Nix smiled wryly, and the motion hurt him, like his lips were going to slice straight through his face. Claire *was* dangerous, because she made him want things he wasn't supposed to want.

Because after fewer than twenty-four hours' practice, she could fade on cue and take a plethora of objects with her.

Because when the two of them touched in the fade, time literally stopped.

Because she'd never believed him about Nulls. Because even if someone was a Null, even if they were the worst kind of monster, Claire wouldn't want them dead. She wouldn't kill them without proof.

She'd ask questions, and she was good at asking the right ones.

Claire was powerful. Claire was smart. She was beautiful, and to The Society, she was a threat.

They only want the ones who don't ask questions. The ones who will kill and kill and kill and feel good about it.

Nix couldn't make himself forget the rush. The adrenaline. The pride and the nausea and the fierce, indescribable, godlike feeling of watching life flicker and fade into nothing.

I liked it.

I hated it, and I liked it, and I did it. I *did.*

Nix saw his targets' ghosts like they were standing there in front of him. Wyler and Sykes and God knows how many of the others. And then there were the bodies, the ones he'd found when he'd entered some of his marks' homes. His marks' victims, still alive and screaming for help from the basement.

And, God, he couldn't regret killing the people who'd put them there.

If they'd only ever sent me after Nulls, I'd be okay.

But they hadn't. And he wasn't. And he couldn't stop seeing Claire's face everywhere, even though the real Claire was only a few feet away. Even though he could have reached out and touched her, if he'd wanted to.

I have to do something. I have to.

Since he couldn't breathe life back into a decomposing body, Nix concentrated on the things that could be fixed.

I hurt Claire's feelings. I made her sad.

He couldn't bear to let himself touch her. Couldn't hold her. Couldn't wipe away her tears. But he could do something to make her smile, to show that sorry wasn't just a word.

Nix walked slowly over to the far side of the cabin. To the books she'd placed, just so on the floor. The ones she'd tried to line up and had settled for stacking.

It wasn't much.

It wasn't enough.

But he could do it for her.

Claire woke to the sound of quiet, muted cursing. Rolling over onto her side, she peeked out from under her blanket and saw Nix . . . speaking very vehemently to a piece of lumber. He had a knife in one hand and he was digging it into the wood, notching it, carving out a . . . what?

Claire had no idea what he was doing. As silently as she could, she propped herself up on one arm, to get a better view. This time, she saw more wood; he must have gotten it from the pile outside.

The pile under the porch, where she'd stashed his weapons two days earlier. Claire's throat tightened. Her heart jumped into it.

I guess he found the weapons.

That explained where Nix had gotten the knife, but it didn't explain what he was doing. He'd carved one end of the plank down to a cube shape, a thick tab that stuck out from the end of the board. A second, identical board sat to his left, and Nix turned his attention to a third, digging his knife in, carving a square-shaped hole.

Claire's heartbeat slowed, and the rush of adrenaline she'd felt the moment she'd seen the knife in Nix's hand began to fade. He wasn't hunting anything. He wasn't hurting anything. He was building . . . something. She wasn't sure what.

Careful not to draw his attention to herself, she lay back down, resting her head on her arms. He'd be upset if he knew that he'd woken her up, and even though she had no idea what time it was—her days and nights were completely turned around—Claire got the distinct feeling that whatever he was doing, Nix had hoped to finish it before she woke up.

I'm not supposed to be watching him.

It seemed right that she was, though. Like turnaround was fair play, because he was always watching her. And in the little motions—the turn of a knife, the appraisal of the boards' positions, the way he fit them together, sliding the tabs into the holes—Claire saw a beautiful, soothing rhythm. Like this was the closest Nix could come to dancing outside the fade.

Time passed. Nix kept working. Claire kept watching. And then he finished. He stepped back, and Claire saw a shelf. A very uneven, unsteady, three-board shelf that sat on the floor, its purpose unclear until Nix crouched back down next to it, and one by one, moved the books she'd stolen from the library into place.

A bookshelf.

He hadn't slept all night, all day. Instead, he'd stayed up and with a hunting knife and rotting old wood, he'd built her a bookshelf.

As he put the last book in place with careful, tender hands, Claire sat up on her knees, the blanket balled in her fist.

He built me a bookshelf.

She forgot to breathe. So by the time he turned around, in addition to being frozen in place, she was a little bit dizzy.

"You're supposed to be asleep," he said, putting his hands into his pockets, averting his gaze.

Claire finally remembered how to inhale. "You built me a bookshelf," she said, because those were the only words—the sum total of words that she had.

"You like books," Nix said, still not looking directly at her. "They shouldn't have to sit on the floor."

"You built me a bookshelf."

"It's not a very good one."

"But you *built me a bookshelf*—and what do you mean it's not a very good one?" Claire felt rather like someone had insulted her firstborn child. "It's perfect."

It was crooked, and the wood was rough, and the books weren't really much higher off the floor than they'd been before, *and it was perfect.*

"I didn't mean to make you cry. At the library." He brought his eyes back to meet hers, slowly, as if he was reserving the right at any point to jerk his gaze away.

"I love it."

"The crying?" Nix asked, his brow wrinkling.

"No. The bookshelf."

He knows I like books. He saw me try to stand them up. He wanted to make me happy. So he built me a bookshelf.

Now remembering to breathe wasn't as much of a challenge as forcing her tightening chest to let her do so.

In.

And out.

In.

And out.

"Thank you, Nix. No one's ever made me anything before." She should have just stuck with *you made me a bookshelf*, because no other words really seemed to do it justice.

"You're welcome. Claire."

There was something in the way he spaced the words that told her he'd debated whether or not he should say her name.

Whether or not he deserved to say it.

Beautiful, broken boy. He built me a bookshelf. He can barely bring himself to say my name.

"You look tired," she said. "You didn't sleep at all."

It wasn't a question, and he shrugged in response.

"You need to sleep." Claire couldn't chase away his ghosts. She couldn't change his past. She couldn't do any of the things she'd hoped that, after a good night's sleep, would magically just come. But she could take care of him.

Make him sleep.

Do a little something that counted big.

She slid over on the couch and gestured that he should join her. He took a step backward, and for the first time, she didn't, even subconsciously, take it as an insult. Instead, she slipped off the couch, so that he could sit down without worrying about touching her.

"I slept. Your turn."

After three seconds, or four, he acceded. Walked over to the couch. Sat down. "I don't sleep," he said, talking to himself as much as to her. "Not anymore."

Claire wondered what—or who—he saw when he closed his eyes. "You don't have to close your eyes. Just lie back."

Nix did as he was told, and Claire, still feeling like there was a land mine in her stomach, like she might explode with bookshelf joy and awe at any moment, walked over to her present. Knelt down next to it. And picked a book up off the shelf. And then she sat down across the room from Nix, a mountain of space between them, and she read.

About the little prince and a rose with thorns and a wild fox that explained to the little prince what it meant to be tamed. She kept reading, the familiar words the closest thing she could manage to a lullaby.

Nix's eyes opened wide as he realized what she was doing, and he listened raptly, as if no one had ever read him a story, as she expected no one had. And slowly, Nix's body relaxed. His eyes closed.

And he fell asleep.

18

White floors. White room. White bed.

Nix woke up calm for the first time in his life, and he wasn't sure why until he realized that he wasn't in his quarters at the institute. The bed beneath him was soft, colored, and technically a futon. Sitting on the floor beside it was a girl, curled up like a cat, reading a book.

Claire. Claire's voice. The Little Prince.

She'd read to him. The realization was sweet—so sweet that Nix couldn't berate himself for having let her.

She'd read to him.

He'd listened.

And he'd fallen asleep. No dreams. No terror. No

waking up underwater. Just . . . nothing. A different kind of nothing than the fade, peaceful to its exhilaration.

"You're awake." Claire said the words shyly, ducking her head. Nix nodded. His eyes flittered toward the shelf he'd built her. She smiled.

It was funny. He'd always thought that the best thing about being a Normal would be talking to other people, having them talk back. But not talking, that had its charms, too.

More of them, maybe, because then you didn't have to find the words. Without making a sound, Claire dog-eared the page she was reading, shut the book, and then put it back in its place, right next to the one she'd read him the night before. Then she went into the kitchen, and when she came back, she offered him a steaming mug.

Coffee.

He took it, their fingers brushing as she transferred it from her hands to his. Then she went back into the kitchen and poured herself a cup.

He drank.

She drank.

It wasn't until the dark liquid in their mugs sank well past the halfway mark that she spoke. "I don't have a plan."

That was the exact opposite of what he'd expected her to say. After the previous night, he would have followed her off the edge of a cliff if she'd asked it.

"But I do have a place."

"A place?" Nix asked, his voice—like the coffee—warm in his throat.

She nodded.

"What kind of place?"

"Sykes's place." She waited, and he realized that she was waiting for him to tell her no. He didn't, and finally, she continued. "His house. Or maybe his office. Everything else The Society has done makes sense, but killing him doesn't."

Nix narrowed his eyes, but she didn't give him a chance to interrupt.

"Everything else The Society did—it's not good and it's not moral and I'd like to take them down for it, one by one, but their motivation makes sense. If The Society wants something and there's someone standing in their way, they take care of the problem. But why would they kill their own plant in the Senate? Even if he was being difficult, even if he was having second thoughts . . ."

Nix was still stuck on the fact that Claire had said she wanted to take The Society *down*. And sounded like she meant it.

"If Sykes was just postponing the vote on Prop 42," she continued, "they wouldn't have killed him, not unless they had a backup plan. So there must have been another reason. Either he had something that they wanted, or he was going to do something that they didn't want him to do."

For a brief moment, Nix entertained a fantasy in which he and Claire really did take The Society down. All of it. In its entirety. The part he'd seen and the parts he was beginning to suspect that he hadn't.

But Claire couldn't kill, and he wouldn't ask her to. Wouldn't let her. If Sykes had something that The Society wanted, and if they could get it first ...

Nix wondered if Ione would bargain for his freedom. For Claire's.

"If Sykes knew something that The Society didn't want him to know, or if he had something worth killing over—maybe we can use it."

It was like she was reading his mind.

"For The Society to kill their own inside man, it would have to be something huge. Something that could threaten the whole operation with exposure, something that could bring the whole thing to its knees."

Understanding washed over Nix. Claire wanted to bring The Society down, but not by killing its leaders. By *exposing* them.

"It would have to be something big to make a difference," Nix said, his mind whirring with the implications. "We're Nobodies. No one's going to listen to us. No one's going to care. Unless it's something huge, they won't look twice at anything we give them either."

"But if it *is* something big ..."

Nix got a taste of the thing she was offering him, and

it warmed him more than the coffee. Hope. Revenge. A future that didn't involve doing that little four-lettered thing he did best.

Maybe, once it was over—

Maybe, if he could—

Maybe. Maybe. Maybe. The possibilities were seductive.

"Going to Sykes's house could be dangerous. The Society has to be looking for us, Claire." Nix tried not to give in to the siren's call of things he could never have. He tried to remember that no matter what he did now, there were some things he could never change.

You are what you are.

"Would the people in The Society ever guess you'd go to Sykes's house?" Claire asked.

Nix rolled the question over in his mind. That was his advantage—and Claire's—in this lethal game: The Society wouldn't know what to expect. They wouldn't be able to guess at his motivations. He'd lived under their rule his entire life, and they would have had better luck profiling a complete stranger.

"Maybe I should go alone." Nix said the words carefully. He didn't want to hurt her again, didn't want her to think that he was pushing her away.

Claire's expression stayed steady, her hands wrapped around her coffee mug. "You can go alone if you want to. I won't make you take me. But I'd rather go with you. We're stronger together, and you won't let anything happen to me." She paused. "I won't let anything happen to you."

It was easy to believe her, easier than it should have been to want her at his back.

She liked my bookcase.

That thought hit him in place of the things he should have been thinking, about who deserved what and, more to the point, who didn't.

"We'll go together," he said.

She smiled, brighter than sunlight ricocheting off a sharpened blade. "Do you know where Senator Sykes lived?"

Nix knew everything about Evan Sykes. Not his hopes or dreams or childhood aspirations, but his date of birth. His last known address. The location of his office in D.C. The office space he rented in Iowa. The places he went for lunch. The streets he walked or drove down to get there.

His allergies.

"I know where he lived." There were some things you didn't forget. Files. Marks. Time of death.

"Okay, then," Claire said, setting down her coffee. "Let's go."

<hr />

The dead senator's home was immaculate. Enormous. But more than anything, it felt empty.

She and Nix entered on the second floor. Walked straight through the Georgian-style windows and the handcrafted moldings on the walls. Landed in a hallway with wood floors and Oriental rugs.

Claire held tight to the fade as Nix led them to Sykes's personal office. She sensed something the moment they stepped into the room. It wasn't a smell or a taste or a sound, but it was something, in the wisps of solidity that made up the furniture: the muted brown desk, the far-away filing cabinets.

Faded Claire wasn't sure why these objects were important. Why she should be looking at them, when her body and Nix's were glowing, iridescent, everywhere. But they'd come here for a reason, and Claire, even though she couldn't exactly remember why, knew it was important.

She closed her eyes. She reached through her brain with both hands and grabbed on to a fleeting image, guaranteed to bring her crashing back to earth.

A towel.

How many times had she had to ask that darn towel boy for one? How many times had she mopped pool water off her face with the back of her own hand?

Crashing. Mayday, Mayday—

Back.

"Triggers," Nix said, as he crossed back over to join her.

"What?"

"You found a trigger. To fade, you have to stop trying to matter. You make yourself feel like nothing and you revel in it. But once you're faded, you can't think about reality. You can't pay too much attention to the solid world, and you can't let yourself remember *wanting* to matter. Triggers are things that make that impossible. They snap you out of the fade. Not exactly pleasant, but they can be useful."

Claire wondered what Nix's triggers were and decided it was probably better not to ask. They needed to move quickly. Two Nobodies. In a dead senator's house. With aforementioned senator's daughter and wife right downstairs.

"They won't hear us," Nix said, picking up on her thoughts. "And if they do, they'll tell themselves it's nothing. But we should be quick."

Even Nobodies could be seen if the situation was compromising enough. Claire *had* talked to people before. She could make them take notice, if only for a few seconds, and something told her that even being maximally inconspicuous might not be enough to camouflage breaking and entering to this degree.

At the very least, she didn't really want to put it to the test.

"You take the computer. I'll case the rest of the room." Nix's words helped Claire focus, and she nodded, heading for the desktop.

What are the chances that Sykes kept incriminating,
top secret files on his home computer?

Claire had a feeling that the answer was slim to none,
and she wasn't anything approximating a hacker, but all
they needed was a lead. A teeny, tiny something to point
them toward the next clue. The next step in dismantling
The Society.

Claire wanted the people who'd raised and trained Nix
to suffer.

She wanted The Society to disappear.

Claire slid into the leather armchair behind the antique
mahogany desk and turned on the computer. She wasn't
at all surprised when it asked her for a password, and
she was even less surprised when "Proposition42" didn't
work.

A Nobody could fool a security system.

Walk straight through walls.

Slip in and out of the most secured buildings unnoticed.

But those abilities didn't extend to firewalls or computer security. The senator's PC had no way of knowing
that Claire didn't matter.

Maybe if I faded . . .

But, no, if she faded, she wouldn't be able to touch the
keys.

On the other side of the room, Nix narrowed his eyes
at a random strip of wall. Claire looked up just in time

to see him fade and walk straight through the barrier in front of him.

A second later, he was back.

"Wall safe," he explained, under his breath. "Nothing there but money and guns."

Wanting some results of her own to report back, Claire made another stab at the password.

Caroline. The senator's wife's name.

Abigail. His daughter.

Caroabby. Abbiline. Frozenlemonade.

The last—Claire's own password of choice—didn't work any better than the first two.

"Abi*gail!*"

The voice that chirped that name was high and sultry— and decidedly not Nix's.

"Oh, like you've never gone there, Courtney. You know *there* better than I know bases one through three, and that's saying something."

Abigail Sykes—the senator's daughter. And another girl—Courtney, apparently. They were close enough to the office that Claire could make out every word of their conversation.

"And you told him you'd bring it? The party stuff?"

"Trust me, Court. It won't be a problem. This juice is way more potent than your mom's zombie pills."

"Those are for migraines!"

"Yeah. Right. And my dad's stash was for his blood sugar."

Claire didn't let herself get caught up in the content of what the girls were saying, even though a part of her brain had registered the fact that Sykes's drug habit was no mystery to his daughter. Right now she and Nix had much bigger problems.

"Abi*gail*!"

"Court*ney*!"

The voices were right outside the door. The knob was beginning to turn.

Claire ducked down behind the desk. Nix followed suit.

"Have you been in here?" The voice—Courtney's, Claire guessed—was subdued. Less overly dramatic than it had been a moment before. "You know, since your dad—"

"Shuffled off this mortal coil?" Abigail snorted, but her next words got caught in her throat. "No. But it's not like things are that different now."

"He was your dad, Abs."

"No. He was the pod person who replaced my father the moment he became the junior senator from Iowa."

"He wasn't that bad."

Claire wondered, absentmindedly, if Courtney was the underage girlfriend that had convinced Nix that Sykes was a monster.

"He didn't care, Court. Not about me. Not about my mom. One day, he did. The next, he didn't. She got drunk, I got pretty, he got dead."

Claire knew what trying not to cry sounded like. Abigail was a textbook case.

"So where did your dad keep his stuff?" Apparently, Courtney had expended her complete capacity for sympathy.

Abigail, sensing her friend had run dry, took several breaths before replying. "There's a safe built into the desk."

The desk?

Claire met Nix's eyes, and an unspoken obscenity passed between the two of them, followed by an urgent mandate: *fade.*

Claire squeezed her eyes shut. Shut her mind down. Thought of what Nix had said. About triggers.

Nothing. You know what that feels like. Reach for it. Grab it. Make it yours.

Instead of thinking about how unimportant she was, Claire thought of the fade. She thought of running. She thought of being nothing.

And the next instant, she was.

Nix couldn't fade until Claire did, and for one horrible moment, he thought that she'd be too held in place by the exchange Sykes's daughter and her friend were having to let go. Nix wouldn't have blamed Claire if she couldn't shrug off reality in the face of Normal girls. For all Nix knew, girls just like them had walked all over Claire at her old school.

Beside him, Claire's eyelids closed and then fluttered. The tension melted away from her jaw. She stopped nibbling on her bottom lip.

She's fading. Three ... two ... one ...

Footsteps approached the far side of the desk, and Nix realized that Claire wasn't the one risking exposure.

Less than shadow. Less than ...

Claire.

Once she crossed over, thinking her name was enough to bring him into unreality beside her. She stayed, crouched behind the desk, but Nix shook his head at her and stood up.

"They can't see us. Can't hear us."

Claire climbed to her feet, her tangled hair looking more like a halo for the light shining off it. "I've never been this close," she whispered, "to ... Solids."

"Normals," he corrected. She took a step toward him, and Nix felt his heart—his transparent, weightless, nothing heart—leap in his chest. If they touched, if her hand brushed his, if he reached for her—they'd leave the time line behind. The world would freeze around them, and nothing else would matter.

Nothing.

Nix wanted to touch her, badly, but he didn't. They

couldn't touch in the fade without stopping time, and if time stopped, the scene unfolding around them—the one they desperately needed to understand—would freeze.

Nix met Claire's eyes, and she nodded to show that she understood, then took a step back.

"Mother dearest doesn't even know this is here," one of the Normal girls was saying. "She went through the other safes when he died. Looking for booze, probably. Or money. She didn't think he'd have hiding spots inside his hiding spots."

"Enough with the soliloquy, Abs. Open it!"

Nix felt the urge to swat at the solid girls, like they were flies or a bad smell that needed to waft away. Listening to them took effort; their words were an annoyance. The need to touch Claire, to shrug off time, was overwhelming.

But he couldn't. He had to let time run its course. Let Sykes's solid daughter saunter over to the senator's desk and press a hidden button. Let the top of the desk shift to reveal a secret compartment.

"Tapes, tapes, tapes ... drugs!" The one called Abigail sang as she rifled through the contents of the compartment.

"What's on the tapes?" The one called Courtney asked.

"Who cares? All I know is this stuff is killer strong. The second it hits you, you don't feel anything."

Don't feel anything.

The words would have made Nix sick to his stomach if he'd processed them, but he couldn't let them be real, didn't dissect their meaning. Not here. Not now.

Now was Claire. *Claire, Claire, Claire* and *fade, fade, fade.* They were invincible, untouchable, eternal.

So long as nothing else mattered.

"God, Abby, what *is* that stuff? It looks disgusting."

Nix didn't look. Couldn't look at the drug Abigail Sykes had pulled from her father's desk. Instead, he looked at Claire.

Hazel eyes.

Freckles.

Lips made for reading out loud.

"It may look like tar, but it feels like heaven. Don't worry, though, there's just enough left for me and Justin. You don't have to get your hands dirty, Miss Priss."

Looks like tar. Feels like heaven.

Nix reached over and touched Claire's hand with his own. A wave of power exploded in the air between them, and the solid girls froze.

Looks like tar. Feels like heaven.

The clock on Sykes's wall stopped moving. Nix ran his thumb slowly over Claire's palm. With his chin, he gestured toward the desk. The compartment. The frozen Normal girls. In a single motion, he and Claire crossed the room, walking on the balls of their feet, silent and deadly, two hunters on the prowl.

Claire's eyes zeroed in on the vial in Abigail Sykes's hand, and she shuddered.

"Empty," she said. "Dull."

Nix concurred. The liquid in that vial was nauseating. The mere sight of it threatened to pull him out of the fade.

"Close your eyes," he told Claire. "Close your eyes and don't look at it. Don't listen to it."

"There's something wrong with that drug," Claire said, eyes still open, voice hoarse. "Do you remember what you told me? When we first figured out what I was? You told me that the world was made of energy, and that there were two kinds of wrong."

Nobody.

And Null.

Don't think it, Nix told himself. *Don't even think the word.*

But the thought had been planted, and even in the fade, even touching Claire, he had to follow it to completion. The Society studied energy. The Society's scientists had used Nix to test countless theories about the way that energy worked. And when Nix had gone back to the institute the day before, he'd seen a Sensor with small round scars—*needle tracks*—on his arm.

Nix dropped Claire's hand, and the world around them fell into motion, as if time had never stopped. Understanding crashed into his body, and he lost his grip on the fade. Gritting his teeth and trying to regain a clear

221

mind, he flashed into physicality one second and back into nothingness the next.

"Did you see that?"

One of the Normal girls blinked several times.

"See what?"

Nix held his breath. He'd only lost his fade for a second. . . .

"Huh?"

"You said you saw something."

"No, I didn't."

"Yes, you did."

"Well, did you?"

"No."

"Okay, then."

Words, words, words. Solid people and their incessant talking. Nix tried not to think about the rest of it. About what Abigail Sykes held in one hand.

About that other kind of wrong.

"Hey, Abby? If your dad . . . if taking this made him all . . . cold and stuff—"

"He did that on his own. This makes it better." Abigail sounded intrigued. Addicted. Drunk on power, just by looking at the vial she held in her hand. The needle. "It's mine."

"Okay, okay, I get it. Your drug. You want to have its narcotic babies. Whatever. Just . . . save some of it for Justin, 'kay? You promised you would."

"Courtney."

"Abigail."

"Abigail!" Someone other than the girls spoke the name. Mrs. Sykes, Abigail's mother, yelled up from downstairs, reminding Nix that the girls weren't the only Normals in the house. "Answer me, Abby! I'm not kidding, young lady. I've had just about enough of . . ."

The girl in question rolled her eyes. She stuck the vial and the needle into the band of her skirt and rolled it over twice. "Mother calls," she drawled. "You better duck out the back, Court. You know how she gets after her afternoon nip."

"Abigail Andrea Sykes!"

"Gotta run." Abigail Andrea Sykes haphazardly slung the top to the hidden safe, setting it on the path to closing, and, Courtney on her heels, flounced out of the room. Moving more quickly than Nix would have believed possible, Claire leapt to catch the hidden drawer before it closed, nothingness melting off her body just in time.

"Gotcha." Claire's word echoed in the now empty room, and Nix's body tensed. If the Normals heard, if they turned around . . .

They didn't. Of course they didn't. And a moment later, he and Claire were alone.

Nix shuddered and let go of his own fade, coming to stand beside her in the real world—in front of the desk, looking down into the hidden safe.

Tapes.

Tiny, tiny tapes and an old-fashioned Dictaphone.

Claire met his eyes. "How much do you want to bet that these have something to do with The Society?"

Nix nodded. "How much do you want to bet that whatever drug Sykes was pumping was their doing, too?"

Now that he was solid, Nix couldn't keep himself from thinking about what they'd seen.

That drug is wrong. There are two types of wrong.

It was impossible. Ten kinds of impossible. And yet, as Claire slipped the first tape into the recorder, turned the volume down low, and pressed play, the unthinkable wormed its way further and further into Nix's thoughts.

This stuff is killer strong. The second it hits you, you don't feel anything.

Abigail's words echoed in his mind, until they were replaced by the voice of a dead man, coming from the Dictaphone.

"You have to give me something to work with here, Ms. Casting."

"I have given you something to work with." Ione's voice. Nix would have recognized it anywhere. "The Society has provided very well for you, Mr. Sykes. Or do I need to remind you just how well?"

"Your previous efforts have been appreciated."

"Without us, you'd be malingering in the state senate."

"And without you, I wouldn't have this pretty, pretty

voice. I wouldn't be so very convincing. And I wouldn't be poised to make your little proposition happen."

"You do not want to threaten me, Senator."

"I'm not threatening you, ma'am. I'm simply . . . requisitioning new resources. Persuasion alone won't be enough to get me appointed to the head of the oversight committee. That's what you want, isn't it? I need to prove that I take a hard line on domestic terrorism. I need to offer the three-letter men something."

"Our deal was for you and you alone."

"You misunderstand me, Ms. Casting. I'm not asking for . . . *refreshments* for the CIA. What I'm asking for, well, let's just call it reconnaissance and threat-removal supplies."

"I don't take your meaning, and you should probably count that as a blessing."

Nix could hear the tension in Ione's voice. He'd never gotten this kind of reaction out of her himself. He never would.

Not even if he found her in a back alleyway.

Put his gun in her face.

Tried to make her beg for the mercy she never showed anyone else.

"What I need to become integral to the CIA is a weapon, ma'am. X-17 would suffice."

"I don't know what you're talking about."

"Your, shall we say, *operatives* aren't as closemouthed

as you think they are, Ione. You've been holding out on me."

"We've been providing you with power and influence. A word from me, and that ends. You saw what happened to Madsen when he resorted to blackmail. Very messy business, that."

Jacob Madsen. Seven. Ione had told Nix to make it messy, and he had. *Knife in his hand. Blood everywhere.* The realization that it was a message—a warning— shouldn't have surprised Nix, but it did.

"If you cut me off, Proposition 42 will fail." Sykes sounded confident. Clearly, the warning had gone to waste.

"There will be other propositions," Ione said, her voice light and cavalier. This was a tone that Nix had heard before; this was the Ione he recognized.

"You don't want to play with me, Ione."

"I made you. I can unmake you."

"Bribery. Murder. Illegal experimentation. Human slavery. I know the location of your little institute. I know what you're hiding in the lower levels there. You will continue to provide me with the serum, or I swear to God—"

"No need to swear, Mr. Sykes. We'll take care of you." She paused. "We always have."

And then there was a dial tone. After a moment, Sykes's voice came on. "If I die, even if it appears to be of natural causes, send an investigative team to 446 Nesturn Avenue,

62145. This is Evan Sykes—and that woman doesn't know who she's messing with."

End tape.

For a moment, neither Nix nor Claire said a word, and then, finally, Claire broke the silence. "It's like something out of a bad movie. 'This is Evan Sykes, and she doesn't know who she's messing with.' He sounds like some kind of egomaniac."

"He sounds like a Null," Nix corrected, but this time, the single word took on new meaning. Because Evan Sykes wasn't a Null—not when he lost those elections early in his career. Not when he paid attention to his wife and daughter. Before he became—how had Abigail put it?—a pod person.

Before he became persuasive.

Before The Society had made him into the perfect plant.

"The drug." He said the words out loud and waited for Claire to catch up, but she didn't know enough about Nulls to see the pattern. Didn't realize how incredibly impossible this was.

"The Society gave him a drug that made him a Null. Or like a Null. Didn't you hear what his daughter said—once she shoots up with it, she can't feel anything. And Nulls don't—they don't feel anything, and they're persuasive, and they have no conscience."

Claire crinkled her forehead, her nose. "They gave him the drug so that he could talk Congress into their corner.

227

Sykes turning into an egotistical maniac who thought he could blackmail them—"

"Side effect."

Nix couldn't believe they were actually talking about this. Like it was actually possible. Like a drug could take a human and turn them into a monster. How long did it last? Abigail seemed human enough, and she'd used the drug before.

A quick survey of the safe revealed that there were no more vials. No more needles.

"He was almost out of the drug when he died."

"And he just assumed someone would find the tapes. His own daughter didn't even try to listen to them. . . ."

"She must have cared about him when he was alive. She was probably crazy about him. Not even angry that he didn't care about her. But once he died, his hold on her disappeared—"

"And now she hates him."

Nix nodded.

"Abigail Andrea, don't you leave this house! You can't talk to me like that! You can't!"

"Oh, go make yourself a Long Island iced tea, Mother. I can do whatever I want."

The sound of a slamming door, reverberating through the large house, broke Nix out of his stupor. "Grab the tapes."

That would give them something on The Society.

But not enough.

"The daughter has the drug. We can't let her take it. Normals aren't meant to be Nulls. Look what it did to her father. And now she's going to give it to some boy?" Nix tightened his fingers into fists.

"We're going after her." Claire beat him to the punch, and he nodded.

"Give me the tapes. We'll have to hurry to catch up with her. . . ."

"We don't need to hurry," Claire corrected, touching his arm softly. "Just fade."

Nix stuffed the tapes into his pocket, hung his future on them, made them an extension of himself.

Five, four, three, two . . .

Nothing.

19

The world can't touch me. The world can't hurt me. The world can't hold me down.

Claire was the same Claire every time she crossed over. No boundaries. No worries. No inhibitions.

The solid girl she and Nix were following would never understand that. They were flaming comets; Abigail Sykes was a firefly with a broken bulb. And as the aforementioned firefly scurried across her little mortal plane, her eyes tearing up and her too-short skirt bouncing as she ran, Claire flew.

Power.

Abigail stopped running. Claire forced her body to still, forced her feet to return to the earth.

"We're back at the cemetery." Nix's voice broke through the hum of nothingness in Claire's mind. "Why would she come here?"

She as in Abigail. A sound clawed through the fog in Claire's brain.

Someone's crying.

Claire grappled with the thought, knowing that it didn't belong in the fade and that if she let herself think it for too long, she wouldn't belong there either. She wanted to stay here. With Nix. Wanted to touch him.

Abigail Sykes is crying.

Claire heard a sound—halfway between the ripping of Velcro and the slamming of a door—as Abigail's tears—and her empathy for them—tore her from the fade. She settled into her physical body, missing the fade so much it *hurt*.

"Hey, baby. You feeling dangerous?"

"I'm feeling like I could do you right here."

Claire tried not to blush. She really did, but Abigail Sykes had chosen that moment to stop crying, and her boyfriend—Dustin? Austin? Justin?—had arrived. They were practically undressing each other with their eyes.

And ... ummm ... their hands.

"Did you bring me something?"

Abigail slowly lifted up her shirt, revealing the syringe tucked into the band of her miniskirt. Claire glanced sideways. Beside her, Nix had eyes only for the drug.

"How are we going to get it away from her?" Claire

asked, keeping her voice to a whisper, even though Abigail and her special friend seemed to be paying absolutely zero attention to the fact that they weren't alone in this cemetery—if they noticed it at all.

"We get the drug by walking up to her and taking it," Nix said.

"Oh. Simple as that."

"Simple as that," he confirmed, but something held him back, kept him from moving. It wasn't until Claire fully absorbed their surroundings that she realized exactly what it was.

Abigail Sykes was standing in front of her father's grave. She leaned back against his tombstone, tempting Dustin/Austin/Justin with her flat, tanned stomach, and the needle lying nearly flat against her flesh. "Some for me and some for you."

Claire felt wrong for watching this. No matter what Sykes had done once he'd gotten in bed with The Society, the man buried under Abigail's feet had been her father. Heavy mascara coated the girl's eyelashes. Instead of tear tracks, black streaks marred her artificially tanned face. And the boy she was with—muscular, leering, clean-cut— didn't bat an eye.

Didn't ask her why she was crying.

Didn't bring her a single thing.

"I'll play first," the boy said instead, reaching for the needle. Abigail ducked away.

"Aren't you going to ask me what it is?" she teased.

The boy shrugged. "Is it good?"

Abigail shot a hateful, happy, *hurting* look at her father's grave. "It's the best."

The boy sank down to his knees. "That's all I need to know." He reached for the vial, and even from a distance, Claire could see something dark and serpentine sleeping in the wry curve of his lips.

Claire couldn't take it anymore. She moved, forgetting how much she'd once wanted the Abigails and Justins of her own high school to remember her name. She stalked toward them. And she beat Justin to the vial.

"This is mine," she said, latching her hand around it and removing it from Abigail's possession.

The dead senator's daughter didn't jump at Claire's touch. She glanced at Claire, and then shrugged her off. The boy seemed to grasp the reality of the situation a little more.

"Where'd it go?"

Clearly, the absence of the drug was bothering him, and he managed to connect it to Claire's presence. "You... you took it."

Claire turned and walked away. The boy wouldn't follow. He wouldn't fight her for it. He'd be pissed that it was gone, but he wouldn't direct that anger at her.

He *couldn't*.

Claire couldn't make people angry. She couldn't make

them happy or sad, she couldn't scare them, she couldn't make them feel even a whiff of emotion toward her at all.

Power.

Stealing clothes paled next to this. She'd walked up to two strung-out strangers, taken a top secret serum from their possession, and walked away without a scratch—and she hadn't even had to fade to do it, because Normals didn't care!

The image of Justin—his hands on Abigail, her face streaked black—came into Claire's mind, and she was *glad.* Glad they didn't care about her. Glad that she wasn't spending her summer trying to make other people take notice, if being noticed meant being . . .

That.

Once the Normal boy figured out that the Normal girl had managed to lose the drug she'd promised him, he came to the conclusion that hooking up on her dead father's tombstone was *sick.* Abigail started crying again, and a heavy knowing settled in Claire's stomach, uncomfortable and disconcerting.

The Society had to be stopped. Not just for Nix and the things they'd made him do or for Senator Wyler or any other innocents they'd ordered dead. Not for Claire, who might have been buried six feet under had she not glanced out her window at exactly the right time.

The Society had to be stopped for Abigail, too. It had to be stopped because of Proposition 42 and whatever was going on in the basement of the institute. For X-17—whatever that was—which Sykes had considered the perfect weapon.

"I'm sorry, Claire." By the time Nix said those words, Abigail and the boy were gone, and Claire tried to remember what Nix—*built me a bookshelf; saved my life*—had to be sorry for.

"You shouldn't have had to do that," he said, nodding his head toward the vial in her hand.

"I shouldn't have had to do what?" she asked quietly.

"Deal with the drug. Take it from them. I should have done that."

"Why?"

Nix's fingers began curling into a fist. "Because if it wasn't for me, that girl's father would still be alive, and she never would have had the opportunity to steal a vial of instant Null in the first place."

Claire brought her hands to his and slowly worked to uncurl his fist, drawing tiny circles on his palm the way she sometimes did on her own.

Nix shuddered, and she sensed something threatening to give inside him. "Sykes wasn't a Null. He wasn't a good person. He willingly turned himself into a monster. But he wasn't a Null. He could have gotten better."

First Wyler. Now Sykes. Claire wondered if Nix would go, one by one, through the contents of all of the folders. All of his kills. She knew, deep down, that he would. And even deeper, in the core of Claire, she knew that she wanted to be there while he did.

She wanted to be the one to put him back together. To rest her hands gently on the sides of his face and say, "Close your eyes. Take a deep breath. Cry. And when you can't hold it anymore—the breath, the tears—let go."

Fade.

—————◆◈◆—————

Nix did as he was told. He felt it—the burn of knowing that he'd been a blade when The Society needed one, the executioner who carried out every death sentence Ione had laid down, except for Claire's. He accepted that the things he'd done would always be there, under his skin. In his skin. Waiting behind every door in every dream.

You are what you are.

He pulled back from Claire's grasp.

"Nix."

His eyeballs stung, and he let the tears fall. Then he let everything else fall away, too. Claire followed him into the fade, and he struggled to remember why he'd pulled away from her touch.

Faded, she didn't seem so very far away.

"It hurts." Claire's voice was high-pitched, frantic.

Nix started forward. "What hurts?" Nothing was

supposed to hurt in the fade. You had to let go of the pain to cross.

Claire looked down at her hand. "It's making me dizzy. It doesn't want to be here."

The drug, Nix realized. *She brought it with her.* In the solid world, the vial and its contents were ugly, but in the fade, they turned his stomach. There were two kinds of wrong, and they weren't supposed to mix. *This* had made Evan Sykes into a temporary Null. God knew what was in it, but every ounce of loathing Nix had ever felt for Nulls was directed at the dark liquid, and the only reason it didn't pull him out of the fade was that—impossibly—it was faded, too.

Claire brought it with her. She was better at this than she should have been. Crossing in and out of the fade. Taking objects with her. She'd picked it up effortlessly—and now she was paying the price.

She shouldn't have brought it here. She shouldn't have even tried.

"It's like a black hole. It's like they liquefied a black hole." Claire wheezed, her features twisted in pain. Standing two feet away from her, Nix could feel it: the drug, the fade's reaction to it, the fact that none of this should have been happening at all.

"Let go of the fade, Claire."

They'd stop fading, and it would be fine. The drug would just be a drug.

Claire shook her head. "It has to come with us." Claire trembled, her hand clenching the serum. Nix reached for it, but she pulled it back. "We have to take it back to the cabin, and we'll travel faster in the fade. I can do this. I should be able to do this. I'm nothing. This vial is nothing. We're nothing."

"It doesn't belong here," Nix said, thinking back to that day on the bus, when he'd covered Claire with his fade. If she'd been a Null, really been a Null—

"It's a part of me. We're nothing. I can do this. I can."

Nix heard the words she didn't speak. *It hurts.*

If she wouldn't leave the fade, and she wouldn't let him take the drug, there was only one thing Nix could think of to do to take that pain away. He put his hands on either side of her face. He forced her eyes to look away from the serum and straight into his.

"Stay with me, Claire."

Her body relaxed under his touch, but he could still see the strain in her eyes. He could still *feel* the drug's unsettling presence in the fade.

"Nix, Nix, Nix," she said his name, over and over again. Nix traced his thumb along the edge of her cheekbone. He'd hate himself for touching her later, remember why he couldn't *later*, but right now she needed him.

To take away the pain.

"That's right, Claire. I'm right here. Stay with me." He

pulled her closer, ignored the warning—*You are what you are. She'll never love you*—as he brushed his lips lightly over hers.

She pressed herself into him, harder. He let her. Nothing mattered, except his lips and hers. His touch and hers. The warmth between them, the power of their fades doubling over and over until the vial in her hand seemed as unimportant as Nobodies did to Normals.

He shouldn't be doing this. He shouldn't touch her, shouldn't kiss her—but it was too late for that. There was no room for *shouldn't* in the fade. Nothing but Nix. Nothing but Claire.

Nothing but the two of them.

For now.

Claire didn't remember running back to the cabin. She didn't remember flying. She didn't remember anything other than the kiss: the way it stilled her mind and grounded her in the fade, the sensation of knowing with a deep and undying certainty that Nix was the only person in the world she wanted, the only person she would ever want, even if he jerked away from her the moment they crossed out of the fade.

No matter what he said or did or how he looked at her—she remembered his smell and his taste and what it felt like, for one perfect moment, to be the thing against which the whole of the universe paled.

She set the drug they'd stolen from Abigail Sykes on the coffee table.

"Nix—"

"No." He didn't let her say any of the things she was thinking. He didn't want to hear it. "I shouldn't have. We shouldn't have."

"Yes, you should have."

He closed his eyes, refusing to look at her. "Don't, Claire."

Condition one, Claire thought. If she reached out to touch him, he'd jerk back. If she tried to talk, he wouldn't listen.

Don't. Can't. Shouldn't. No. Claire's eyes drifted over to the bookshelf. *Her* bookshelf. No matter how tired she was of being pushed away, no matter how much she wanted things he would never let her have—she couldn't bring herself to hate him for it.

"The drug's a different color now." Claire gestured to the liquid inside the vial. If he didn't want to talk about it, they wouldn't talk about it. "Before, it was the color of tar. Now it's like onyx. Still dark, but ..."

She couldn't make herself say the word *beautiful.*

"Do you think taking it to the fade changed it?" Claire focused on that question instead of asking him how he could think, even for a second, that kissing her had been a mistake.

Nix flicked his eyes toward the Null drug. "You're right. It does look different. Nobodies and Nulls are polar opposites. I felt it when you brought the drug into the fade. Something happened." He paused. "I don't know exactly what's in that drug, but whatever it is, it's not compatible with the fade. They reacted to each other."

"Like matter and antimatter?" Claire wasn't even sure what the words meant, but at least she was talking, and at least she wasn't saying what she was thinking.

Tell me you want to be with me the way I want to be with you. Tell me you felt it, too. Faded or solid, today, tomorrow—

"Yeah," Nix replied, and for a moment, she pretended he was responding to the thing she hadn't asked. "Something like that."

20

Claire's being quiet. Her knees are pulled up to her chest. Her hair is falling into her face.

Nix didn't want to think about what bringing the drug into the fade must have cost her. To bring something into the fade, you had to consider it an extension of yourself. The strength of will it must have taken to look at the drug, to know what it could do and absorb it into her sense of self was incredible.

"Claire?" He reached out and touched her shoulder. He'd kissed her to stop the pain—and it had worked. But that hadn't been his only motivation. He'd wanted her, wanted so many things that he knew he would never have. "Are you okay?"

"What are we going to do with it?" She answered his question with a question. "The drug, the tapes, the fact that The Society killed a senator—will it be enough? If we gave it to the police, or the FBI, or the media—would it be enough?"

Nix tried to picture himself giving the Null drug to someone, telling them what it did. If they heard him, they wouldn't particularly care. And if they cared—if he and Claire could send a letter or an email or find someone else to deliver the message and the proof—what would happen? Would the government shut The Society down . . .

Or would they take it over?

The Society had three purposes that Nix knew of now. Killing Nulls. Studying energy. Preserving and extending the power of The Society. Maybe there were other initiatives, and maybe there weren't, but the government would almost certainly have plans of their own. They wouldn't be able to resist the temptation to use The Society's means for their own ends.

Wasn't Sykes proof of that?

"If we're going to expose The Society for killing Sykes, we have to do damage control first." Nix glanced at Claire. "No one can know about the Null drug. We can't run the risk that someone else will take it. And no one can know about us."

"We have to destroy the drug." Claire spoke the truth

that he had been dancing around. "Not just this vial. All of it."

"All of it," Nix agreed. They couldn't risk The Society, or the government, or anyone else giving themselves the power to manipulate others—and becoming a psychopath in the process. They had to destroy the drug. The research that went with it. Any chance of making it again.

And that meant that they were going in.

<hr />

A part of Claire had always known it would come to this. Nix had already returned to The Society once, and he'd come back bleeding. No matter how much evidence they gathered, no matter what they learned about The Society's purpose and their plans and the lies they'd told Nix—at the end of the day, the enemy still had to be taken apart from the inside out.

Only this time, Nix wasn't going in alone.

He's going to tell me I can't come. Claire knew that. She also knew that he was wrong. *He's going to say that it's over and that I'm not a part of this, that it's something he has to do alone. But I'm not going to let him leave me behind. Not again. Not now.*

"I bet my parents haven't even realized I'm gone." That was the only thing Claire could think of that wouldn't give him an excuse to run. "I disappeared, what, three, four days ago? They probably haven't even noticed I'm gone. What if I never go back? Will they just forget I existed at all?"

I'm never going back. Claire knew it was true the second the question left her mouth. *Even if Nix says it's over, even if he tries to send me away. Knowing what I know, knowing that they'll never care—*

There was no coming back from something like that.

<hr />

From the moment Nix had realized that he was going back to the institute, he'd known that this would be goodbye. This was *his* fight. *He* was The Society's executioner, its weapon.

He had to let Claire go. But as he looked at her, really *looked* at her, he realized the obvious: that Claire didn't have anywhere to go.

"They won't forget you right away," he said, a lump rising in his throat. "They'll realize you're gone, but they won't look for you. If you went back this week or next or six months from now, you could probably jog their memories."

"But a year from now? Or two? Or ten?"

They'll forget about you. Nix didn't have the heart to say it out loud. The only reason The Society's members would remember that Claire existed was that they had protocols in place to prevent them from forgetting. They had files. Reminder alarms set to go off to prompt them to read those files and recall what it was that they were after.

Claire's parents didn't have any of that.

"You ever heard of Roanoke?" Nix wasn't sure why he decided to bring that up, other than the fact that the story didn't involve talking about going back to the institute, and it didn't involve telling Claire that the people she'd called Mom and Dad would probably forget they'd ever had a daughter.

"That's the lost colony, right? The one that just sort of disappeared?"

"Sir Walter Raleigh—the guy who funded the expedition that landed at Roanoke—was Society. Most of the people on the ship were Nobodies. A few were Nulls who Raleigh wanted away from the Crown. A half dozen Sensors. I guess The Society wanted a claim on the New World, the power that would come with it."

Claire snorted. "How'd that plan work out for them?"

"The Nobodies killed the Nulls. The Sensors forgot the Nobodies existed. Raleigh and the Queen neglected to send supplies for a few years." Nix shrugged. "Didn't go well."

"So there were more of us back then?" Claire asked, and the idea was as strange to Nix as it was to her.

From dozens to two.

"There must have been."

"And now there's just you and me. You. And me." The words burst out of her mouth with enough force that he realized she'd been holding them in the whole time. While they'd discussed the drug. While they'd been making plans.

"I never would have been normal, Nix. I never would have been Abigail with her Courtneys and Justins. I won't ever have a normal life, no matter what I do, and I swear to God, I don't know whether to be sorry for them or for me. Because I know—I *know* what's going to change and what's not going to change, and I know that you're the only one who will ever see me. And that's enough, because you're the only one I want to see."

He couldn't quite process the words, but he read their meaning in the set of her body, the tilt of her chin.

You're the only one I want to see.

She knew what he was. She understood. Maybe he should walk away, maybe he didn't deserve her, but Nix knew—suddenly and irrevocably—that he couldn't.

Wouldn't.

You're the only one I want to see.

She wouldn't ever have a normal life. If she'd never met him, if he walked away and never darkened her door again—

She'd be alone. And it would kill her, the way that walking away from her would kill him.

"I'm not going to leave you, Claire." He'd never made a promise before. The words had a taste to them—sweet like lavender, solid like steel.

"Ever?"

Nobodies didn't think about the future. Nobodies didn't have futures. All they had was an ability and a responsibility. To kill.

"Ever."

Claire took a step forward then, a tiny, hesitant step that Nix found hard to match up with the way she'd wrapped her arms around him at the graveyard. The way she'd asked him—commanded him—to let it out. The way they'd kissed the rest of the universe away.

Now she was asking him, one tiny step at a time, to let that be real. To let it be lasting and solid. Nix didn't pause. He didn't hesitate. He didn't give a single moment to shoulds. He forgot about the vial on the coffee table. He closed what little space remained between them, and as his arms enwrapped her, his mouth descended, and condition one went the way of condition two.

What happened before can't happen again.

When I say you're done, you're done.

His lips brushed hers. She closed her eyes. Pushed to her tiptoes. Locked her hands behind his neck. Trailed her thumbs down its sides.

This won't ever be over.

He kissed her. The rest of the world didn't fade away;

power didn't explode between them; but he couldn't keep himself from crushing her body to his.

This is real.

In the fade or out of it, solid or immaterial, she was his.

Touch me, he whispered, from his mind to hers, and as she did, he lost himself to her. Together, they sank in and out of the fade. In and out of time. Physical. Transcendent. Nothing. Everything.

Nix-and-Claire.

21

Claire stared up at the ceiling, eyes wide open, Nix asleep beside her. If she closed her eyes, he might disappear. Not because he chose to—he'd said he wouldn't leave, and she believed him—but because Happily Ever After didn't happen to girls like Claire.

Until now.

If you believe in something long enough. If you want it hard enough...

There was still The Society. The people who wanted her—and Nix, too, by now—dead. The Null drug sitting on the coffee table. The fact that, sooner or later, they had to venture into the belly of the beast. The fact that they were just kids...

But they weren't. They weren't kids. They were Nobodies, and Claire had been on her own for a very long time, Nix—so peaceful in his sleep, so quiet—for even longer. Claire thought of her parents. About the fact that she probably wouldn't ever see them again, because seeing them and knowing they hadn't missed her would make the times she'd missed them, missed everything that they could have been so much worse.

Claire wondered if she'd always feel this way. She wondered whether she and Nix would make it in and out of The Society's stronghold alive. But mostly, despite the stakes and everything that had happened and was about to happen, Claire wondered what Nix was dreaming about. What had put the soft, boyish smile on a face that had never looked so soft. So vulnerable.

Claire thought of *The Little Prince*. Of a wild fox that had asked to be tamed. Claire knew the story. Knew it by heart and didn't need to pick the book up off her shelf.

Nix's shelf.

The most important things in life were the things you couldn't see with your eyes. The things you saw with your heart. Claire closed her eyes, saw Nix's image against the backdrop of her eyelids. Felt the heat from his body, lying next to hers. She curled into his torso, laying her head on his chest. He shifted in his sleep, enveloping her, curving to meet the curves of her body.

You understand the things you tame, she thought,

reworking the fox's words to the little prince, making them hers. *When you tame something, it is wholly and uniquely yours.*

<hr />

Nix woke up to the feel of Claire's breath on his face. She needed toothpaste. He smiled.

We can stay this way, he thought. Maybe not forever. Maybe not past noon. But for a few soothing seconds, as he felt her heartbeat. For a moment of exhilaration as his beat faster in return.

The vial on the coffee table stared back at Nix the moment he tore his eyes away from Claire's face.

We're going in.

To a place crawling with Sensors. To destroy files and hard drives and every trace of the Null drug they could find. But first, Nix had to figure out how they'd kept it hidden from him to begin with. He'd been inside their labs. He'd walked their hallways. He knew every inch of that building.

Unless they had other buildings. Other labs. Nix was beginning to suspect what he knew about The Society only scratched the surface. They'd taught him not to ask questions, to never expect answers. He'd known only what they wanted him to know.

We'll have to find someone with inside access, make them talk.

Nix heard Claire stirring beside him, and he turned to watch her eyes open, to see the recognition in them the moment they locked on to his.

We need a plan—but not today.

The thought surprised Nix. *Vacation* wasn't a word in his vocabulary. Nobodies sat and they waited and they bled and they killed. Over and over and over again, until they died. No variation. No vacation.

That's not Claire's life. It's not mine—not anymore.

"Good morning." She greeted him with a smile. So simple. So sweet.

It was perfect. So perfect that for a moment, he wished he could freeze it, the way the two of them could stop time from the fade.

"What are you thinking?" Claire asked.

Nix smiled back, banishing the drug to the back of his mind. "I'm thinking that we should go somewhere. Like . . . on a date." The word felt inadequate and silly to the extent that Nix actually wondered for a split second if he'd mispronounced it. "We should go out," he amended.

Before we play David and Goliath with The Society, we should have at least one day, just for us.

Claire glanced toward the coffee table, but he put his hand on the side of her cheek, brought her eyes back to face him. Claire tilted her head into his palm.

"Okay," she said, with another smile—almost shy, twice as sweet. "Where do you want to go?"

Not the graveyard.

Not a dead senator's midwestern mansion.

Nix's lack of experience with the outside world was limiting when it came to brainstorming ideas for dates. "Once we fade, we can go anywhere," he said, hedging to give himself more time to think.

Claire's smile grew to almost blinding proportions. "Anywhere sounds nice."

"Anywhere it is."

Nix cleared his mind. He let everything but Claire trickle out—no drug on the table, no weapons under the porch. No Society. No Sensors.

Just Claire.

Shadow. Air. Nothing. Claire.

A new mantra. New words, pumping through his veins, forming a strange duet with the old one.

Less than—
Shadow—
Less than—
Air—
Nothing—
Claire.

Nix opened his eyes just in time to see Claire slip from reality, and he realized that it didn't matter how many times he watched her do this. He'd always be completely absorbed in it, entranced by the way the light shined through her body, from the inside out.

The expression on her face would always be new to him, precious.

Amazed. Awed. Ecstatic. Blissed.

"Let's run." Nix purposefully used her words from that first day, from the first time she'd crossed over.

They ran. And as the world bowed down at their feet, as Nix passed through the forest, as Claire blurred beside him, he accepted the fact that they'd never be Normal. Not even for a single date. Not even for just one afternoon.

They were more.

Anywhere ended up being a boardwalk in a small, touristy town—far enough away from their hideaway that they couldn't have run there weighed down by solid limbs, but close enough to remind him of the town where he'd found her standing on the sidewalk in stolen clothes.

The two of them stopped running at the exact same moment, in the center of a modest crowd. Eventually, they'd cross back to the solid world. Do normal things. Eat lunch. Play games. Enjoy the view—but not yet.

Like a dancer moving through motions choreographed long before his time, Nix flowed toward Claire, closing the space between them. She met his eyes. Caught his hand, and the moment they touched, time stopped.

We shouldn't be able to do this. The Society doesn't know that Nobodies can do this. If they had, they never would have sent me after her, never would have risked—

Nix couldn't finish the thought. He belonged to the fade and to Claire. There were no worries here. No thoughts. There was only light. And excitement. And the incredible rush that came with absolute power.

All around them on the boardwalk, there were people. Normal people on Normal dates, frozen in the middle of their Normal lives. A woman screamed at her child, her face contorted at an angle so unnatural that it looked like her skin was melting off the bones. A man was using his briefcase to part the crowd. An old man smelled a hot dog, his eyes closed. Nix wouldn't have given the man a second glance, but for the almost imperceptible light around his face.

Around his nose.

Moving on instinct, Nix put himself between Claire and the man and scanned the perimeter of the boardwalk.

There—a woman walking with her hands held out slightly in front of her body. And there—a twenty-something with his left ear turned toward the crowd. Nix found the remaining two by looking for the energy their powers gave off, visible only from the fade.

Five of them. Seemingly harmless. Spread out across the area. But Nix knew. He *knew*. He'd seen lights like those before. In the halls of the institute.

Don't think it. Don't worry. Don't. Lose. Your. Fade

Claire, sensing something was wrong, put her free hand on the back of his neck, pulling him closer, forcing him to look at her and only her, as he'd done for her the night before.

"Claire." He gave the word its due and let himself absorb their closeness, breathe it in and out until he could form the words he had to say. "There are Sensors here. I should have known. The Society never stopped looking for you. For us. I knew they were searching. I *saw* them—"

Any second, the two of them could lose their fade. Any second, these Sensors could make a move toward completing the job that Nix had left undone.

"We're here, we're together, we're safe." Claire's words took on the rhythm of a song. "Just you and me."

Nix couldn't shake the fear, the crippling, solid, undeniable fear that Claire was in danger, that they might hurt her.

I can't let them find her—hurt her—

"I'm going to lose my fade." He spoke the words directly into her ear. "And when I do, you will, too, so you have to leave."

"I'm not leaving you here."

He struggled to hold on for just one more minute, just long enough to tell her what to do. "Sooner or later, we would have gone looking for a Sensor. We need information; they might have it, but five on two . . . the odds . . ."

Less than shadow. Less than air. Claire.

"Run. Get away from me so I don't bring you back, too. Go to the cabin. Hide the serum. Bring me a gun."

Nix held on. Closed his eyes. Concentrated on her smell. Remembered the way she tasted—and the whole time, he prayed she'd do what he said, because he couldn't forget the limp body he'd carried onto that bus; the way a cleanup team had almost killed her once before.

"Okay."

The word was the only warning Nix got before Claire pulled away from him and ran. The moment they broke contact, Nix could hear the sounds of time speeding up around them. He felt her absence and knew it was only a matter of seconds before he lost his fade. Weight began returning to his limbs, but he fought it, fought tooth and nail to keep his mind clear, his body immaterial, just long enough to give her a chance—

Nix solidified on the boardwalk. Life went on all around him. The Sensors continued searching, and Nix took a step back. To think. To plan.

He and Claire needed information. The Sensors might have it. But they also might sense him, and they undoubtedly had orders to kill him—or Claire, when she returned—on sight. Five on one, five on two—either way, Nix didn't like the odds.

They want to hurt Claire.

The thought—the same one that had made it impossible for Nix to stay faded with her by his side—brought the predator inside him to the surface now. The Society had trained him to hunt. They'd trained him to kill. They'd made him the perfect assassin.

Time to even the odds.

Claire felt Nix's absence the second he left the fade. If she'd been standing next to him, if she'd seen it happen, she wouldn't have been able to resist following, but she was running, through people and shops and trees, and she refused to allow her limbs to slow down, refused to let her mind think about the half of her soul that was missing.

I'm nothing. I'm Nobody.

She was Nobody, and she was running.

Situation: What if he were here beside me? What if we were racing? Floating, blurring, blending—

The wind can't touch her body, but his breath can. She can feel him behind her.

"Winner takes all," he whispers into her neck. Claire laughs, pushing down the desire to turn around, to take everything she wants, to allow the power to explode out from her body and connect with his.

He streams past her, and she lets out a gasp, full of mock outrage.

Faster, farther, more—

They run, neck in neck, their steps in sync. His heart beating in unison with hers. Faster, farther—

There.

"End of Situation." Claire whispered the words as she made it back to the cabin, and the moment she let go of it, her mind processed the reality she'd kept at bay: Nix was gone. She'd left him with the Sensors.

As far as triggers went, it was a good one.

Bones crunching, skin screaming, pores weighted down with cement.

It was all Claire could do to stay on her feet. Physicality had never been so brutal. It was like she didn't fit in her own body anymore. She forced herself to straighten, to lift her eyes from the ground to the bookshelf in the corner.

"Hide the serum. Bring me a gun." Claire repeated Nix's orders like a prayer. "Hide the serum. Bring me a gun."

She allowed herself the time it took to take one breath, then two, and then she moved, grabbing the Null drug off the coffee table. Her limbs became accustomed to movement again, and she walked out the front door and crawled under the porch, where she'd hidden Nix's weapons. Digging her fingernails into the dirt, she made a small hole and dropped the onyx-colored drug in, before covering it again. Then she turned her attention to the weapons.

An eternity ago, Nix had laid his weapons out on the counter and told her to choose. He'd put a gun in her hand and told her to use it, and she'd refused.

That Claire was a different Claire.

She picked up the gun, the one Nix had aimed at her chest the day they met. The weapon was heavy in her palm and it made her hands feel tiny, but she kept a grip on it. To bring an object into the fade, you had to consider it an extension of yourself. After bringing the Null drug into the fade, imagining this gun—*Nix's gun*—as an extension of her hand, her arm, her body, was nothing.

And an instant later, so was she.

22

Nix wove his way in and out of the crowd, putting distance between himself and the Sensors, choosing his vantage point carefully. If one of his targets managed to approximate his location, fine. Nix would see them coming. Otherwise, he'd wait for them to split up and then he'd deal with them, one by one.

Individually, Sensors walked past him in the hallways of the institute every day, barely registering his existence. As a team, they were far more dangerous, and yet they didn't have the good sense to stay together, which told Nix that though they were prepared to find their targets, they had no reason to believe that he and Claire were actually in this town, on this boardwalk. This team was one of many. Ione's protocols and her threats and her team of scientists could only do so much.

They don't know I'm here.

The thought—and the fact that Claire was out of immediate danger—made it easier for Nix to concentrate, to regain the certainty that if he had to fade, he probably could. For now he watched as the five Sensors transitioned from scanning the streets to canvassing the tiny boardwalk stores, split off into smaller units.

These people want Claire to die.

Nix registered their movements and memorized their faces.

One male, late sixties, large body, beady eyes.

Two females, middle-aged. Most remarkable thing about them? The guns holstered under their shirts.

One male, young. Twenties, maybe. Smiling. Excited. This one, Nix recognized innately as a killer. This one liked killing. He wanted Nobody blood.

Claire's blood.

Nix ground his fingernails into his palms, leaving bloody half-moons in their wake, but he forced himself to concentrate, to track the last Sensor as he stepped out of a store and began walking in the direction of Nix's perch at the edge of the crowd.

I should probably kill him. He can't kill Claire if he's dead, and we only need one of the Sensors alive to talk.

The thought wasn't as natural as it once would have

been for Nix, but it still formed far too easily in his mind, as the Sensor in question came within fifteen feet of Nix, and then ten.

"Nobody."

The Sensor's voice was familiar, but Nix couldn't quite place it.

"I know you're here, Nix."

Nix didn't move. He wasn't armed; the Sensor probably was.

I could kill him.

"I know you're here," the Sensor said again. "I can taste you. Or rather, the lack of you." The Sensor in question was looking near him. Not directly at him, but near him. "We don't want to hurt you."

Nix placed the voice. One of his trainers. The one who'd had him from age six to ten. The one who'd watched him drowning and never moved to loosen the straps. The one who'd pressed a knife into his palms and shown him how to cut up a corpse.

Ryland.

"We don't want to hurt you," the ghost from Nix's past said. Older. Grayer. Lying.

"You're confused. I know this is confusing," the man said, velvet voiced and oozing sincerity. "You have to trust that we're doing the right thing. For everybody."

Nix took stock of his situation:

No weapons.

Five feet away from one of the people who'd taught him to kill—*made* him kill.

Unable to move without risking full exposure.

Nix smiled. They thought they could talk to him. They thought they could bring him back. They thought he'd latch on to any sliver of false hope that he was wanted. Needed.

They were wrong.

"Less than shadow. Less than air."

The Sensor probably thought Nix was throwing the words he'd been taught back in his teacher's face, but he wasn't. Nix didn't care about this man. Or The Society. Or Nulls.

Or anything.

Claire was there, at the periphery of his consciousness. She'd always be there, but right now there was something bigger in his mind than even her. This man wasn't his teacher anymore. Nix wasn't his student. He wasn't nine years old.

This was graduation.

Slipping into the shadow world was as easy as it would have been if Claire had been standing beside him, and Nix was greeted by the awareness that somewhere, she was faded, too.

She's safe.

And she was about to get safer.

Sidling forward, Nix approached the man who'd placed

weapon after weapon in his small, pudgy hands. Who'd drugged him and buried him, six feet under, in the name of science. In the name of the greater good.

Lies.

It didn't matter.

There was no room in Nix's head for memories. He was Nobody. Nothing. Immaterial.

And Nobodies never got caught.

Nix's old mentor straightened the moment Nix slipped into the fade. Disconcerted, but not afraid, the man took a step backward, and he moved his head slightly, to speak into his wrist. Nix sprang forward. He thrust his hand into Ryland's body, and it went straight through his neck. Unaware that Nix was *inside* him, the Sensor continued giving even-keeled orders into a communication device on his watch. From his tone of voice, he might as well have been talking about the weather. "The boy is here, but he slipped away. The girl will follow. Use him to trap her, and then terminate both."

That was what The Society did to those who stood in their way. Wyler. Sykes. Nix.

That should have made Nix angry, but Claire wasn't in immediate danger, and Nix managed to wall off his emotions, the way he had before they'd met. Instead, he concentrated on cold, hard facts.

Fact: Ryland had taste buds that allowed him to taste

energy—or the lack thereof—a skill that was useful for locating Nobodies in the real world, but not in the fade.

Fact: Ryland was heavily armed: two knives, two guns, possibly a grenade. None of which could touch Nix until and unless he became physical again.

Fact: Nix had no weapons. No physical body. No weaknesses, and no strengths.

Faded, Nix couldn't push Ryland, and Ryland couldn't push back. Nix tilted his head to the side and looked into the man's eyes, dragging his ghost of a hand over his target's chest in the shape of an X.

Until he'd met Claire, Nix had never thought much about the way that energy worked, the ins and outs of a Nobody's powers. For her, he'd put everything he'd learned into words.

He'd told her that you could take a physical object with you into the fade if you considered that object an extension of yourself. Dragging his immaterial hand over the Sensor's chest once more, Nix considered the reverse. *Stands to reason that if you don't consider something part of you, it stays behind.*

Nix pushed his hand into Ryland's body and moved it down, down, down—his wrist in between the man's rib cage, his fingers behind it. Nix knew human anatomy. He knew how to put bullets into hearts to stop them from beating, and into skulls, directly between the eyes.

They taught me that.

Nix knew where to find the Sensor's heart.

And based on what he'd taught Claire, he knew how to grab it. How to squeeze it. How to stop its beat, without any weapons at all.

This hand isn't mine. I have no hands.

Claire had always been able to imagine anything, to convince herself of anything. That was how he suspected she'd survived on her own, before he'd told her what they were. She'd had imaginary friends, imaginary inter-actions. That was why she'd picked up fading so quickly. All she had to do was imagine something, and it became real to her.

When Nix thought of Claire, it was easy enough for him to do the same.

This hand tried to kill Claire. It isn't mine.

Nothingness slipped away from the appendage, one finger at a time, and though Nix couldn't feel his own hand, though it was as gone to him as it would have been if he'd spontaneously transformed into an amputee, he could see it.

He could see it, solid and wrapped around the Sensor's heart.

Ryland, blind to what was happening, stopped speak-ing into his watch. He stumbled. He gasped. He clutched at his chest.

Squeeze. Squeeze. Squeeze.

Nix cheered on the hand that wasn't his.

Nobodies don't need weapons. We are weapons.

At the word—*Nobodies*, plural—Claire's face came unbidden into Nix's mind. Her eyes, bright, inquisitive, tearing up. Her eyelashes—long and not quite black. Her heart-shaped face. The way her bangs never fell in quite the same way from one day to the next.

This hand brushed Claire's hair out of Claire's face. This hand has held hers. This hand is hers, and so am I.

Nix felt his fingers, one by one, slipping back into the fade as he reclaimed them. Wholly immaterial once more, the Nobody pulled his hand out of Ryland's chest. The man fell to his knees. Nearby, a woman screamed, and a ripple effect spread through the crowd.

"Somebody, quick! Call nine-one-one! I think this guy's having a heart attack!" Pedestrians rushed to the Sensor's side. Nix took a step back.

I didn't kill him. I could have killed him, and I didn't.

In Nix's mind, the words were tinged with equal amounts accusation and awe. Killing Ryland might have made Claire safer. It would have weakened The Society by one one-hundredth, or one one-thousandth or some margin, trivial or not.

If I'd held on a little bit longer, I'd have killed him. He'd be dead.

"He's still breathing. That's right, buddy, just breathe. The ambulance is on the way. Can you talk? Are you okay?"

The pedestrian leaning over Ryland had no idea who

or what he was talking to. Maybe, if he'd heard the casual manner in which his "buddy" had ordered Claire's death, Mr. Good Deed wouldn't have been so keen to save his life.

The life Nix hadn't snuffed out, because he'd thought of Claire. Because he had a choice.

I am what I am. I am what I want to be.

The Sensor's face sagged on one side, and as Nix watched, the man's tongue crept out of his mouth, limp and useless.

He's trying to taste for me, and he can't.

"Oh, man. I think he's having a stroke!"

"Don't worry," Nix whispered to the Good Samaritan, backing away and into the crowd as the paramedics swarmed the sidewalk. "He'll live." The words were battery acid on his tongue, even as his insides warred. "He'll live, and he'll recover—mostly anyway."

But he wouldn't be tasting for Nobodies anytime soon.

Nix slipped back through the crowd unnoticed.

One down, four to go.

<hr />

Claire knew the second Nix stepped into the fade. And she knew the second he left it. The sensation was a cousin, twice removed, from the one she'd had the first time he looked at her. A faint chill, a subtle shattering of things that were.

Her feet touched down on the boardwalk, but she kept her fade. The gun in her hand felt lighter than it had in the solid world, and she found herself drawn to the weapon. She held it up in front of her face, staring.

She knew, in the back of her faded brain, that she'd brought this weapon for someone else to use, but there was another not-quite thought that was just as insistent—*protect Nix, always tries to protect me, can't let him use it*—that made faded Claire think that maybe she'd brought the gun for herself. Her hand warmed the metal until they were the same temperature, and Claire concentrated on the sleek angles of the gun, the muted power of the bullets that bided their time in the belly of the beast. She'd brought the gun to the fade.

It was hers.

Claire kept her eyes trained on the gun as she walked through the crowd, barely conscious of the fact that she was passing through people in a way that would have thrilled her the day before.

Nix.

She couldn't let her mind fully form the word, couldn't think about the fact that he was close and solid without feeling the pull of reality at the edge of her consciousness. She could, however, give in to the magnetic pull of Nix's presence. Claire had always had a horrible sense of direction, but faded Claire had a perfect sense of Nix.

Her feet—touching the ground in only the most cursory

manner—propelled Claire toward a tiny tourist shop, the kind that sold plates with cartoon lobsters painted on them, and wind chimes made of fake seashells, and shirts emblazoned with statements of various levels of cheese and impropriety. The sign on the door—BACK IN TEN— was crooked, and there was a smiley face at the bottom. This was the kind of place that would have made her smile when she was just plain Claire, but now she was Nix's.

"Come on," she whispered to the gun. Light on her feet and giddy with anticipation, Claire flowed through the walls of the shop and into the back room.

Nix was there, but she refused to look for him. She closed her mind against the beacon of his presence, refused the rush of blood to her heart.

If she crossed over, he'd want the gun, and if he had the gun, he might use it. If she stayed in the fade, she could cover him. Protect him—from the Sensors, from himself.

Claire listened—not for Nix's silent footsteps, but for the reason he'd come to this shop. The Sensors. With steely effort, she managed to focus her eyes and mind on the material world and was overcome with a vague sense that this particular duo, two women, midforties, were not what she had imagined they would be.

"Which one's which?" Claire whispered, unsure whether she was talking to herself or the gun. "What do these Sensors do?"

Claire watched and she listened the way that only

someone who had spent a very large amount of time people watching could. The woman on the left scanned the room in a gridlike pattern. The one on the right walked with her hands held out in front of her body.

Extrasensory sight, extrasensory tactile sensations—and neither one of the Sensors had any idea that there was a boy lurking behind them, or that Claire was standing in the fade, a hair's breadth away from their paltry, solid bodies.

"Ryland has gone out of contact," the woman holding out her hands said.

"Do you think they got him?" her companion asked, after a single beat.

"Who?" The first woman wrinkled her brow and then touched her forehead, and the touch seemed to anchor her thoughts. "The Nobodies?"

The women did not seem bothered by the prospect that one of their colleagues might have been "got." They weren't scared. They weren't agitated. They were neutral.

Claire hated neutral. Neutral was being ignored and stepped over and having the same thing written in your yearbook every summer.

Triggers.

Claire stayed away from those hated thoughts and re-centered herself in the fade. She closed her eyes and breathed in the not-quite air. She was powerful. Wispy. Nothing.

Nothing with a gun. Nothing that could step out of the fade and shoot that gun, if she had to.

Nix chose that moment to cross into her peripheral vision, and Claire had to force herself to look away. She knew that he could see straight through her fade, the same way she'd always been able to lock her eyes on to him, but she couldn't let their gazes meet. She had to stay invisible to the Sensors. She had to be the one with the gun.

Nothing. I'm nothing. Stay nothing.

Claire eased herself back, away from the Sensors, into the wall. Now she was part of this place—unnoticed, unwashed, unloved. Back in reality, the boy she couldn't think about was moving, silently and smoothly. He had a wind chime in one hand, a lobster plate in the other.

I can't let him kill them.

The urgency of that thought undermined the even calm of Claire's mind, but she fought against solidifying, a deeper instinct telling her that it wasn't time yet. That before she could save him, she had to give him a chance to save himself.

<hr />

Claire's here.

She'd brought him the gun, the way he'd asked her to. He could fade and take it from her, shoot the Sensors.

Once the bullets left the faded gun, they'd solidify. Two shots, two fewer Sensors.

I am what I choose.

Nix knew, in that instant, that if he let himself fade, he'd take the gun from Claire, and he'd shoot them. He'd kill them without a second thought. If he wanted to stay in control, whatever he did—or didn't do—had to happen on this side of reality. He couldn't fade.

Nix tightened his grip on the items he'd liberated from the front of this shop.

The Sensors meticulously scanned the piles of boxes and excess inventory all around them, looking for some sign that a Nobody had been there, unaware that if they'd turned a little to their left, they would have seen him, plain as day.

And these are the people who decided my life. Who gave Ione her information, so she could tell me who to kill.

Sensors weren't all knowing. They weren't all-powerful. These two had no idea that Claire was faded, just out of reach, and they had no idea that he was now standing directly behind them.

"Looking for me?" Nix wasn't sure why he said the words. Maybe to get them to turn away from Claire. Maybe because he wanted to see their discomfort when they realized that they were his prey, and not the other way around.

The one whose ability rested in her hands went immediately for her gun, but to Nix, the pace of her motion was laughable. Adrenaline gave Nobodies an edge. The Sensors' presence threw Nix's body into fight mode, while his did nothing to theirs.

Emotions? Useless in a fight. The biochemical jolt that came with them? Gold.

Lightning quick, Nix feinted to the left and turned to block the woman's movement toward her gun. He caught her wrist in the strings of the wind chime, and twisted viciously—first to trap her hand and then to break it. Meanwhile, the woman's partner managed to get her gun unholstered, but Nix spun and lashed out with his left leg, knocking it out of her hands.

"Some of us have spent every day of our lives being molded into the perfect weapon," Nix said, his voice high and light. "And some of us haven't."

He backed up his words with action, pinning the first Sensor's good hand to the ground with his right foot and sending the commemorative plate he held in his left hand crashing into the second woman's face.

Kill.

The impulse was strong, and it would have been so easy. He dropped the remains of the plate, except for a single shard.

I could slit their throats.

One motion, two dead Sensors, two fewer problems down the road. Nix wanted to do it. He needed to do it. Wanted desperately not to. He couldn't think straight.

But Claire was there, in his mind and in the wall. Watching.

I can't.

So he didn't kill them. Instead, he shifted all of his weight to his back foot and felt the crunch of the first Sensor's bones under his heel.

No more hands. No more sensing.

The logic was elegant, the reality ugly, and Nix found the two sides of justice satisfying and nauseating both. Course set, he turned to the second woman, the one who'd scanned the room's energy with her eyes instead of her hands.

Her face was already bleeding. And, having seen what he'd done to her partner, she knew what to expect. But still, the Sensor's face was blank. Neutral. Her pupils weren't dilated with fear.

She didn't even seem to have a desire to run.

"You would have killed me," Nix said, considering the shard in his hands as he mentally replaced the *me* with *us.* "But I'm not going to kill you."

"Why not?" The woman's interest seemed entirely academic, even as Nix brought the shard to her throat.

Nix looked over his shoulder, to the wall, to Claire standing there, visible to his eyes only.

Because I don't want to, he thought, but out loud, all he said was, "Because." And then he slashed the shard across the woman's face.

No more eyes. No more sensing.

Done.

23

Claire couldn't dwell on the liquid ease with which Nix moved, the way his eyes narrowed in an almost snakelike fashion as his limbs fell into a blur of motion. So instead, out of the corner of her faded eye, she watched the Sensors. Not their bodies, but the light around one's hands and the other's eyes. It was a glint, a glare, a flickering aura—the kind of thing that couldn't be seen from outside the fade.

Power.

Claire held the gun, loose and ready at her side, but she didn't take aim, didn't pull the trigger. She watched the lights—the *power*—that had marked her view of the Sensors go out, like a firefly's bulb pinched between two fingers, as Nix attacked them.

He didn't kill them.

Claire stepped out of the wall, pulled by a force she couldn't deny.

Nix could have killed them, but he didn't.

He threw the shard in his right hand roughly to the ground. Walking toward her, he faded, and an instant later, they were beside each other, standing eye to eye with only a fraction of space between them.

"How many of them are there left?" Claire asked. Nix brushed his hand lightly over her cheek. The world froze around them.

"Two." Nix moved his hand from her hair to the back of her neck, keeping contact. "We need to find them before they find us."

Claire let her eye travel away from Nix's to the Sensors on the floor, broken and bloody. Powerless. One of them was unconscious, but the other lay frozen mid-action, her mouth open, as if she were about to speak.

"What do you think she's saying?" Claire asked.

Nix rubbed his thumb over her neck. "One way to find out."

Claire nodded and took a step away from Nix's touch. The moment they broke contact, the world around them fell back into motion.

"Target is gone. The Nobody just disappeared. I'm hurt. My eyes. God, my eyes . . ."

Claire glanced at Nix and lifted one invisible hand to

the woman's eyes. "Here," she said and then she turned to the unconscious woman. "And here," she indicated the woman's broken hands. "There used to be light. There isn't anymore."

Nix looked away. "They used to be Sensors. Now they're not."

Faded, Claire wasn't horrified. Her eyes didn't linger on the broken bones, the blood. She was a step removed—and all she could think, over and over again, was that Nix hadn't killed them. He could have—but he hadn't.

The fox asked the little prince to tame him.

"Stay where you are, Elena. We're about three minutes out. We'll be there soon."

Claire forced her faded brain to process the words coming from the Sensor's communicator. *Three minutes.* The other Sensors would be here in three minutes. Moving on instinct, she grabbed Nix's hand, her palm brushing lightly against his, their fingers interlocking.

"They're close," Claire said. "They're on their way here, and now"—she glanced meaningfully at his hand, at hers—"they're frozen."

"Two left," Nix said again. "We'll need to talk to at least one of them."

Claire brushed her lips against his, grounding her thoughts—and his—in the fade. *Here, now, them*—that was what mattered.

"Two left," Claire repeated. She lifted the gun and

rested it against his chest between them. "I like our odds."

<hr />

Pulling away from Claire was hard.

The smell of her hair. The curve of her lips. The way her hand held the SIG P226. Claire was more than the sum of her parts, but even the tiniest details of her body drew Nix like a planet toward the sun.

Forget the Sensors. Forget what they'd come here to do. Forget everything. Why go back? Ever? What had the real world ever done for them?

But Nix knew he couldn't do it. They had to disable the last two Sensors. Had to leave one of them in shape to talk.

Nix took a step away from Claire, pulling space in between them, but keeping a tight hold on her hand. Together, they walked through the walls of the store, through the dozen or so wind chimes out front, frozen where the wind had left them.

The boulevard was silent, motionless. The remaining Sensors had taken to one of the side streets, but they weren't hard to find. The older man had a nondescript nose and a pockmarked face, and he carried himself in a way that reminded Nix of a bloodhound—snout first.

Beside him, the younger man, the one Nix had

recognized as the kind of person who *liked* playing the role of predator, had one ear tilted toward the ground and the other turned toward his partner.

The two men must have been talking—to each other, to the frantic, blinded Sensor via their comms—at the moment that Nix and Claire had stopped time.

"Lights," Claire said, nodding toward their faces, her voice dreamy and rough, as if the owners of those faces did not want them dead.

"I see them." The lights. The Sensors. The enemy.

"You see the lights," Claire murmured, and Nix heard something in her voice that told him that concentrating on the sheen of energy that marked these men as Sensors kept her from thinking about them as people, thinking about what he—*they*—were about to do.

Nothing. No fear. No emotions. No hate.

It wasn't a bad strategy, and Nix wondered if it was that simple. See the lights. Put them out.

Nix stepped forward, hand still in Claire's. He couldn't touch the Sensors from the fade, but there was some chance he might be able to touch the light.

To Normals, a Sensor's power is invisible. It's nothing. So am I.

Nix reached out his free hand and for a moment, he expected to be able to catch the light in his hand and pull the powers out of the Sensors' bodies—no muss, no fuss, no blood. But the moment he made contact, a violent jolt traveled up his arm, from hand to shoulder.

Fuzziness.

Confusion.

Pain.

Is this what Claire felt when she brought the Null drug into the fade?

Nix barely had time to finish the thought before he realized that he'd dropped Claire's hand. They were still faded, still invisible to the outside world—but the second they parted, time sped up.

"—rash and inadvisable." The old man's words picked up midsentence. Nix kept himself from reaching for Claire.

"Nix, what happened?" Claire asked. "Why—"

Nix held his index finger up to his lips, in part because he didn't know the answer to Claire's question, but also because he found himself wanting to hear what these Sensors had to say.

"Elena is out of commission. So are Margaret and Ryland. Either we find these Nobodies and we neutralize them, or they neutralize us." The younger man was adamant—not because he was angry or scared.

Because he was titillated.

Because he wanted blood.

Nix concentrated on maintaining his fade. It was his fault they'd fallen back into the time line. He'd dropped Claire's hand, and now that the Sensors were talking, he couldn't bring himself to stop time again, not when eavesdropping might reveal something useful.

"If Ryland, Margaret, and Elena couldn't neutralize the Nobodies, what makes you think you can?" The old man's words were mild, as if his partner didn't provoke any more emotion in him than their targets did.

"This!" The younger withdrew a small vial. At first, Nix thought it might be the poison The Society favored for inconspicuous kills, but one look at his adversary's eyes corrected that assumption. A killer might romance their weapons, but they didn't hunger for them, and the look in the younger Sensor's eyes was akin to starvation.

Looks like tar. Feels like heaven. Nix thought of the drug Sykes had used. But this one looked different—lighter in color.

Almost transparent.

Back at the institute. Nix recalled what he'd seen in the laboratory the day he went back, his insides going ice-cold. Ione asking for a status update on Claire—and then demanding one on their "defense mechanism." The needle tracks he'd seen on one of the Sensor's arms.

"We've already taken the maximum dose of this particular drug, young man." In the present, the older Sensor's voice boomed. "Enough to partially inoculate us to our prey's powers. Enough to tell me that our targets could be close, listening to every word we say."

A breeze blew directly through Claire and Nix, and

even though it didn't affect them, when it reached the old man's nose, he tilted his head back, just a bit.

"If they were listening to us, we'd be dead." The young man, cocky, took a needle out of the inside pocket of his jacket, inserted it into the vial in his hand, and pulled back, filling the needle with a strange, nearly clear serum that glowed a light rose pink in the sunlight.

Not a poison.

A drug. And not the one Sykes had been taking. Not a Null drug.

Nix thought of the first Sensor he'd taken out. Ryland. His old trainer. The one he'd left, gasping for air on the pavement.

A man who never should have been able to get a lock on him, faded or not.

Maybe The Society's current head of research *wasn't* a complete waste of space. Maybe the Null drug wasn't his only achievement.

"Erikson, don't do this." The older man stepped forward to grab the younger man's arm, just before needle met skin. "You're not approved for another dose for twenty-four hours. The side effects—you're messing with forces you don't understand. The drug doesn't just protect you from their powers. It affects your own energy, alters the metaphysical building blocks of your entire—"

The old man's words were lost as his partner shook him off. Needle slid into vein, and the younger man—

Erikson—squeezed his eyes shut, the edges of his mouth pulling tight and tilting upward.

Pain.

Ecstasy.

And then he opened his eyes, and they were red. Not the light, translucent pink of the serum. Dark and bloodshot.

I wonder what Sykes looked like when he took the Null drug. Nix shook off the thought. He had to stay faded. With Claire.

"They're here," Erikson whispered, his pupils pulsing with some kind of artificial high. "I can't see them. I can't hear them. But they're near."

"Yes, yes, they are, faded most likely, and I would wager to guess that if they wanted us dead, we'd be so already." The older man looked upward—probably because he didn't know where exactly they stood. "They didn't kill Ryland or Margaret. Elena either."

The blood-eyed Sensor was too far gone to listen to reason. "I think I'll kill the girl first. Make it watch."

It as in Nix.

The words had their expected effect on him, and Nix felt a rush of unwanted emotion.

—*Protect Claire, save her, even if I have to kill him, it's my choice, mine*—

"I hear you," the object of Nix's hatred sing-songed. "You're here. You're close. You're hiding."

Nix reached for Claire, counting on her presence in

the fade to ground his. She glanced at him, but stepped back from his touch, and Nix realized that she didn't want to stop time. He wondered why.

Claire wrapped her left hand over the base of the gun she held in her right.

"Stop baiting them, Erikson." The old man's nose crinkled of its own volition as he spoke.

"Isn't that what The Society teaches you?" Erikson sneered. "The best way to deal with a Nobody is to taunt them. Lure them. Pretend to care, and they'll step right out into the open." His hand went back into his jacket pocket, producing another vial of translucent liquid. "Ione and her ilk need to get with the times."

Nix's heart thudded in his ears. With another dose of the drug, would this Sensor be able to see through the fade? Would he become a Nobody, the way Senator Sykes had taken on the characteristics of a Null?

No.

It was impossible, and it was wrong. But not as wrong or as impossible as the idea of Claire, her eyes locked on their target, lifting her arms. Lifting the gun. Steadying her aim.

Ready to fire, just in case.

<hr />

From the moment the smirking, sneering man started talking, Claire felt herself losing it—not the fade, but the ability to think and see things clearly. Whenever Nix got upset, he started flickering between the real world and the fade, but in that moment, with Nix at her side, Claire's grip on nothingness was so perfect, so complete that she faced the opposite danger.

She felt like she might never go back. Like the rules and morals that governed the real world didn't apply here.

Power. We have it. They don't.

The more ugly, meaningless word-sounds poured out of the young Sensor's smirking, sneering mouth, the less Claire felt like Claire, and the more she felt like something else. A girl with a gun.

Nobody.

Smirk-Sneer was holding another little pink-tinted vial, but Claire couldn't talk her eyes into looking at it. She couldn't parse the man's voice into words. All she could do was watch the flecks of light around his ears.

Moving faster.

Growing.

Claire barely felt her arms floating upward. She barely registered taking aim.

"Claire. No." Nix's voice cut into her thoughts, but only slightly.

What Smirk-Sneer was doing to his body and the flicker surrounding it—his energy, his aura, his power—was wrong.

It affects your own energy, alters the metaphysical

building blocks of your entire being. Claire remembered the older man's warning and finished it for him. *There's no telling what might happen.*

The lights surrounding Smirk-Sneer's ears grew brighter. They bubbled up on themselves, like blisters rising on the surface of burned skin.

"Give me the gun, Claire," Nix said softly. For a moment, Claire considered his request, but then the younger Sensor—*bad man, ugly-solid man*—stuck another needle in his skin and the flicker of light around his face exploded outward, doubling, tripling, quadrupling in size. Light. Swarming the bad man's body. Not just his ears.

Eyes.

Nose.

Mouth.

It spread down his body with the speed of a lit fuse. Each tiny fleck of light split in two and then in two again, and the whole time, they were growing, growing, growing. . . .

Claire's arms stiffened. Her finger slipped easily around the trigger of the gun. She was faded, and the bad man was looking directly at her. He was *talking* to her. "I see you," he said, his lips twisting maniacally as he went for his own gun.

"Claire!" Nix yelled.

Claire didn't care. She didn't hear it. All she could think about, all she had room in her mind for, was the light.

Claire could stop this. Stop the man who wanted to hurt them.

"Hide-and-seek is over," her target said, ignoring Claire and her gun and speaking directly to Nix. "How much do you want to bet I can make her lose her fade? A few well-placed words and a little pull of the trigger—she dies."

Claire didn't look away, and she didn't fire her gun. She watched as the bulging flecks of light wound themselves around and around the Sensor's body. Attacking his skin. Pushing their way in, and then back out. So many of them, in and out.

Everything in this world has an energy.

Maybe our energy is different. Maybe it's weaker. Maybe it's just set to a different frequency.

Nobody and Null. Nobody and Sensor and Null. Different kinds of wrong aren't supposed to mix.

With sudden clarity, Claire knew what was going to happen. She dove for the ground. The Sensor, mistaking her reasoning, adjusted his aim, training his gun on her. Nix threw himself at Claire. And then, before Nix's body could collide with hers, before the two of them could stop time, the Sensor who'd injected himself with three times the limit of The Society's experimental Nobody drug smirked and sneered, one last time. He went to pull the trigger, and his entire body exploded in a ball of light, the forces he'd been playing with devouring him whole.

The explosion, and the shock at what had happened,

knocked Claire back into the physical world, and she and Nix fell the last inch to the ground, their limbs tangled together in a mass of arms and legs. Outside of the fade, there was no trace of the explosion: no light, no energy, no corpse.

It took Claire a moment to realize that the gun was still in her hand. That it hadn't gone off, and that, with instincts she'd never been aware of possessing, she was aiming it at the remaining Sensor.

Unfaded. In public.

A passerby slowed down, his eyes on Claire sprawled out on the ground and holding a weapon, his brows furrowed, as if he couldn't quite process what he was seeing.

"Claire?" Nix whispered. "Gun?"

Claire bit her bottom lip and then nodded. Nix placed his hand over hers, and without ever changing its aim, he transferred the weight of the gun from her palm to his.

The Sensor—the last man standing in this team of five—nodded and closed his eyes, waiting for the axe to fall, but instead of putting a bullet between his eyes, Nix spoke, his words the sweetest sound that Claire had ever heard.

"Why don't we go someplace a little more quiet?" Nix stood and stepped in front of Claire, placing his body between hers and the Sensor's. "I think we have some things to discuss."

24

Society operatives had standing orders to self-destruct rather than risk exposure. Hidden somewhere on his person, their captive doubtlessly had a small white pill—deadly and discreet, for situations such as these.

"Hands where I can see them," Nix said softly, his gun resting on the small of the older man's back, reinforcing the point. There was no way was he letting his captive fall on the metaphorical sword before explaining what exactly had just happened and how the hell it landed on the *possible* side of the possible-impossible divide. And that wasn't even taking into consideration the information they needed to destroy the Null drug and associated research, to bring The Society to its knees—cripple it the way he'd personally crippled most members of this man's team.

Moving quickly and drawing little attention, Nix forced the Sensor into a back alleyway, Claire on their heels.

Revealing yourself to a Nobody probably doesn't even count as exposure.

If this Sensor did attempt to take his own life, Nix doubted it would be because The Society's secrets had been compromised.

It would be because the Sensor had failed.

Three members of this man's team were incapacitated—permanently. The fourth was dead by his own hand. And yet, the Sensor seemed remarkably unconcerned.

We can't scare him. Nix realized that this might make torturing information out of the man difficult. Nobodies were assassins, not specialists. They trafficked in death, not fear.

"I imagine that you're coming to realize your predicament, much as I've come to realize mine." The Sensor's tone was completely conversational.

"You shouldn't be able to imagine anything about us," Nix replied evenly. "My words should fall deaf on your ears. You shouldn't care enough to wonder what we're thinking."

"Oh, I don't. Not concretely. But abstractly? Well, I've always found the idea of Nobodies fascinating."

Nix rolled his eyes. It was just his luck that their hostage was one of *those*.

"So, no. I don't care what you, personally, are thinking. I can't bring myself to really pay much attention to you at all. But if I take a step back from the situation and think about an abstract, pretend Nobody who is in an abstract, pretend situation very much like yours, then with some mental wrestling, I can come to conclusions." The man paused. After a long moment, he continued, "I imagine that most people in your situation would have certain questions."

"You think we're people?"

Nix felt his heart clench at Claire's question. Her tone of voice told him that she was all too ready to believe that of all the members of The Society, they'd somehow found the one who thought Nobodies were human, same as anyone else. Nix angled his body, wanting to shield her from the inevitable response.

"Do I think you're people?" The Sensor repeated the question and shrugged. Clearly, his ability to put himself in others' shoes didn't extend quite that far.

"The Society considers us monsters," Nix said, willing Claire not to take the man's apathy personally. "They use Nobodies to kill Nulls, but if there weren't any Nulls, they'd be using the Sensors to kill us."

On some level, Nix had always realized this. It was just that before, he hadn't cared.

"Frightfully hard to kill, Nobodies. Not much cleanup work, which is nice, and the police never seem to follow up on leads, but your kind is damn hard to get a lock on. Makes extermination difficult."

Nix closed his eyes, unsure whether he should take advantage of the Sensor's chattiness, or put him out of his misery now. "That's why The Society sent me to kill Claire. The best chance they have of killing a Nobody is using another Nobody to do it."

"I can't say that I was involved with that decision, but the logic seems sound. . . ." The Sensor trailed off. Clearly, the gun wedged into his back wasn't quite incentive enough to keep his attention from wandering.

"What happened back there?" Claire asked him tentatively. "With the—"

Nix knew she was going to say *with the lights*, but he didn't want Claire to tell this Sensor that they could see the source of his powers. Maybe The Society knew about the flicker that indicated a Sensor's power in the fade and maybe it didn't, but Nix wasn't going to be the one to let that information slip.

And neither was Claire.

"What happened with your partner?" Nix said, finishing her question without giving anything away.

The question wandered in and out of the Sensor's mind, until he seemed to come to it on his own. He obliged Nix, intentionally or otherwise, by speaking his thoughts out loud. "Erikson was young and stupid. This generation—they have no respect for the old ways. The principles on which The Society was founded. *Protection. Invention. Discretion.*"

Nix snorted. At one point, he'd believed in The Society and its principles. Now the only thing he believed in was standing beside him, her nose crinkled and her hazel eyes opened wide.

"The Nobody serum was designed to make Sensors more sensitive to Nobodies. In small doses, it allows us to catch a whiff, so to speak, of things that might otherwise escape our notice."

"Us," Claire said, caught halfway between bluntness and blatant curiosity.

"Nobodies are—in the abstract, mind you—quite terrifying. The Society of Sensors has been around for thousands of years, and this serum is the first step we've successfully made toward immunizing ourselves against your powers."

Immunization? That was what they were calling it?

"This serum," Claire said slowly. "With it, people can . . . see us?"

Nix heard the hope in her voice, and his own chest tightened in response.

"See you? Yes. Remember you? For the duration of the dose, yes. Care about you? No."

For someone who was dealing only in abstracts, the Sensor was remarkably astute. And cruel.

Nix dug the gun farther into the man's back, leaving marks, bruises. Physical effects to match the wounds of Claire's the carelessly uttered words had picked open.

The Sensor gave no visual indication that he felt the barrel digging into his back. "In answer to your earlier question, I suppose that I don't believe that Nobodies are monsters. Or animals. I believe your lot in life is incredibly sad and that in most cases, termination in childhood is a mercy."

Termination in childhood?

"There were others?" Claire asked. "Like us? And you killed them?"

"Me, personally? No. I've been off active duty for a decade and the only reason I've been recalled is that Ione and her people deduced that my academic fascination with Nobodies might make me more willing than the average Sensor to pilot the serum."

Which serum? Nix wanted to ask, but he held his tongue. All in due time.

"But there *were* others, like Nix and me, and The Society killed them?" Claire's tongue moved freely.

The Sensor looked vaguely uncomfortable. "The Society has existed, in one form or another, for most of recorded history. The majority of our mandates were written in a harsher time."

Nix ground his teeth together and bit back the urge to smash the butt of the gun into the back of the man's head.

"And you can't change the mandates?" Claire asked softly. Nix could tell by the look on her face that she was picturing little Nixes, little Claires.

Terminated in childhood.

"Nobodies are quite rare. Relatively speaking, our discovery of their existence was quite recent. The things we could have accomplished with that information during the Crusades! But, alas, it wasn't to be, and when the Roanoke experiment went south, your numbers dwindled. As far as The Society has been able to tell, there haven't been more than a handful of Nobodies per generation since. Not enough to merit a large-scale revision of well-established precedent."

"You kill us because you're too lazy to revise the rules? Because the effort just isn't worth it, for just a few lives?"

Nix wove his free hand through Claire's. In the fade, the gesture would have stopped time; outside of it, the physical contact served no purpose but comfort. Nix had been given a lifetime to get used to The Society's attitude. It wouldn't have mattered how common Nobodies were. No one at The Society would have cared enough to change procedure.

"We don't kill all of you," the Sensor said, quite cheerful. "Consignment is an option for Nobodies located before the age of five."

Consignment.

White walls. White bed. White floor.

Life in a lab.

Trained to kill as soon as they could walk.

"Traditionally, once they reach a certain age, Nobodies become more recalcitrant. Hardly worth training . . ."

"Stop." Nix couldn't take watching Claire's face as she heard the Sensor's careless words.

This was the big mystery they'd set out to solve. The reason Nix had begun looking into his previous kills. Because he couldn't imagine why The Society wanted Claire dead. And even though they'd considered this answer on their own, even though they'd considered it likely—

Hearing it out loud was different. Especially for Claire.

"You must be thinking about killing me," the Sensor said, turning around, so that Nix's gun was pressed into his stomach instead of his back. "I would imagine that, in the abstract, someone in your position might want to kill someone in mine. But you're not likely to meet a more knowledgeable source on The Society's infrastructure, or one more sympathetic to your cause."

Nix gouged the man in the side, and beside him, Claire winced.

"*Sympathetic* was perhaps the wrong word," the man wheezed. "Forgive my imprecision of language and allow me to rephrase. I feel nothing for either of you, but my feelings toward Ione and the heads of the South American and European institutes are not what one would call positive. The Sensors they're producing are subpar at best and dangerous to Normals at their worst."

"Like the one who blew up," Claire said blithely.

The Sensor inclined his head. Nix tried to follow the conversation, but found himself stuck on the idea that there was more than one institute. That there might be more to The Society than he had seen.

That there might be no place on earth outside The Society's reach.

What I knew was the tip of the iceberg. This isn't David and Goliath. This is David versus Goliath and a few dozen of his closest friends.

"We have a drug." Nix hadn't meant to admit that out loud, not yet, but he had to know. "It gives Normals some shade of a Null's powers—and their indifference to others. A U.S. senator was killed because of it. If you're so familiar with The Society's infrastructure, you can tell me where the drug is made, who knows about it, and how far this thing has spread."

"Ahhh . . . the senator would be Evan Sykes, I suppose?" the Sensor said, thinking out loud. "I'd heard he got issued the first dose of the Null-2."

"Null-2?" Claire asked.

"The Nobody serum is at stage one: it helps inoculate us to your powers, but doesn't give us any of our own. As you saw with my impetuous young partner, trying to distill the ingredients into higher concentrations proves somewhat . . . fatal. But the scientists have made significantly more progress with the Null drugs. Null-2 is the second stage: it doesn't just protect against powers. It induces them."

The Sensor wasn't telling them anything they didn't already know.

"Nulls are easier to study than Nobodies, you know. Especially once they started piloting Null-1."

"What do we do?" Nix issued a very specific question. "About the serum?" *To destroy it and take The Society down?* Nix didn't say the last part out loud, but figured that it was implied.

He figured wrong.

"Well, I wouldn't advise taking it. Energy is tricky. Nulls and Nobodies . . . I'm not sure what you'd get if you mixed them. The results would be unpredictable. Anything could happen, really."

Nix thought of the feeling of unease and disgust that had rippled its way through the fade when Claire had crossed over holding a vial of Null-2. The way that vial had changed colors, reacting to the fade.

"What do we do with the serum *to destroy it and take The Society down*?" This time, Nix was explicit. "We're going to eradicate the serums, and then we're going to expose The Society. You're going to tell us how. The government? The media? The police?"

The Sensor shook his head. "The Society has plants

everywhere. It's strong, boy. Old. Many branches, many powerful people. And even if you could expose us—ask yourself this: do you really want the government to know that you exist? That Null-2 exists?"

The Sensor wasn't asking Nix anything he hadn't already asked himself, but still, it rankled. Nix had been The Society's assassin for three years. He had no desire to play that role for the U.S. government and no confidence that it would be able to resist using him in exactly the same way.

"If we can't expose The Society, what will it take to make them stop coming after us?" Nix asked, trying not to sound desperate. Not to feel it. Everything they'd done, everything they'd discovered—and still, they weren't safe.

Weren't ever going to be safe.

The Sensor didn't reply, and Nix sighed. "In the abstract, what would it take?"

"Ione's removal as the head of the North American unit. The physical destruction of the North American institute, along with any physical or electronic files on either of you. The eradication of the serums and with it, the memories of those files."

"Why are you telling us this?" For once, Claire seemed properly suspicious. Nix narrowed his eyes at the Sensor as the man shrugged.

"I'm dissatisfied with the current quality of—"

"No." Nix interrupted him. That wasn't a reason to

hand over a plan for The Society's destruction—partial or otherwise.

For a long moment, the Sensor was silent, and then he reached slowly into his pocket. Nix's pulse jumped in his throat, but Claire held him back, staying his trigger finger and allowing the man to withdraw a file.

A file, Nix thought. Someone from The Society was giving him a file. That could only mean one thing.

"You want us to kill someone?" he asked dully.

"No, I don't want you to kill someone." The man swallowed, his Adam's apple bouncing like a buoy on water. "God help me, I want you to save her."

Claire took the file gingerly from the Sensor's hand. There was a part of her that wanted to forget how little she mattered to the outside world, and that part wanted to hurt this man for reminding her, but the moment his face began to crumble, Claire knew that she wouldn't be able to do it.

It wasn't the Sensor's fault that he didn't care about Nobodies. That was just the way things were. And this man, this dear old man who the granny inside of Claire was already sizing for a scarf—cared. Not about her and not about Nix, but about someone. About a *her*. And he cared about this her enough to risk everything for her safety.

"You knew your partner would overdose on the Nobody serum." The conclusion was one that Claire spoke a millisecond before she actually reached it. "You wanted to talk to us. You planned this."

"I warned him not to do it," the old man said. "And I may have also been the one who left the extra serum unguarded in his presence."

With shaking hands, Claire opened the file. There was a picture clipped to the front. A little girl, about seven or eight, with bright red hair and a scattering of missing teeth.

"Your daughter?" Claire guessed. "Or granddaughter?" She revised her guess for the man's age.

"No," the man said. "Subject N-632. Natalie."

Claire flipped through the papers attached to the file. More pictures of the same child. She had wide green eyes and appeared openly fascinated with the world around her. The last picture gave Claire pause.

There were two other small children in the picture: dark-haired, blue-eyed children, being held underwater by gloved hands. Adult hands.

And the little red-haired girl was just watching, the same bright smile on her face.

Nix glanced down at the page and blanched. Claire felt him leaving her, going deep into his own memories, and she scooted closer to him in protest. She ran her hand up and down his arm, and slowly, he came back to her.

"They're Nobodies," Nix said.

"Natalie?" Claire asked.

"No. The other two."

They couldn't have been older than five, maybe six. One boy. One girl. Their resemblance to each other was obvious.

Their resemblance to Nix was a bullet straight to Claire's heart.

"This must have been what you looked like," Claire said softly, leaning into his body, forgetting that Nix still had a gun drawn on the Sensor. "The black curls. The eyes." Claire swallowed, hard. "They look so scared."

"Can't fade when they're scared," Nix said, his throat closing in around the words and forcing them out as a grunt. The sound—anguished and gruff—turned Claire's heart inside out. "Their trainers are holding them under, forcing them to fade, and they can't, because they're scared."

Claire wished that she could melt into Nix. Physically become a part of his body and take away even a single layer of his pain.

"Who are they?" Nix asked. Claire felt his body tense with each labored word.

The Sensor shrugged. "Natalie is—"

"I don't care who Natalie is. Tell me who *they* are." Nix jabbed a finger at the dark-haired pair.

"Subjects X-17 and X-18," the Sensor replied, pointing first to the little girl and then to the boy.

"X-17," Claire repeated. That was what Sykes had demanded for his continued cooperation. What he'd wanted The Society to give him.

A weapon. A Nobody. For "reconnaissance" and "threat removal." An assassin, a spy—

A child.

The Sensor cleared his throat. "I believe their trainers call them Nix."

This time, Claire was the one who had to be restrained. She threw herself at the man, tearing into him—scraping her nails down his face, digging her teeth into his shoulder, kicking him, screaming.

Nix dragged her away.

"I thought you said Nobodies were incredibly rare."

"Well, naturally, yes, they are. And rarely identified before the kill point, as you can imagine. But about Natalie—"

The man's eyes were desperate.

"No," Claire said, struggling against Nix's hold. "Not about Natalie."

It was one thing for this man to be cold toward her, and to Nix. But to children? Kids who'd never get to be forgotten at Walmart or left out of a school play or abandoned on a field trip to the zoo, because their caretakers were too busy attempting to drown them?

Claire knew suddenly what it was like to really, truly want to hurt another person. The instinct was overpoweringly strong, and if she hadn't given Nix the gun, Claire might have done it.

"Please," the man said, unaware of the reaction he'd provoked. "You have to listen to me. Natalie—"

Natalie, Natalie, Natalie. It was every other word out of the man's mouth, and Claire wondered how he could justify it to himself—betraying everything for one little girl, and not being bothered in the least by the systematic torture of another.

"Tell us about these children, and we'll listen about Natalie." Nix's voice was dull, and Claire wondered how he could be so calm. She curled up against his body, and he settled his free arm around her stomach.

"They're Nobodies. Still quite young. Haven't made their first kill. When The Society acquired Natalie, Dr. Milano insisted all three be housed together." The man's voice took on a reverent note every time he mentioned the little girl's name. "They've been serving as donors, for the serum."

"Donors?"

"To inoculate a Sensor against a Nobody's powers, you need Nobody blood, among other ingredients. Powerful stuff, Nobody blood."

Claire pictured these little ones. Crying. Bleeding. Not crying, once they'd learned their tears were worthless. Claire bent her lips inward, holding them in place with her teeth and trying desperately to hold everything together.

For Nix.

"Why do they look like me?"

The question laid Nix out bare. Claire could see all of his hurts, all of the things he'd never let himself want. She could see him as a little, little boy.

This boy.

"As I said before, Nobodies are notoriously hard to locate in the first few years of their lives. We haven't managed to harvest one before the kill point from the general population since the mid-fifties. But they do have their uses, so in the past two decades, certain members of The Society have provided us with Nobody infants in exchange for positions of wealth and power within the organization."

"And how exactly do they do that?" Claire asked, knowing from the rhythm of Nix's heartbeat that he was suddenly terrified of the answer and incapable of asking it himself.

"Nobodies suffer from a rare birth defect. It has been found over the years that certain mothers—although Normal themselves—are more likely than others to produce defective children. The Society has been known to recruit these women. To offer them incentives."

Claire couldn't take listening to this. Not because it meant that her own mother might have had a genetic part in making her the kind of child a mother couldn't love, but because every word the Sensor was saying indicated that Nix's mother had willingly given him to The Society.

She'd sold him.

And based on the family resemblance between Nix and the children in the picture, Claire was willing to bet that she'd sold his siblings, too.

———◆◆◆◆———

Nix hadn't realized that it was possible to hate a nameless, faceless woman. But he found, in retrospect, that it was actually quite easy.

Hating his mother—*I had a mother and she gave me away*—was easier than anything except for loving Claire. Just as natural. Just as inevitable. Just as sure.

I hate my mother. And it doesn't matter, because my hatred doesn't count.

The thought reminded Nix of the other people he'd hated, the other emotions he'd wasted on recipients who never looked at him with anything other than vague indifference.

His mentors.

His marks.

And Ione.

Ione, who was Normal, but had somehow climbed to the top of the corporate ladder to head The Society—or at least, the North American branch. Ione, who had never spared him more than a passing second. Ione, who had dyed her dark hair blond, to better match her light blue eyes.

Dark hair. Light eyes. *Certain members of The Society have provided us with Nobody infants in exchange for positions of wealth and power.*

"Ione is my mother." Nix tried to process the idea. *Mother* was an abstract term to him. He'd never had one. He'd only seen one, or two, only allowed himself a few stolen moments watching and listening to their lullabies, from the shadows. "And these two." He laid first his index finger and then the pinkie of his free hand on the picture Claire held. "Ione is their mother, too."

"If you'd like to kill her, I have no objections. It will be necessary, if you want to truly free yourselves—"

"And the children," Claire added. "We have to free them, too." Nix marveled at her ability to think ahead. To plan. To believe that there was a better life for this Nix and that Nix than there had been for him.

Do you know why we call you Nix, child?

Because that was what they called all Nobodies. It wasn't even a name. Not really. And these little ones, they deserved names. They deserved naps and stories and hugs. And Claire.

They deserved to be loved.

"Yes! Yes! The children. Once the North American institute is destroyed, and the serums and formulas along with it, you can take them. Hide them. Give them a fresh start."

"I know the institute. I lived there. If there were other Nobodies on the premises"—*brother, sister*—Nix's voice caught as he tried not to think the words—"I would have known."

"The way you knew about the serums?" the Sensor asked. "The North American institute has two parts: one is aboveground, one is below. They have separate entrances, separate staffs, separate mandates. It's a typical safeguard against Nobodies—you walk through walls, you rise through ceilings, but you don't, as a general rule, attempt to sink down to the center of the earth and stumble across things buried four stories underground."

The words began pouring out of the man's mouth faster, his eyes glowing with an almost feverish insistence. "I'm giving you information you didn't have, information you need. You want to destroy the drugs, the research, to weaken The Society and fall off its radar. I can help you, and all you have to do is *save the children*."

At first, Nix wondered why the Sensor seemed so desperate to save "the children," and then he remembered the desperate repetition of the red-haired girl's name— *Natalie, Natalie, Natalie*—and Nix recognized, finally, the manic glint in the Sensor's eyes and the root of his willingness to throw everything away for Subject N-632.

"She's a Null."

The Sensor's lips trembled. "She's eight years old. She's beautiful and she's bright, and it's not her fault she's different. She could be good. She could be different. You have to save her. You *have to.*"

Eight years old, and already capable of manipulating a full-grown Sensor into crippling The Society's reach in North America.

Nix stared at "Natalie." In the picture, she looked on, vaguely interested, as his little brother and sister struggled against the hands that held them in the baby-size dunk tanks.

Her indifference wasn't because they were Nobodies.

It was because she was a Null. Discovering that some of his victims had been Normals hadn't changed Nix's feelings toward those he'd killed who weren't. Murderers. Serial killers. Psychopaths.

I've killed, but I can stop. They can't. They can't ever stop.

"You realize she's a monster," Nix said evenly, trying not to let his thoughts show on his face. "That she's doing this to you."

"She's not. She's a child! And she's sweet. She is . . ." The man—who didn't seem like a Sensor any longer—was equal parts adamant and broken. "If you want them, you have to take her. I can give you the North American institute. I can give you weaknesses, blueprints, anything you want or need. Just promise to make her safe."

Nix could do that. He could lie. And The Society could come apart at the seams, just like that.

"We promise." Claire beat him to it, and Nix cursed himself. He knew her well enough to know that she wouldn't lie. Not about this. She'd made the promise with every intention of keeping it, and she would never understand that a little, little girl could be dangerous.

So dangerous that The Society should have known better than to think it could keep her caged.

"If she's as sweet as you say," Nix said slowly, "then why don't the other Sensors see it? Why don't the scientists?"

Claire arrived at the answer before their captive actually articulated it. "If there's a Null-2, there must be a Null-1, right? A serum that protects people from a Null's powers? Are you taking it?"

The man shook his head.

"*Were* you?"

He nodded. Nix felt something, akin to pity, in the pit of his stomach.

"And when I stopped taking Null-1, that's when I met Natalie. The real Natalie, not Subject N-632."

Nix looked back at the little girl. She was small. And powerful. And sooner or later, she'd be dangerous.

But that wasn't his problem, and it wasn't Claire's. It wasn't the little boy Nix's or the little girl, Nix's—and if this Nix had his say, it never would be. They'd never feel a large hand in the small of their backs, pushing them toward that first kill.

Terrifying. Horrifying. Addictive.

Nix ground his teeth. The Nulls of the world weren't his problem anymore. They weren't his responsibility, and if this Sensor wanted little Natalie, the ticking time bomb, he could have her. It took Nix less than a second to come to the decision that for Claire and the little ones, he'd gladly sell his soul. Go against everything he'd believed in once.

Not. My. Problem.

"Fine. The Null lives. The Society—this portion, at least—dies. Now tell us everything we need to know and get the hell out of here."

25

Claire let out a breath that she hadn't realized she was holding. She'd promised to save the Sensor's Natalie before it had occurred to her that Nix might not agree to do it, and that realization had cut her nearly in two. Because Null or not, manipulative or not, born wrong or not, Natalie was just a little girl.

A little, little girl who couldn't help what she was any more than little Claire had been able to help being left and forgotten and ignored.

Null drug. Black hole. Hurts. Wrong.

Claire thought of Evan Sykes's miracle drug. Null-2— made with little Natalie's blood—had turned Abigail's father into a pod person. Uncaring. Manipulative. Cruel.

For a moment, Claire was overcome with a still-frame daydream, chilling in its simplicity: Natalie smiling.

She's just a little girl.

"The institute is extremely secure. You're familiar with the upper level; it's nearly identical to the sublevels. For both, Sensors are scanned by an entire team before being allowed into or out of the building, and only a handful of Normals have the kind of access necessary to travel past the first floor. Besides Ione and Dr. Milano, no Normals have access to the sublevel entrance at all. You'll have to fade to get in unannounced, and with a subset of the security team on the serum, there is an increased chance that your presence will be detected."

Claire focused on what their informant was saying. He sounded as if he'd practiced these words many times, as if he'd whispered them to Natalie as a bedtime story when he'd promised, again and again, to get her out.

"You weren't able to see through our fades," Nix cut in. "You didn't stop taking the Nobody serum, correct? Just the Null one?"

Claire knew what Nix was really asking. They needed to know just how potent the serum was. Their informant hadn't been able to see them in the fade. His partner had only been able to do so after his third dose. If this was the serum's normal efficacy, it wasn't much of a threat.

Yet.

The Sensor cleared his throat, a gargling sound that

reminded Claire that he was human. And old. "I'm still on the Nobody serum. It's probably the only reason that I was able to integrate the information I've been able to gather about the two of you. I have a horrible attention span, and my senses and memory aren't what they used to be—"

"What are the chances of someone at the institute pulling an Erikson?" Nix asked, cutting the man off and moving on to his next question without segue.

The Sensor was nonplussed. "Erikson was remarkably stupid. One does not obtain a position on the institute's security force with that kind of stupidity. No one else will double up doses—not without Dr. Milano's approval, and he won't give it until the full effects of a single dose are documented. No one will be able to see through your fade, but they might be slightly more aware of your presence on an instinctual level, and once you stop fading, they will be more likely to explicitly register your existence and less likely to ignore you than they otherwise would be."

For what seemed like the hundredth time, the Sensor shrugged. Claire felt Nix seething beside her, and she leaned into him, trying to intuit why.

He wants answers. He wants to be alone.

Nix couldn't stand to feel emotions around other people. He'd been taught that he didn't deserve them. Sensors were the ones who'd imparted that lesson. And right now Claire could see, in the lines of Nix's body and the set of his jaw, that he was trying very hard not to feel anything.

Not to think of the little girl Nix and the little boy Nix being turned day by day into weapons.

Not to think of the things that little Natalie might do once they let her go.

"Thanks for the warning, but we don't need it." Claire was surprised to find her voice textured in complement to Nix's. Lower. Darker. Even. "We want the real information. What's The Society's Achilles' heel? How do we destroy the institute? Both levels, all of the drugs."

The Sensor ran one of his knuckles up the bridge of his nose, like a person who'd worn glasses for many years before switching to contacts. "The Society has a fail-safe mechanism. An insurance policy against exposure. If any individual branch is threatened with imminent and widespread exposure—if the press break in, or the police start making arrests, or anyone infiltrates the security far enough to get ahold of classified files, the directive to meltdown is given."

"Meltdown?" Claire found herself sickly fascinated with the idea.

"The entire institute is equipped to self-destruct within a five-minute window. Once activated, the self-destruct mechanism cannot be undone. Five minutes after activation, the building and anyone inside are dust." He paused. "Both levels."

"What's the catch?" Nix asked the question before Claire could get to it. "Why would The Society make it that easy to take the institute down?"

"Who said that activating the self-destruct mechanism was easy?" The Sensor shook his head and clucked his tongue. "I assure you, it's not a simple matter of pushing a red button. Were that the case, I would hardly have to enlist Nobodies as help."

Claire didn't respond to those words. Neither did Nix. Eventually, the Sensor elaborated.

"To activate self-destruction, you need two keys. The keys are in the possession of the two heads of the institute, who must agree that the breach of security is severe enough to merit meltdown."

"Ione." The muscles in Nix's throat visibly tightened as he spoke the name, and Claire felt her own clenching in empathy.

"Ione has one key," the Sensor agreed. "And Sergei has the other."

"Sergei?"

Claire arched an eyebrow at Nix, surprised that there was someone at the institute who he'd never met.

"Sergei is an All Sensor. The only one in North America. He's a bit of a recluse, but his powers are unparalleled, so his position at The Society has never been in question. He lives in a penthouse on the top floor of the institute. If you explored it, you probably didn't find it to your liking.

Very plain, very severe. Sergei is a dangerous man, and he finds Nobodies rather ... aversive."

Claire thought of the four Sensors she'd seen since coming after Nix. "I'm guessing that by *All Sensor*, you mean that he—"

"Is gifted in all five senses? Yes, quite. He's from an old Society family—the bloodline goes back to the old country and then some. He's also remarkably lethal. He doesn't leave the institute and he doesn't enjoy being around people—sensory overload, you see. You'll need to infiltrate his quarters and find his key. It will likely be on his person; Ione wears hers around her neck."

Situation: What if your boyfriend's evil mother was wearing the key to the kingdom around her neck, and you had to get it to save the world? What if you knew that he couldn't do it, because seeing her would tear him apart and make him vulnerable?

What if you had the chance to kill her?

Claire shook her head. Actually, physically shook it. Because as much as she wanted to hurt The Society and the people who'd hurt Nix, she didn't want to be the type of person who could think of murder and smile.

"So we get the keys," Nix cut in. "What do we do with them?"

The Sensor started talking about the location of the self-destruct trigger, and Claire, with no frame of reference with which to ground the directions, found herself tuning out, picturing Nix's mother. His little brother and sister.

Natalie.

"I know the location you're describing." Nix's voice broke into Claire's thoughts, and she forced herself to concentrate on the present. "Never knew what it was, but I know where it is. Getting to it won't be a problem."

The Sensor replied, addressing his comments to the space just over Nix's left shoulder. "It's not getting to the mechanism that's the problem, although I assure you that no one besides a Nobody would have the ability to do so without the proper security clearance." The Sensor paused, and Claire prepared herself. If getting to the mechanism wasn't the problem that meant that there *was* a problem. And problems, when they involved The Society, tended to be deadly. Just ask Senator Wyler. Just ask Evan Sykes.

"The chamber in which the trigger is housed is rigged. The moment one of the keys is inserted, poisonous gas is emitted into the room. It reacts to flesh like acid, can eat through any protective materials you might wear in an attempt to circumvent your skin's melting off your body, and a single breath is fatal. Death is instantaneous to anyone inside the fail-safe chamber when the key is inserted."

After she got past the mental image of a skeleton leaking skin, Claire could not help but see the flaw in the logic of such a system. "Why would Sergei and Ione ever agree that a meltdown was necessary if it meant they had to die?"

The Sensor chuckled. Nervous laughter that Claire suspected had nothing to do with the fact that he was talking to people who mattered no more than the average ball of dust and everything to do with the fact that he was planning the destruction of all that had ever mattered to him. At the request of an eight-year-old girl. "Ione and Sergei are immune to the poison. They've been taking it in very, very small doses since they ascended to power. It takes two years to develop the immunity, and it's part of the screening process for promotion. If you die because of the treatments, you're fired."

The Society doesn't care who dies, Claire thought dully. *It kills Nobodies. They kill Nulls. They kill their own without a second thought.*

Claire was caught between wanting to shiver and wanting to growl. She was fifteen. Nix wasn't much older. The Society had been around for thousands of years, and there was no one else to stop it. Stop *them*.

Nix and Claire had to do this.

They were going to do this.

"Gas can't poison what's not there." Nix's voice regained a bit of its edge, and Claire felt it on every inch of her skin. "The mechanism isn't Nobody-proofed."

The Sensor shrugged. "Design flaw, I suppose. Though,

of course, one must solidify to insert the keys, and then fade again within an instant to avoid certain death."

Clearly, the idea of putting a Nobody in danger wasn't a problem for the Sensor. *Shocking,* Claire thought. Out loud, she said, "So we activate the mechanism. What next?"

Nix laid his hand on the back of her neck, and Claire felt his appreciation that she could be his voice when he didn't have one and ask the questions on the tip of his tongue.

"While one of you initiates the self-destruct sequence, the other will need to go to B-4. The children's quarters."

I know what you're hiding in the lower levels there. Those were the words that Sykes had used to threaten Ione. The ones with which he'd signed his own death warrant. The Society kept children in the lower levels of the institute, and Sykes had wanted a slice of the Nobody pie. A pet assassin of his very own.

The Sensor continued, "I've snuck a look at Milano's files, and the math is straightforward enough. Three Nobodies should be strong enough to cover one Null for a very short period of time, if the Null is willing. Natalie has been practicing with X-17 and X-18. She'll be ready."

Taking the Null drug into the fade had sent a shock up Claire's arm. It had stirred something in her stomach, made her nauseous. She wondered what taking a live Null with her would do.

"X-17 and X-18?" Nix hissed, enmity dripping from

each syllable like blood from the tip of a blade. "They're not numbers. They're kids. And there's no way I'm taking a Null to the fade. You said it yourself: Null blood and Nobody blood are powerful, tricky things. What do you think is going to happen if we take a body full of Null blood into the fade?"

<hr />

Nix tried to calm the revulsion in his gut. He'd taken Claire into the fade, back when he'd thought she was a Null—but that was before he'd felt what it was like when Claire brought the Null drug with her. Nix couldn't push down the surge of disgust he felt, just thinking about it now.

He hated Nulls, and the fade was sacred, and The Sensor had called his little sister X-17.

I can't even look at Null-2. Claire had to hold the vial. I have a sister.

The thoughts blurred together in Nix's mind. Claire pressed her body lightly to the side of Nix's, and all up and down the left half of his body, Nix felt the gentle reassurance of her presence. The fury simmering beneath his surface calmed, still ready, still hot, but contained enough that he could put it into words, feel it without putting his body into motion.

All the Sensor cared about was the little Null. Demented

by the girl's powers, he was willing to sell out the principles for which Nix and his siblings had been bought, trained, tortured, and enslaved.

I believe their trainers call them Nix.

X-17. X-18. Nix and Nix. Nothing. Nobody.

Nix hated this. Hated that The Society could still hurt him. Hated that he wanted to scream. Hated that he couldn't get the children's cherubic faces, distorted by the dunk tanks, out of his mind.

Nix had never had a family before. And now he had one, and all this man cared about was the Null. The Null who'd been practicing God knows what with his little brother and sister. Nix couldn't think about the fact that the children were probably as Null-struck as this pathetic excuse for a man beside him.

Saving Natalie might be a necessary evil—but that didn't mean Nix wanted to think about it. About what Natalie could do. About what she might do, if she grew up into a bright-eyed, red-haired woman.

Necessary evil or not, Nix couldn't swallow the idea of bringing *that thing* to the fade. The one place that Nobodies mattered. The only place where the real world couldn't touch them or hurt them or mess with their minds. Sanctuary. Paradise.

"Covering Natalie with your collective powers is the only way to get her away from the scientists. Do you know what they do to her? They make her bleed. They hurt her. They make her hurt things. She doesn't like it. She wants out."

For a moment, the Sensor's face changed, and his tone and words became someone else's. Nix could almost picture the girl from the photograph saying these things.

They're hurting me. They make me hurt things. I don't like it.

And then the Sensor snapped out of it, and his words became his own again. "You need me if you want to destroy the institute."

"Why?" Nix kept his voice even. "We know about the keys. We know where the children are. We know about the self-destruct mechanism. Why do we need you?"

Beside him, Claire's mouth dropped open slightly, and Nix realized that the idealistic part of her *wanted* to save Natalie. Wanted to believe that she was just a little girl. And that was exactly why Nix couldn't let Claire anywhere near the Null. Tender hearts were child's play for Nulls, and Claire was an open book.

The Sensor clearly didn't—*couldn't*—feel betrayed that Nix was already reneging on his promise. Instead, he continued speaking in the same calm, neutral tone. "You need me to destroy the institute, because I can make your files disappear from the mainframe. The computer systems are set to automatically upload all content to off-site backup hard drives the moment the self-destruct sequence is initiated. Milano's possessive enough of his research that he hasn't uploaded it to the mainframe yet, so destroying the institute will destroy the formulas for the serums. Your files, on the other hand, are in the computer, and Ione has activated certain security protocols to remind us of your existence and the threat you represent. After the institute is destroyed, there will inevitably be some kind of investigation, most likely spearheaded by the European office. They'll go through everything, talk to everyone. The people involved will likely forget about you and almost certainly won't be able to provide any kind of details, but unless I destroy the electronic trail, you'll have the whole of The Society nipping at your heels."

With great effort, the Sensor flicked his eyes to Nix's face and then to Claire's, and Nix got the message loud and clear.

"Tonight, when I go back to the institute, I'll remove your files from the computers and upload them on to an external hard drive. If you bring me Natalie, I'll give you the disk. Ione and Sergei will go down with the blast, and in the chaos of reorganization, the two of you and X-17 and X-18 will almost certainly be forgotten in the aftermath."

Unless, of course, the Sensor saved the files and gave them to the remaining branches of The Society, which he would gladly do if Nix didn't give him Natalie in return.

"We give you Natalie. You give us—all of us—our freedom." Claire put the terms of the agreement into words.

"Yes. Save Natalie. You must." The Sensor's eyes took on that fevered look again. "And the only way you can save her is to make her fade. She's bright, so bright, so beautiful, that she'll be hard to hide. The world won't want to let her go. But there are four of you. Unprecedented. Absolutely unprecedented. You're strong. You can save her. I know you can."

Nix's lip curled upward, and his fingers curled down, driving his nails into the skin of his palm. Fading was power. Energy. Release. It was his. The one thing that no one could take away. The only thing the universe had given him to make up for all it had taken away when he'd been born terminally unimportant.

Null. Faded.

To Nix, it was blasphemy. Like sleeping with a dead animal. Like rolling over and exposing your soft under-belly to a beast that wanted to tear out your entrails. It was stupid, and it was wrong.

Necessary evil.

Nix gritted his teeth and clamped down on the roar of emotions circling each other in his gut.

It's not my job to kill Nulls. Not anymore. It's not my responsibility to turn myself into a monster so the rest of humanity can live free and clear.

Numbly, dispassionate, Nix nodded his assent. If this was the cost of freedom, so be it. Nix met the Sensor's eyes, even though the old man didn't quite reciprocate the gaze. And then he said the one word that set things fully and irrevocably in motion. "Tonight."

The Sensor nodded. "Tonight. The information I gave you says where. And remember: no Natalie, no files."

Null. Null. Null.

Refusing to look at the Sensor or at Claire, Nix turned and slipped into nothingness, feeling like he'd left a chunk of himself behind.

Claire nibbled on her bottom lip, trying to find the right thing to say—like there was a right thing to say in a situation like this. Nix hadn't uttered so much as a single word to her since they'd let the Sensor go.

He'd headed back to the cabin. Claire had followed.

He'd lifted one of the panels on the wooden floor, revealing a weapons cache much bigger than the one Claire had kept under the porch. She'd silently knelt beside him, laying out the spread as he unearthed wires, rope, and needles. Knives. Guns. Darts. An ice pick, several bags of white powder, and a variety of explosives.

"Take off your clothes."

Nix's voice washed over Claire's body. Deep. Reassuring. It wasn't until the words disappeared from the air that she realized their content.

"Take off my ... ?"

"I would give anything to leave you here. To keep you safe. But one of us has to initiate the meltdown while the other one gets the children. This isn't a job for one Nobody. It's a job for two. And even if it wasn't, you'd come. Where I go, you follow. Even if I could keep you safe, you wouldn't want it. I know you—you won't even stay away from the Null."

Null. Null. Null.

If Claire hadn't already known how Nix felt about Nulls, the venom he put into that word would have told her more than enough.

"Take off your clothes," Nix said, repeating the order. He stood and stalked out of the room, returning a moment later with two pairs of pants and two shirts: one for him and one for her. Not bothering to expand on his earlier command, he followed the advice he had given her, stripping off his shirt.

Sleek. Stone cold. Hard. His stomach looked like it had been carved from marble. Every muscle was tensed. Taut.

Ready.

Biting her bottom lip again, Claire brought her fingers to the end of her own shirt. Nix wrapped an Ace bandage around his middle, and with expert fingers, he began to weave and tie knots in it, twisting and turning the fabric to form pockets. Claire watched the motion, hypnotized, her own limbs still frozen.

Dagger.

Darts.

Some kind of double-edged blade.

Nix tucked the weapons into his makeshift halter. One wrong move, and he'd slice himself open.

Guns were strapped to his ankles. Wires were wrapped around his wrists. Claire stared down at her own hands—miniature compared to his. After an elongated moment, she lifted up the end of her oversized shirt, revealing an expanse of suntanned skin underneath.

Without a word, Nix came to stand behind her. Wrapping his arms around her body, he strapped a knife to her side, his fingers brushing against the flat of her back as he did.

"Do you know how to use this?" he asked.

"It's a knife," Claire replied. "You stab it."

Nix almost smiled. Almost. He tapped her jugular. "Slice," he said, and then he trailed his hand over her shirt and down her chest, until it rested inside her rib cage. "Stab. If you can't reach the torso, go for the femoral artery. Here." He indicated the place on her leg, his touch light. Then, carefully, he turned her around to face him.

"Hopefully, you won't need to use the knife. From the fade, you won't be able to." And with those words, he went and picked up two guns. One for each of her ankles. Finally, he gave her back the SIG.

"Do you know how to shoot?"

It had never occurred to Claire that it might be more complicated than pulling a trigger. She said so, and moments later, they were outside, and he was going through the steps, one by one.

"Close one eye. Look down the barrel. Grip steady. Arms straight."

It took her three tries to hit a tree. He showed her how to reload, and they fell into a pattern: shooting, reloading, his hands steadying her body against the kickback.

"If you shoot from the fade, the bullet crosses into reality once it leaves the gun—unless you actively try to keep it immaterial. Assuming you let the bullet go, you can take out a target without ever giving them the opportunity to lay a single finger on you."

Claire thought back to aiming the gun at the rogue Sensor as he injected himself with the serum for the second time. She hadn't thought about killing, or mechanics, or what any of it meant. She'd moved on instinct.

And if he hadn't killed himself, she might have done it for him.

Nix doesn't want me to do this. I don't want to do this. I don't want him to do this.

It had to be done.

"So that's the plan?" Claire asked softly. "We go in, guns blazing, and pick them off one by one? Shoot Ione and Sergei, take their keys, and be done with it?"

She'd do that. For the little black-haired boy and the

little black-haired girl. For Natalie, who couldn't help what she was. For Sykes and Wyler. For Nix. For herself. For their future.

Nix shook his head. "If we shoot Ione or Sergei, someone will figure out that we're there, the entire place will go into lockdown, and we'll lose our chance to grab the children. No one can know we're there. The weapons are just a precaution."

As far as precautions went, Claire thought the artillery strapped to their sides was rather extensive, but this wasn't her realm of expertise. It was his.

"In an ideal world, we wouldn't ever shoot a gun, and everything else would stay sheathed. So long as we're in complete control, all we need to do to get the keys is stop time, find the keys, and materialize just enough to take them."

Claire noticed that Nix said that they needed to find the keys. Not that they needed to find Sergei and Ione.

Ione. His mother.

Claire almost said something, but she decided against it. She knew, better than anyone, that there were some hurts you couldn't afford to feel.

Nix closed his eyes, and his body grew bright with the fade. Claire's lips softened, as they always did, and the impulse to join him, to let go, to forget about what they were doing and why, was incredible.

But she didn't.

Instead, she watched as he spoke. "This isn't my hand. It's not me. It's not mine. It doesn't belong here."

Claire watched the fade slowly recede back from Nix's fingertips, and when he knelt to the ground, he plucked a single blade of grass from the forest floor.

"You try."

She did. The warmth of the fade came easily and quickly, and with a serene smile, Claire said good-bye to the digits on her right hand. It was much easier than shooting a gun. What was a hand anyway? It didn't have thoughts or feelings. It didn't have memories. She'd raised that hand in class, again and again, and been overlooked. Really, in the grand scheme of things, hands weren't such a very big deal.

"Good," Nix said, once she'd accomplished the task. "We might lose timelessness when we partially solidify, and we'll definitely lose it when we split up, but we'll just have to cross that bridge when we come to it."

Claire saw many bridges in their future, not the least of which was Natalie the little Null. Their future was full of crossings, but for now there was only one detail to be settled, one point on which Claire had no intention of giving in.

"You can't go anywhere near Ione."

Nix whipped his head up, but she didn't give him the chance to stare her down.

"Thinking about my parents makes me lose my fade. She's your mother, Nix."

"She's not my—" Nix's words caught in his throat as though someone had closed a hand around his throat, and the real world—the solid world—pulled at him.

"You lost your fade," Claire said, matter-of-fact about the force that had jarred him into silence. "Just now talking about her made you lose your fade. And when you lose your fade, I lose mine. And if we lose it in the institute, then these weapons won't be for show." Claire dragged her free hand down to the knife at her side. "Slice," she said. "Stab."

She knew how his mind worked. He didn't want her to kill, and he certainly didn't want her fighting for her life.

"Fine," he said. "You take Ione. I'll take Sergei. If we split up, we won't be able to freeze time, but we won't lose our fades either. We'll meet back, and then—"

Claire saw the moment that it occurred to Nix just how much he abhorred what had to happen next.

"One of us has to go get the kids, and one of us has to initiate the meltdown," Claire said, picking up where he had left off. "Both of which will require leaving the fade, at least for a moment, and both run the risk of tipping the powers that be off to our presence. If we stick together and go for the kids first, they'll find a way to block the meltdown mechanism. If we initiate meltdown, the first thing they'll do is go for the kids."

"We'll have to split up. Again." Nix spat out the words.

Claire knew that neither one of those jobs would be

one he'd willingly have given her, if he had the choice. Nix hated Natalie. Hated Nulls. And he didn't want her anywhere near one. But the alternative involved partial solidification in a room with gas that could kill her, stripping her flesh from her bones in a heartbeat.

Whatever decision Nix made, whatever task he set her, he'd hate himself for it eventually. And right now they really didn't have time for the luxury of self-loathing.

"I'll get the kids," Claire said quietly. "They'd do the same thing to you that Ione would. And no offense, but I'll stand a better chance of bringing Natalie into the fade."

Claire didn't have Nix's history with Nulls. She'd already taken the Null serum with her. And she'd survived, basically intact.

"I don't want you near the Null," Nix said.

"And I don't want you to risk losing your hands or your life if something goes wrong when you insert the keys."

Claire saw the second her words registered on Nix's face. Both jobs were dangerous, but only one had caused the Sensor to make reference to *instant death*.

Nix closed his eyes in defeat, and for a second, Claire was terrified that she'd lost him. That he'd retreat, close down, block himself off from her in every way that mattered.

Don't leave me, she told him silently. *Stay. Fight.*

As if he heard her silent plea, Nix opened his eyes, and placed his hands on either side of her waist, under her shirt and over her weapons, sending a jolt of heat through her body.

Be careful, he told her with his eyes, but out loud, he said other words. Massive, undeniable, un-take-backable words that she'd stopped expecting to hear. "Claire?"

"Yes?"

Her heart was beating. She was scared. Not of The Society. Not of tonight. Of this moment. Of now.

"You tamed me."

Something gave inside of her chest, and it almost felled her. And just when she thought she might have imagined the words, he repeated them.

"You tamed me, Claire. I love you, just so you know."

The dam inside her broke, and Claire repeated the words back to him, felt them, meant them.

Maybe they'd come out of this, and maybe they wouldn't, but they had to try, and as Claire brought her lips to his and lost herself in the smell, taste, feel of *Nix,* she knew that it was worth it.

Live or die, succeed or fail, for better, or for worse—it was worth it.

26

White walls. White floor. White bed.

Even from the outside of the institute, Nix could smell the pungent odor of disinfectant and feel the walls closing in. Gravel crunched beneath his feet, but there were no flashbacks today. No memories. Just him and Claire and the knowledge that they might not make it out of this alive.

"Ready?" Claire whispered.

Nix nodded. He bowed his head, let reality fall from his body. *Fade. Fade. Fade.* Slowly, he lifted his eyes to Claire's. Her face was bright with the power of the fade, and the rest of the world paled in comparison. His hands moved to touch her petal-soft skin, and she reciprocated the motion. They moved in tandem, coming closer and closer to each other, their bodies in perfect sync.

"Ready," Nix said, his lips an inch from hers. He caught her hands in his. He felt her breath on his face and warmth spread out over his body. The smell and sound and feel of Claire faded banished everything else from his mind. The world went still around them.

Fade. Touch. Stop time.

"Now or never," Claire whispered.

They turned, and without another word, they flowed hand in hand toward the building. Past the gates that kept visitors out, through the thick wooden doors, through the foyer, through the dozens of Sensors, frozen in the process of screening everyone who entered. The glints of light reflected in the Sensors' faces and hands flared in reaction to the presence of two Nobodies, but the Sensors themselves remained motionless.

Step one, Nix thought, tightening his grip on Claire's hand, *infiltrate the institute.*

Claire squeezed his hand. The last time he'd come here he'd lost his fade, but there was no danger of that now—not when they were together.

Step two: acquire the keys.

"We have to split up," Claire whispered. Those weren't the words he wanted to hear, but even as she dropped his hand and took a step back away from his body, he could still feel the ghost of her touch on his face, his arms. Nix felt himself sliding back into the time line as easily as they'd left it, and as the world sped up around them, the urge to reach for Claire's hand again took on a life of its own. But if Nix did that, if he took hold of her and refused to let go, they'd have to go together to get the keys, and that would mean seeing Ione. Nix couldn't risk doing that. Couldn't look at the woman who'd bartered away his life. Couldn't think about her. Couldn't allow her name into even the deepest recesses of his mind.

Nix turned his back on Claire, took one step away from her and then another. He pictured her face, like an artist sketching it onto a blank page. He was faded; so was she. No matter where they went or what they did next, Claire was his.

For the rest of his life, for the rest of hers, they belonged to each other and nothing could touch them. Not gravity. Not physics. Not Sensors.

Three steps. Four. Five.

The pace of Nix's steps built, until he was running. Through the walls and the hallways, the rooms and the labs and the corridors. This was the institute he knew, the one he'd paced, a ghost in the shadows, for years. Only this time, as Nix ascended from the first floor to the second, from the second to the third, he moved with purpose. He was going to find the All Sensor, to get his key. Nix wasn't an eavesdropper, an interloper skulking in the walls of the apartments The Society kept for people who mattered. He was a man on a mission.

Keeping Claire with him in his mind—the way she looked when she slept and the way she looked when she danced through trees and crowds and the way she smiled, more with the left half of her mouth than the right—Nix felt a surge of power. Like The Society was playing on his territory, instead of the other way around.

We're not David. We're Goliath.

Moving quickly, Nix pushed himself through the door to the top-floor apartment, his feet forming no impression on the thick, lush carpet under his feet. He'd snuck up on targets this way, looked into their eyes, and solidified only long enough to deliver The Society's death sentence, again and again.

If he'd been anyone or anything else, Nix's heart would have skipped a beat and pounded against his rib cage to make up for it, but he was calm, cool, detached. He walked through the foyer, through the living room, through the kitchen, and back to a bedroom, crossing invisible lines he'd never crossed and bringing himself face-to-face with his prey.

Sergei.

Nix observed his target for one second, possibly two. He couldn't tell, from the fade, whether Sergei was short or tall, fat or thin, because the halo of light that ringed his face was more than just a sheen of energy. It was blinding.

Everything in this world has an energy....

Nix allowed the light to wash over him and forced himself to look through it. All Sensor or not, powerful or not, his target was a man. A solid, pitiful man, sequestered so deep in his own burrow that this was the first time he and Nix had ever been in the same room.

Dispassionately, Nix scanned the man's body, staring through the light, refusing to blink his immaterial eyes. He was looking for a key. Small. Black. Star-shaped end, embedded with microchips.

Gotcha.

Nix saw the outline of the key—little, unimportant, solid—and it took him a moment to realize where exactly the object he was searching for was. He'd half expected Sergei to wear it on a chain around his neck, but this wasn't a man who took chances. The key was there; Nix could see it, but instead of lying under Sergei's shirt, it was embedded under the skin of his neck, just above his collarbone.

Small. Black. Star shaped.

A thin white scar betrayed the surgery that had placed the key under a thin layer skin, and even faded, Nix's mind did the math. Grabbing the key, tearing it from this man's flesh—that was an act accomplished easily enough with fingers that slipped in and out of the fade. But as the bulging flecks of light around his eyes, ears, nose, mouth, and hands testified, this man was more in touch with energy than anyone Nix had ever met. The chances that he wouldn't notice a pair of hands, even if they belonged to a Nobody, as they tore open his throat—

Slim to none.

Nix took a single step back from his target. The gun strapped to his side tempted him.

Shoot him. Kill him. Take the key.

It would be so easy; the Sensor couldn't see Nix coming if he was dead, couldn't raise an alarm that might tip the rest of the building off to Claire's presence before the game had even begun.

Nix closed his eyes, picturing Claire. Feeling her. Seeing the world through her eyes.

Somewhere in this building, she was key hunting as well. He could feel her, in his blood and in his mind.

I am what I choose. I won't kill unless I have to.

In one lighting-quick movement, Nix thrust his arm through the dense flicker of light and into Sergei's neck. The fade fell from his hand and Nix closed his fingers around the key and pulled. The skin that held the treasure in place gave way with a sound like the tearing of wet cardboard. Nix set his mind to reclaiming the hand—and the key—but before he could bring them back into the fade, a massive, calloused fist caught those five thieving fingers in a bone-crunching grip.

The hand has the key, Nix thought. *And Sergei has the hand.*

In the fade, Claire couldn't hate Ione. Not for Nix, and not for herself. She couldn't let herself feel anything about the woman standing in front of her. All she could do was stare at her, very pointedly *not* wondering how it was that someone so clearly *unspecial* could have given birth to someone like Nix.

Ione wasn't a Sensor, and she wasn't a Nobody. She was Normal. Plain. And she had something that Claire wanted, very much, hanging on a solid chain around her solid, insignificant neck.

The key was small and delicate, and from the fade, Claire had a very hard time seeing it as important at all.

I need it. We need it.

Claire, her mind full of Nix, her body aching with the remnants of their last kiss, remembered why she'd come, and like a dancer stretching herself into an arabesque, she moved forward on tiptoe, her feet barely touching the floor. Ione paused to straighten her skirt, and Claire sidestepped, eyes on the key. She reached out one faded, iridescent hand, placing her fingers just above the key's surface.

This isn't my hand. I don't have a hand. I am a handless, fingerless Claire.

The digits in question solidified and grasped the key.

That key is a part of that hand. That key is like a finger to that hand, and THAT HAND IS MINE.

344

Under her emphatic declaration, Claire's hand re-entered the fade, and for the millionth time, she was grateful for the amount of time she'd spent convincing herself of one thing or another, playing games inside her head that made fading and all that went with it a piece of cake.

Ione, completely unaware that she'd been robbed, continued on the path she'd been on when Claire had found her, tossing dyed-blond hair over one shoulder and power-walking down the hallway.

Straight through Claire, who had her key.

Get the key. Give it to Nix.

Claire let his image fill her mind, until she was propelled unerringly and irresistibly toward him.

Up through ceiling. Up through floor. Up, up, up.

To Nix.

Nix should have been concerned. Sergei, who Nix had now ascertained was roughly the size and build of a bear, had a crushing hold on his hand.

Except, of course, the hand wasn't Nix's.

Fade, fade, fade, Nix told himself. *Don't look at him. Don't think about him. Just reclaim the hand and be done with it.*

"Tricky little Nobody, aren't you?" Sergei's voice was rough—more like a chain saw than gravel. "Partial solidification. Impressive."

If Sergei noticed that he was bleeding profusely out of the neck, he didn't give any visual indication of it, and Nix found himself drawn to the Sensor's eyes and incapable of blocking out the man's voice.

"I assume you're Nix. One of them anyway. You lived here. Tried to kill yourself once. Typical." Sergei's words were hard-won. Even for the most powerful Sensor in North America, it took a great deal of effort to remember specific facts about someone who didn't matter in the least. Those four sentences were probably all Sergei had on Nix—

And they were enough.

Enough to make him think about things he didn't want to think about—

Make it messy, they'd told him—and he had. And then he'd come back to the institute and turned the knife on himself.

"Claire." Nix said her name out loud. If he could think about her, he could stay faded. Out of Sergei's reach. Invincible, but for his solidified hand. "Claire."

The second time he said her name, she appeared, rising up through the floor like an angel, or a ghost. She was on him in an instant, wrapping her arms around his waist, burying her head in his chest, giving him every reason in the world to stay exactly where he was.

"You're mine," she said, banishing Sergei's venomous words as time froze around them. "You belong here. You belong to me." Claire grabbed his arm, his solid arm, and then she met his eyes.

"I love this arm." She trailed her eyes down the length of the limb. "I love that hand."

This hand has touched Claire. This hand is mine, the way that I am hers.

Nix's hand faded, and so did the key. Because that key was their future. His and Claire's. It was a part of them. A part of the only *us* he'd ever have. Claire locked her hands around his elbow and pulled, and together, they stumbled backward, Nix whole once more.

His hand should have hurt. It was doubtlessly bruised, possibly broken, but there was no place for pain in the fade.

"Key." Nix stated the obvious, staring down at his hand.

"Key," Claire replied, removing her hand from his arm and holding up the key she'd retrieved.

In reality, Sergei, frozen one second and moving the next, sensed that he'd lost his grip on Nix's psyche and roared, an enraged bull seconds away from storming through the china shop.

Nix's first impulse was to reach for Claire and stop time again, to buy himself precious seconds to think, but any way you sliced it, eventually, the two of them would have to split up again, and Sergei's motion would pick up right where it left off, alerting the rest of the institute to their presence. There was no way of stopping him. No way of keeping him contained.

The Society can't know we're here. The first thing they'll do is hide the children. Or eliminate them.

Nix moved quickly. In one fluid motion, he withdrew a gun from his side. He took aim. And he fired.

My choice this time. Mine.

Nix didn't dwell on it. He didn't look to Claire for her reaction. They'd set this thing in motion together, and he knew without asking that they were going to see it through.

The feel of cool metal in his hand brought Nix fully into the present.

"Here," Claire said, pressing her key into his palm and using her fingers to close his around it. "Now you have both of them."

That was all she said. She didn't say the other things, the obvious ones. Nothing about what he had to do next: initiate the meltdown; nothing about where she was headed: to the sublevels hidden deep underground and the little ones Nix couldn't allow himself to think about.

Nothing about the dead man on the floor.

Because at this point, there was nothing left to do but finish it.

27

Claire pulled herself away from Nix. Without a word—*no good-byes*—she willed herself downward—down through floors and ceiling, ceilings and floors and layers and layers of earth to the sublevel basement that had existed under Nix's feet for years.

Maze.

Labyrinth.

Claire knew a dozen words that would have been appropriate for the sublevels of the institute. Natalie's Sensor had given Claire a good idea of where the children were housed, but faded, Claire couldn't concentrate on words or paces or north northwests.

This way.

Claire didn't need directions. She didn't need a plan. The same thing that had always allowed her to feel Nix set her on an unmistakable path.

Toward them.

Three steel doors, locked from the outside. Five armed men, standing guard. Two-way mirrors. White noise, layered with a sound that Claire couldn't pinpoint, blared from speakers. If she'd been solid, she might have found it distracting, but the fade had its own kind of music.

This way.

Layer after layer, door after door, Claire made her way toward those Like Her. The institute had its treasure buried so deep that trying to get to it in solid form would have been like getting to the innermost layer of a set of Russian stacking dolls.

Cage inside a cage inside a cage.

For Claire, it was nothing. And for the first time, it occurred to her that if they could fade, all of these safeguards should have been nothing for Nix's siblings, too.

Unless there was something—someone—they weren't willing to leave behind.

Unable to fully entertain the thought, Claire walked through a final steel door and into a large room with four white walls. In one corner, there were three white beds; the opposite wall was lined with mirrors; and in the very center of the room, three silent children sat in a triangle formation, their backs to one another. Natalie was facing the door.

The little Null's eyes didn't register Claire's presence, but as Claire came forward, the other two occupants of the room whirled around.

They can hear me through the fade, Claire thought. *They can see me. Just like Nix.*

Natalie, unaware of what had caused the other children's reaction, noted her objection to such behavior. "Don't move. That's the rule. If you break the rule, you'll get punished. If you get punished, they might break you. We can't play when you're broken, and I don't want to turn the jump rope myself." Natalie's voice was high and clear, and even from the fade, Claire realized that it had a sweetness to it, a quality that would have been compelling if Claire had been solid.

We can't play when you're broken.

Claire found herself wondering what exactly *broken* meant. And why exactly Natalie's biggest concern with her playmates' potential for *breaking* was that they might be too battered to turn her rope. For the moment, though, Claire couldn't think about Natalie, couldn't ponder her words. All she could do was look at the little boy and little girl who flanked her side. And the moment she met their eyes, Claire knew that she was going to lose her fade.

She said a brief prayer that up on the main floor of the institute, Nix didn't lose his. ·

If he does, he's dead.

That was the thought that greeted Claire the moment

she became solid. It was terrifying, paralyzing, and all consuming, and she didn't have time for it. The guards watching this room might not register her presence immediately, but if they were taking the Nobody serum, if they'd been partially inoculated to her powers, they'd notice her eventually, and all hell would break loose. She had to get the twins and Natalie back to the fade before that happened.

And the sooner she got back to the fade, the safer Nix would be.

"Who are you?" Natalie demanded, not bothering to look Claire in the eye.

Claire smiled at her. "I'm Claire," she whispered. "I'm here to take you all away." And then, to Natalie's absolute shock, Claire turned her back on the little girl and brought one hand up to gently touch Nix's siblings—shoulder, arm.

Brush the hair out of their faces.

Look them in the eyes.

"I'm Claire," she said again. "I'm here for you."

"You're here for me," Natalie said helpfully. "I told him to get you. I don't want to play this game anymore. I want to leave."

"We're all going to leave," Claire said. "All three of us. And to do that, we have to work together."

"They have to leave, too," Natalie agreed. "They have to leave because they're mine. I don't like it when they're gone."

The two little Nobodies—Claire couldn't bear to think

352

of them as Nix and Nix—moved closer to Natalie, their little bodies nearly touching hers.

They love her.

To Claire's surprise, Natalie closed the gap, grabbing each of the other little ones by their arms, a little too hard.

"They have to come, too. They're mine."

Like they were toys. Or dogs.

It didn't seem to have occurred to the little girl that Claire might want to get her companions out of her own accord. Then again, chances were good that the children had never met a grown-up—or almost grown-up—Nobody. Natalie had never seen anyone who would have given either of the Nixes the time of day.

"I would never leave them behind," Claire told Natalie solemnly, and then she made eye contact with first the little girl and then the little boy. "Never, ever, ever."

The distinct sound of rattling—locks churning, doors opening, yelling—interrupted Claire's promise.

"We're going to go away now," Claire told Nix's little siblings. "We're going to go somewhere no one can ever hurt you, and Natalie's going to go, too."

"We tried," the little boy said. "We tried and tried, and Dr. Milano got mad, because we couldn't do it. But if we do it, they'll take Natalie away."

"Nobody's taking Natalie away," Claire said, and then she was struck by the double meaning of the sentence she'd just uttered.

Nobody is *taking Natalie away.*

"I can fade, too," Claire told the children. "And if all three of us fade, and if we make Natalie a part of us, the very most important part—"

Natalie smiled, and the expression, though aesthetically adorable, was chilling to Claire. Natalie was used to being the most important part. She couldn't fathom being anything less.

Doesn't care about anyone else. This could end badly. This could end very—

"Let's close our eyes," Claire said, her tone making her feel like either a preschool teacher or a drill sergeant, and unsure of which. *"Less than shadow. Less than air."*

It wasn't her motto, but she was betting it was theirs, same as it was Nix's. The Society would have taught it to them, made them believe it, the same way they'd taught it to him.

"Less than shadow, less than air." The children's reaction was instantaneous. Nix's brother and sister joined hands and closed their eyes, and Claire willed them to succeed at shutting out the rest of the world.

"You're nothing," she said, hating herself for telling them a thing they'd already heard said too matter-of-factly, too often. "You're Nobody."

From outside the children's chamber, Claire could hear the muffled sound of yelling.

"They watch me," Natalie said blithely. "All the time,

every day, they watch me. They know I'm talking to you. They know my Nobodies moved, and now they're going to break them again!"

She stamped one foot, and Claire could feel the compulsion to make Natalie happy worming its way into her blood. She blocked it, thinking of her Nix and these little Nixes. Claire forced her own mind to still and spoke words designed to make the little ones do the same.

You can do this, she told them silently, unable to praise them out loud. *You're strong. You can do this.*

"Be nothing," she told them out loud, but even as the words exited her mouth, she accepted that she couldn't heed her own advice. The voices outside their chamber were getting louder, closer, and the locks she'd walked through, the precautions that had to be more for Natalie's benefit than the twins' were being quickly undone.

Click. Click. Click.

The sound of the innermost door's lock, more suited to a bank safe than a bedroom, told Claire that she didn't have much time, and in a single motion, she thrust the children—all three of them—behind her. Her right hand went for her gun, and her left managed to grasp the knife Nix had strapped to her side, just as the guards burst into the room.

"Keep going," she told the children, her eyes flashing, weapons at the ready.

"Less than shadow, less than air," the tiny, childish

voices chanted behind her. "Less than shadow, less than—"

"I'm scared!" one of the children—Claire couldn't see which, though she knew immediately that it wasn't Natalie—said.

"Don't be. Don't be scared," Natalie instructed. "I just said not to." Clearly, to Natalie, that settled things. Claire found herself hoping that the little Null was right.

They aren't faded yet, Claire thought. *The guards will kill them before they let me take them.*

And that was the last conscious thought Claire had, because the second she heard the first gunshot, instinct took over. Claire threw her arms out to the side, gun in one hand, knife to the other, and within a breath—less than— she fell into the fade and pushed it outward from her body.

This space is mine. The bullet is in this space. It's mine.

She couldn't let the guards shoot Nix's siblings, and the only way to protect them was to—

Fade.

She felt the power burst out of her body, covering the space around her. You could take an object into the fade with you if you considered it a part of yourself. A gun in your hands. The clothes on your back.

A bullet.

Claire didn't have time to marvel at the fact that she'd done it—taken the bullet with her into the fade—because now there was an immaterial bullet barreling straight for her immaterial head. Frantically, Claire pictured her mother—ignoring her, talking through her, forgetting her. *A trigger*. The half-completed thought that jerked Claire out of the fade—

But somehow—impossibly, improbably, miraculously— she left the bullet behind.

Harmless. Immaterial.

The guards continued their onslaught. More bullets, more fading and unfading. Claire moved side to side, twisting and turning, disappearing from one spot and reappearing in another, pushing her fade outward, creating a shield for the children.

Nothing gets past me.

That realization occurred in the curves of Claire's lips as she smiled, darkly. This was a Nobody's true power. This was why The Society couldn't risk a Nobody coming into their powers unless they were Society trained. This was why they'd sent Nix to kill her. This was what made Nobodies more dangerous than Nulls.

She faded again and focused on her adversaries' weapons. She urged her fade outward. *My guns. My tasers.* Within seconds, she'd disarmed the guards, bringing their weapons into the fade. And then she solidified again.

As more guards poured into the room, the rush in Claire's blood, the excitement, the thrill of absolute power had her greeting them with a single raised arm, holding a gun.

"How much you want to bet I can get mine to fire almost as quickly as I can make yours disappear?"

Behind her, Claire felt the exact moment that Nix's younger sibling slipped into the fade. She felt them, pulling at her, pulling at Natalie, and as the guards eyed her weapon and slowly lowered theirs, Claire faded again, joining the little ones who already held her heart.

"Natalie is ours," she told them. No room for doubt in her voice. No room for doubt—about what Natalie was and what she might be capable of—in the fade. "We belong to each other, and she belongs to us. She's like an arm or a leg or the clothes on your body. She's a piece of your heart."

And with those words, Claire pushed everything she had, every ounce of absolute power toward Natalie.

Slippery, supersolid Natalie.

Claire's brain rebelled the moment her fade touched Natalie's body, revolted, and a shock went through her body—

Just like touching the drug, only worse, reversed, turned inside out—

But Claire clung tight to the power, the joy, the limitlessness of being nothing. She held on to her Nix and to his siblings and to everything that mattered more than the real world, with its bullets and Sensors and cages inside cages inside cages.

The whole world is a cage. Everything that's not this, not now—

Claire took that thought, that feeling, and she wrapped it around Natalie, coating the little girl in it, like a servant mummifying a pharaoh, one strip of cloth at a time.

"Our Natalie," she said.

Just a kid. Can't help the way she was born. Can't help it.

"Our Natalie," the twins replied.

And then the impossible happened. Natalie the solid, Natalie the Null, Natalie who mattered—

Joined them in the fade.

<hr />

Nix had seen the fail-safe chamber before, but hadn't realized what it was. He'd never noticed the security lock on the door or the fact that a solid person would have had to scan some kind of identification card to enter. The ceiling, floor, and walls were lined with vents, and in the very middle of the room, there was a small activation pad.

Faded, Nix walked toward the center of the room, Sergei's key in his battered right hand and the key Claire had given him in his left.

Two keys. One activation pad. No margin for error.

Nix went still, less than an arm's length away from the console that held the means to destroying this building and everything in it. Transferring both keys to his right hand, he took a shallow breath and set his left on the console's cover, poised to pry it open the moment he allowed it to regain solid form.

Nix forced himself not to think about the poison that would be released into the air the second the cover was removed. He didn't think about anything other than the fact that his right hand had killed people. Had made it messy.

Not my choice. That wasn't me.

He squashed down the part of him that would never fully believe that the blood on his hands was anyone's responsibility other than his own, and instead concentrated on the appendage itself. The fingers. The nails. The palm.

Not mine. None of it's mine.

Solidity oozed over his fingertips and Nix watched as they gripped the plastic, threw it back.

Touching Claire's face, her hair, laying that palm against hers.

Nix reclaimed his hand just as a thick white fog began to creep out of the vents in the ceiling, the floor, the walls.

The poison.

Nix took a deep breath. As his lungs filled with air, he could feel Claire slipping out of the fade. The sensation reminded him of pulling back from a kiss, but he couldn't think of that or of Claire. He cleared his mind of her influence. Of her current objective. Of everything but the two keys in his right hand and the uncovered activation pad with two identically shaped holes.

Nix raised his hands outward, his right hand—battered and broken—loosely gripping Sergei's key, his left liberating Ione's from its partner's grasp.

Can't let the keys fall.

Nix coaxed the muscles and the bones in his broken hand into holding tighter to the key. Looking at the mangled appendage was disconcerting, but Nix felt nothing. Pain didn't exist here, and he had no time for it. No time for the fog growing thicker and thicker in the solid world around him.

With careful precision and a mind as blank as an unused chalkboard, Nix maneuvered the keys into place. In the fade, they couldn't touch anything, but once they crossed over, they'd activate the meltdown sequence. Hands steady, keys in position, Nix began the process of disassociation. The only way he could turn the keys once they'd solidified was with hands that had done the same. Once he'd completed the action, he'd have to bring his hands back. Before, when he'd triggered the poison, he'd a second to think, to concentrate, but now a single second was a luxury he couldn't afford, assuming he wanted to walk out of this with hands and not just useless scraps of skin on bones. The poisonous gas would eat through his hands, burn them, devour them whole.

Nix didn't think that. He wouldn't. Blank slate. No emotions. No hopes. No fears.

Nothing. Nix breathed in, and then he let go. *These*

keys belong to those hands. Those hands are not mine. Those hands kill people. Those hands tried to kill me.

They. Are. Not. Mine.

Activation was instant. So was the pain. Though Nix couldn't feel it, it was hard not to imagine. Skin bubbling. Acid ravaging. Sirens roaring.

Meltdown initiated.

Those are my hands. They took care of Claire. They've brushed her lips. They've spared people who deserved to die.

Nix welcomed his hands back into the fade and cradled them against his body, even though he couldn't feel the searing agony they were owed.

Time to get out.

Nix turned and walked toward the far wall. The sooner he left this room, the safer he'd be. The room was airtight, the gas contained. Once he made his way into the east hallway, he'd be fine. He'd meet Claire, and they'd escape before the building self-destructed.

Claire.

Down in the sublevels, she was faded. He could feel her, the way he always had. Her presence pulled at him, propelled him through fog that couldn't touch him, through poison that wanted nothing more than to strike him dead.

Claire.

He felt her power. Bathed in it. Drank it. Made it his own. With liquid fluidity, Nix strode toward the east hallway, closer and closer to the chamber's edges. All around him, the air grew more opaque as the poison snaked out of the vents at steady speed, but Nix didn't think about the airborne acid or what a much lower concentration of it had done to his hands. There was no pain in the fade, and Nix's grip on it, his mind's connection with Claire's, was rock solid.

Null.

The wave of nausea was instantaneous. It was a thousand times worse than the sensation of watching Claire bring the Null drug into the fade. *Not just a drug this time. A Null.* Nix stumbled, and the word—snide and ugly and permanent—permeated every cell in his immaterial body. One foot shy of the chamber wall, he forced himself forward, tried not to dwell on what his senses were telling him.

Claire had succeeded. She'd brought the little Null into the fade, and the girl's presence was every bit as toxic as the poisonous gas. Like a stone tossed into a lake, her energy rippled through the fade. Nix felt it—in every pore, in the air he was breathing, in the pit of his stomach.

Null. In the fade.

Nix couldn't move. He couldn't take that last step to the wall, through it, and in the moment he realized he'd lost his fade, the thick haze of acid in the air became—like his own body—all too solid, all too real.

Less than shadow. Less than air.

Nix had to think the words, had to fade before the poison ate clear through him like termites through wood.

Less than shadow—

Agony. Hands burning. Clothes dissolving. Can't take a breath. Not a single breath. Skin melting. A thousand knives. A thousand knives for every square inch of skin.

LESS THAN SHADOW. LESS THAN AIR.

It hurt. And then the next second, it didn't, and Nix, welcoming the relief like an old lover, stumbled through the wall of the fail-safe chamber, out into the east hallway, where it was safe. No more poison to eat its way through his skin. Still, Nix didn't let himself think about the Null in the fade, or the angry, gaping redness of his wounds.

Fade. Fade. Fade.

Claire. Claire. Claire.

It was nice here. Peaceful.

ClaireClaireClaire.

And then he saw her, waiting for him in the east hallway. Not Claire.

Ione. She was standing there, waiting for him, like she somehow knew beyond a shadow of a doubt that he was the one responsible for the sirens now echoing through the hallways, the mechanical voice advising evacuation.

A shadow.

That was all he'd ever been to her. Killing targets or being eaten alive by poison, that was all he'd ever be. An afterthought. Less than human. A means to an end.

This time, Nix couldn't fight it. Couldn't conjure up Claire's image, couldn't even remember the searing, all-consuming pain that awaited his solid form. All he could see was Ione. His mother—and as Nix's tortured limbs solidified and he collapsed on the ground at her feet, he realized in the screaming, bleeding, cavernous hallways of his mind that his *mother* was holding a gun.

<hr />

Nix is gone.

The knowledge that Nix had left the fade weighed Claire down. It tore at her and picked at her seams, but she couldn't let herself unravel, couldn't let go of her grip on the fade.

On Natalie.

On the twins.

The dark-haired little duo anchored her here: their similarities to Nix, their differences. Already, she knew them. Knew their solemn smiles. Knew that she wanted to rock them and push them on swings and read them stories. Bandage skinned knees, put training wheels on their bikes.

They were hers. And they were faded, and Claire clung to that, even as her other self, the girl she couldn't be, stopped breathing, heart rate accelerating as the possibilities, horrible possibilities, wormed their way into—

A small hand wrapped itself around Claire's. She looked down, and the little boy—*like Nix, so like Nix*—refused to meet her eyes, as if he expected, fully expected her to pull away.

"Thank you," she whispered, refusing to remember how much Nix, her Nix, had always wanted to hear those words.

Nobodies don't get thanked.

Claire's mind settled enough to notice that when the little boy had taken her hand, time hadn't stopped. Whatever otherworldly connection she shared with Nix didn't extend entirely to his siblings; either that, or the little Nobodies just didn't have that kind of power yet.

"Are we leaving?" Natalie asked, bouncing on the tips of her toes. "I want to leave. Let's leave."

"Almost," Claire said. "First, we have to run."

Run to meet Nix in the eastern hallway. Where he'd lost his fade. Where he was waiting for them. Where he'd be okay.

"Let's run," Claire said again, anchoring herself on those words, not allowing herself to consider the possibility that Nix might not be okay, that something might have gone wrong.

"Run?" Natalie asked, her curiosity piqued.

"Run." Claire didn't give any more explanation than that, and the children, in the way of the very young, didn't seem to need it. Claire ran, the little boy's hand in hers, the girls on their heels—

Straight.

Toward.

Nix.

She didn't hear the sirens, didn't notice them, didn't register the fact that they meant that Nix had succeeded in his mission, the same as she had at hers. Because suddenly, the things Claire couldn't think in the fade became a reality, one that wouldn't be denied by any amount of pretending or imagining that it wasn't so.

Nix wasn't the only one in the hallway. Ione was there, and Nix wasn't, wasn't—

Claire couldn't move, couldn't even remember the word *run*. Thoughts tore through her brain like lightning, searing her body from the inside out.

Nix. Ione. Bleeding—him, not her. Holding a gun—her, not him.

Claire didn't even try to hold on to the fade. Nix's body wasn't his body anymore. It was—*holes, full of holes.* His skin was the color of a scream, stuck in someone's throat.

Brutal.

Agonizing.

Red.

Like someone had turned him inside out. Like he was dying.

Bang.

It took Claire a moment to realize that the sound was a gunshot, and by then the bullet had already caught Nix in the shoulder—*God, he was already so hurt, why would anyone*—Claire turned her anguished face toward Nix's mother and she saw the answer in the neutral set of her lips, the uneven focus of her eyes as she took aim at Nix again.

She wasn't aiming for his shoulder.

Even though Nix wasn't faded, even though Ione could physically see him, she couldn't quite focus on him enough to tell exactly where he lay—so she was just going to keep shooting until a bullet found his heart.

Claire cocked her own gun, unaware of the fact that she'd even raised it. Behind her, the kids scattered, the Nobodies frightened by the fact that she'd ripped them out of their fade the moment she'd lost hers, and Natalie upset with the turn their little game had taken.

"Shoot him again, and you die," Claire said, her voice low. She meant the words. She meant them, but when Ione turned and aimed her gun back at her, Claire found herself staring into blue, blue eyes.

From the fade, Ione hadn't looked this much like Nix.

"If *it* could move, *it* would shoot me," Ione said, her tone conversational. "Because of you."

It, as in Nix. Ione's *son*.

Claire felt her grip on the gun tighten.

"But you, *you* won't shoot me. That's the problem with Nobodies after the kill point. They get used to thinking of themselves as human." Ione glanced down at her watch, unafraid and making a show of it. Mere feet away, Nix writhed, and Claire knew that this woman's words were eating away at him, same as the poison.

Shoot her, Claire. Just shoot her. But she couldn't. This woman was Nix's *mother.*

"This whole building is going down," Claire said. "In—"

"Two minutes," Nix croaked.

Claire kept her voice even, choking back a sob. "If you leave now, you might make it out."

Ione shook her head. "I was responsible for this building and everyone who works here. I was responsible for all of you. My superiors take responsibility very seriously, and I have no time to construct a cover story of the appropriate depth. Whether I make it out or not, I'm dead." She smiled. "If I kill him, you'll be distraught. You won't be able to look away from his body. And as long as you're looking at his body, you won't be able to fade. And if you can't fade, then you'll die, too. This is my mess. The least I can do is clean it up." She paused. "Oh, what the hell. I'll just kill you now."

I need to fade. I have to fade. Power, remember the power. You're invincible, you have to be invincible, but how can I—Nix lying there, Nix hurt, God, hurts so much can't leave him can't move can't—

Claire heard the sound of a gun cocking. The sound of a bullet firing. It took her a second to realize that the gun in question wasn't Ione's, and it wasn't hers. The bullet sliced through Ione's skin, burying itself in her skull, and the woman fell backward, crumpling to the ground, empty eyed, and unaware that she had lost.

Slowly, Claire turned in the direction from which the bullet had come. Nix was lying on the floor, his hands still useless, struggling to make it to his knees. And standing beside Nix, an oddly neutral expression on her face, was Natalie.

Holding a gun.

She just saved my life, Claire realized.

"I liked it better before," Natalie said, the beginnings of a pout on her face. "When we were running and things felt funny. The lady's gone now. Can we go back?" In a single, dainty motion, Natalie sat the gun back down beside Nix and bounced back to her toes.

Can we go back?

Such a sweet voice. So innocent. So happy, for someone who'd just killed.

Not important. Doesn't matter.

Claire ran to Nix. She knelt beside him. "We have to go—"

"Can't. Hurts."

Talking was agony for Nix, and listening to him was agony for Claire. She couldn't do this. She couldn't leave him.

Nix coughed. "One minute. Have to go. Get them out—"

"I'm not leaving you." Claire bit back the urge to hit him, to hug him, to cover his body with hers and absorb his pain.

I can take it away. I can take it all away.

Sudden light pressure on her shoulder made Claire jump and dragged her away from her thoughts. The children—the little Nobodies—had placed their hands on her shoulder, their eyes on Nix.

"Less than shadow," the little girl said, her eyes seeing everything, taking in too much.

"Less than air," the boy said, looking at Claire, only at Claire.

"Less than shadow," Claire said, saying the words for Nix, because he could not. "Less than air."

Her own mantra went unspoken. She didn't need it. All she needed was Nix, and that need exploded in her head like an aneurysm, until she couldn't see or feel or hear anything else. She faded to nothing, absolute nothing, and she pushed it outward to Nix, pulling him home, where he belonged.

In unison, the twins joined her in the fade, and when they reached out to Natalie, Claire pressed her lips to Nix's forehead.

"It doesn't hurt here," she whispered.

He didn't move. But with his last wisp of energy, he embraced the fade and pushed it outward.

To Natalie.

Nothingness was sweet relief. The silence was absolute. And when the institute exploded around them, Claire didn't feel it or see it or wonder at the fact that an entire building could be reduced to dust in a heartbeat.

Instead, she picked up Nix and gathered the children to her side, and together, they left the ruins behind. Not flying. Not running. Just floating—silently, slowly, delicately, like ashes on the wind.

28

Nix was about ninety percent sure he was unconscious. The world was hazy, and the taste on the tip of his tongue was sweet. An abandoned road stretched out on all sides of him, and no matter which direction he turned, there it was, a path to nowhere.

A path to nothing.

A path to a wall of light.

Energy. So bright.

The words were familiar, but Nix couldn't quite place them. Couldn't remember what brightness looked like.

His senses collapsed onto each other. Nix tasted blue. He heard yellow. He smelled music. Sunscreen and cinnamon, the sweetest melody.

Claire.

The single word stopped him in his tracks

I don't have feet. I don't have a body, but I was walking. Toward something.

He began moving again. He had to. It was time to go.

Brighter. Light. Blue.

Quiet. Peaceful. Still.

Everything.

As he moved, Nix's memories collapsed the same way his senses had, until the past and the present and the future were all one thing.

I don't have a body.

He didn't even have a head. And as his own voice got quieter and quieter in his mind, that sweet melody wafted back into his consciousness.

Claire.

And that was when Nix knew. He knew what he was walking toward, and he knew that he wasn't just unconscious. He was dying, and this was the end. Infinity. Everything.

It was soothing. Tempting. Painless. Free. And it had its jaws clamped around him.

Death had him, and it wasn't letting go.

Nix forced himself to think. To imagine. To picture Claire. Her eyes were brown, flecked with amber and green. Her hair was light brown, but shone golden in the sun. She never made the exact same facial expression twice. She fit perfectly under his chin.

Claire.

Death did not roar. It did not fight him. Because death knew that it was going to win. That he was going to die. And that the best he could do, the only thing he could do, was picture Claire and hold fast to that picture and force himself to wake up one last time.

To say good-bye.

<hr />

By the time they landed at the rendezvous point, miles away from the remains of the institute, Claire's psyche had been stretched past its limits. The strain of holding Nix in the fade, when his mind had left his body, was compounded by the concentration it took to keep Natalie immaterial.

He's okay. He's okay. He's got to be okay.

The fear that he wasn't was absolute, and Claire couldn't fight it any longer. Solidity came like a rush to the head, and she collapsed onto the ground, Nix's body too heavy for her now that they'd crossed from weightlessness into gravity's sordid grip.

Nix is dying.

Claire refused to believe it. His shoulder was bleeding. His entire body was covered with burns. There wasn't an inch of skin left untouched by The Society's poison.

It ate him.

But Claire didn't see it that way. She refused to see it

that way. She saw Nix. Her Nix. The way he'd looked the first time she'd seen him, standing outside her bedroom window with a gun. The way he looked as he'd painstakingly fashioned firewood into a bookshelf.

Nix wasn't dying.

He wasn't going to die.

He just wasn't.

Claire cradled his head in her lap, arranging his body on the ground. "You're going to be fine," she said. "Miracles happen. They do. And we won. We did everything right. We got the kids. We got out, and the institute is gone." Her voice got louder and higher. "We won, Nix." Her tone sank back to a whisper that got caught in the back of her throat. "You're going to be okay."

As if he'd heard her, as if she'd believed him into existence, Nix's eyelids fluttered.

Claire sobbed—a strangled, broken noise that told her that despite her best efforts to the contrary, she hadn't really believed she'd ever see him awake again.

"You're okay," she said.

He couldn't talk. Not really. But he could look at her. His eyes—those beautiful, Nix-blue eyes—were miraculously intact. He could see her.

And she could feel him in that gaze. Everything she loved about him. Everything she would miss.

"No," she whispered. "No. You're going to be okay. You're going to be fine."

Nix struggled to open his mouth, his eyes going vacant with pain as he did.

"Don't talk," Claire whispered, her own voice breaking. "Don't talk. Just get better."

She didn't want him to talk. She didn't want him to say it. She didn't want him to leave.

"Love you," Nix managed, the words as mangled as his body. "Always love you."

It wasn't clear if he meant that he always had or that he always would, but Claire didn't want to hear it either way, because she knew what he was saying. She knew what came next.

Good-bye.

"No," Claire said vehemently, the tears dripping from her eyes onto his face. "You're not going to leave me. You're not allowed to leave me. Not ever."

Good-bye.

"You're the only one, Nix. The only one who matters. The only person I've ever mattered to. You're everything. You're mine. You can't die. You just can't."

"Love you."

He loved her, and he was leaving.

"Stay," she whispered, hating herself for holding him in such agony, unable to let him go. "You just have to believe you can. You have to believe you'll get better, and you will, Nix. You have to." The words came out faster and faster, picking up momentum as they came. "Situation:

what if the person you loved most in the world, what if the only person who ever loved you was dying? What if you were dying, and you loved someone on earth enough to stay? What if love is magic? It feels like magic, what if it was? What if all it took to heal someone was a kiss?"

What if?

What if?

What if?

"What if we could make it? What if we could have a house and a lawn and a life together, forever? What if happily ever after is real? Say it, Nix. Say it's real."

Love you.

He couldn't even say it anymore. Not with words. Only with his eyes, over and over and over again, as he slipped away from her.

Forever.

I'll fade. I'll fade and take him with me, and then he can't die. He can't die in the fade. I can do it—I can.

Claire broke down, hunching over, her body no longer her own, her grief a beast of its own accord.

No.

She thought about kissing him. Kissing him and making it all better. Kissing him and stopping time, but she couldn't.

Couldn't save him.

Couldn't let him go.

Couldn't say good-bye.

But she had to, because she couldn't let him die without hearing it from her lips, one last time. "I love you, too."

Feeling like she'd signed his death warrant, Claire broke. She shattered. And she barely noticed as Natalie knelt beside her, leaned forward, and put her hands on Nix.

"I don't like this," Natalie said, her face blank as she looked at Nix's. "I don't like you like this."

Claire felt the compulsion to make the world exactly as Natalie wanted it to be, but, no.

Nix, Nix, Nix, Nix.

All that mattered was Nix.

Not Natalie, standing up and turning, with an oddly neutral expression on her face, toward Nix's little brother and sister. Not the knife Claire couldn't remember dropping on the ground, not the way Natalie picked it up.

Nix, Nix, Nix, Nix.

Not the knife, which cut into the little boy Nobody's skin. Not the almost imperceptible flicker of energy that flared out from his blood as it began to flow freely down his arm.

Claire knew she ought to say something. To stop her. Natalie. But she couldn't move. Couldn't care. Couldn't drag her eyes away from Nix's, or the single speck of light still there.

Her expression just as blank, Natalie turned the knife on her own arm and sliced it, too. And then she came to stand beside Nix, perfectly confident that the boy she'd just knifed without asking would follow.

He did.

Claire wanted to yell at them. To tell them to leave Nix alone. He was hers, and this was good-bye. They didn't have a right to . . .

Bleed on him?

Powerful stuff, Nobody blood.

Claire watched as the blood flowed from Natalie's arm and the little Nix's.

Nulls and Nobodies . . . I'm not sure what you'd get if you mixed them. The results would be unpredictable. Anything could happen, really.

The steady streams of blood intertwined midair, and Claire watched as the lights, pearl white and black-hole dark—which could normally only be seen from the fade— broke their way into the real world.

Light. Pure light. Dark. Whole.

Like matter and antimatter.

Expanding.

Moving.

Growing.

And there, in the middle of it, was Natalie, her eyes alight with pure force of will, as if the power of her stare could send the physical world to its knees.

The light grew brighter. More intense, until it actually had a sound: a high-pitched humming and a low rumbling and everything in between. The opposite of white noise.

"Do it," Natalie whispered. Through the light, Claire saw Nix's skin shuddering, saw the flesh bubbling and flowing, like water boiling over the edge of the pot. Spreading, morphing, and then—

Silence.

The light around Nix pulsed and then imploded. It was like watching the death of a star. And there, in place of that star, that conglomerate of power and beauty and the will of an eight-year-old girl—was Nix.

He's okay.

He was better than okay, Claire realized with a start. He was alive, and there wasn't a mark on his body: no ink, no scars, no wounds.

Impossible.

———◆✕◆———

What if magic were real? What if love could heal? What if there really was such a thing as happily ever after?

These thoughts, clearly, weren't Nix's. Happily ever after had never been an option for Nix. He'd never wanted it. He'd never thought about it. He'd certainly never deserved it.

And yet.

"You're okay."

He'd heard Claire saying those words before, through a haze of pain. Pain that was gone now.

Wrong.

Pain didn't just go away. You felt it. You owned it. You let it go in order to fade, but it was always there, waiting, when you got back. Pain was an old friend. Pain was real.

And now it was gone.

"You're okay. You're okay. You're okay."

The fourth time Claire said it, Nix realized she was crying. The fifth and sixth times she said it, he sat up and pulled her to him. The seventh time, they kissed. And the eighth and the ninth and again and again, until an imperious little voice broke into their two-person world.

"Stop that. I'm hungry. You should feed me."

Nix found himself strangely compelled to feed the person speaking. She was important. She needed food. She was so sweet and he wanted to feed her—and that's when Nix remembered—

The Null.

The eight-year-old Null who'd saved Claire's life by shooting Ione. The one who'd saved him, by cutting into her own flesh and that of his little brother.

She was still holding the knife.

She looks comfortable with it. She's not bothered by the blood. She likes it.

"You saved him," Claire said, her voice reverent, her eyes shining in a way that told Nix that even if Natalie hadn't been a Null, Claire would have been defenseless against her, from this moment on. "The blood, and the energy, and . . . *what did you do?*"

Natalie scuffed her foot into the ground. "I thought. I thought real hard. I wanted it to go away, and it did." She smiled, the expression curving slowly over her cherubic features. "I always get what I want."

Nix stifled a shudder. Nulls were dangerous because they were incapable of forming emotional attachments to other people, of caring about anyone other than themselves, and they were dangerous because it was all too easy for them to manipulate others. But they couldn't manipulate the physical world. It wasn't possible.

The same way that walking through walls wasn't possible. *Nobodies and Nulls are opposites. Oh, God.*

"Can you make things do what you want them to, Natalie?" Nix forced himself to say her name, to not recoil at the idea of Nulls, even small ones, even one who'd just saved his life, having that kind of power.

"Things that aren't people, or things that are?" Natalie asked.

People aren't things. Nix didn't try telling her that, knowing it wouldn't do any good. "Things that aren't," he said instead.

"Things that aren't people are hard," Natalie said plaintively. "I couldn't used to do it. The bad doctor taught me. He taught me lots."

Claire swallowed, hard, and Nix's eyes were drawn to her lips as they parted to ask the question on the tip of his own tongue. "And the blood?"

Natalie's blood, his little brother's. Nix could remember, barely, seeing the little girl pick up the knife, but the haze of pain had been so thick, and all he'd wanted was to look at Claire, at Claire's eyes. To let the last thing he saw be *her*.

"Energy," Nix's sister answered the question, and he wondered where exactly she'd learned that there was energy in her blood.

Where else? The Society had raised her. It had used her as a lab rat. They'd taught her.

Natalie, sensing that she was losing attention, cleared her throat. "The mean doctor talked a lot. He did things I didn't like. I didn't like him. I'm glad he's dead. I wish they were all dead. Maybe I'll kill them. I'm hungry. You will feed me. I like hamburgers."

"Hamburgers?" Claire repeated. "You can have all the hamburgers you want. Do you understand what you just did?"

Nix watched as Natalie's eyes flicked back toward him, and then she shrugged. "It looked bad. I didn't like it. His skin was ugly. His voice sounded funny. You were crying too hard to get me food. I didn't like it, so I made it go away."

Saved by a Null. An eight-year-old Null, in search of a hamburger.

"Natalie!"

It took Nix a moment to recognize the voice, and then he realized that somehow, between his losing consciousness, almost dying, regaining consciousness, and almost dying again, Claire had managed to get the five of them to the rendezvous point.

The Sensor—the one who'd handed them the key to the institute's destruction—was beaming, like he hadn't just initiated the complete demolition of everything he'd ever believed in. "Natalie, sweetheart, I'm so glad you're okay. I told you I'd get you out. I told you. I did just like you asked."

Nix forced his brain to actually function, and then he climbed his way to his feet. "You did just as she asked, and we did just as you asked." Nix nodded toward Natalie and then looked back at the man. "Our files, please."

The man's eyes lost their focus for a moment, and Nix felt a pang in his stomach, tinny-tasting fear that the Sensor might not have held up his end of the bargain. But after a long moment, and several more beaming smiles directed at Natalie, the man fished through his pockets and pulled out a flash drive.

Small.

Black.

Freedom.

Nix took it from the man's hand. The man didn't even notice. He had eyes for Natalie. Only for Natalie. Nix wondered what he'd do with the little girl now.

"We're going home, Natalie. I bought a house, just for you. It has everything you like. You'll love it there."

Natalie smiled, but then, after a long moment, she turned. "Can I bring my stuff?" she asked.

"Of course, sweetheart."

Nix watched as Natalie gestured to his younger brother and sister. "They're mine. They have to come, too."

"No." Four people said the word at once, and Nix was struck by the way their voices played off one another's—the little ones' whispers, Claire's high and loud, and his own, a rumbling growl.

"I don't like *no*," Natalie said. For a moment, Nix felt something—a pull to let Natalie have exactly what she wanted. And then his eyes were drawn, again and again, to the knife.

Make her happy. Have to make her happy. Give her what she—

No.

The pull from Claire and from the dark-haired pair was stronger. Nulls might have an increased ability to affect people, but nothing was as strong as the pull of like to like.

"Take her and leave," Nix told the Sensor. The man wrinkled his brow, confused, trying to reconcile himself to the fact that Nix didn't want to give Natalie exactly what she'd asked for.

"But I want them," Natalie said, pointing to the other children.

"You can't always have what you want," Claire said softly, not looking at the little girl. Looking at Nix.

"I can," Natalie said. "I do. I wanted the mean people dead, and now they are. I wanted that boy's uglies to go away and they did. The mean doctor was right. Sometimes, with enough energy, things that aren't people are almost as easy as things that are."

Things, like his body. Energy, like the result of mixing a Nobody's blood with a Null's.

She saved my life. A Null saved my life.

And we saved hers. Nix felt the second half of that revelation with foreboding and guilt—and the tiniest sliver of hope that maybe Natalie was different. That she'd somehow come to care about his little brother and sister. That she'd saved his life and Claire's because deep down, she wasn't a monster. Nix even entertained the idea that being in the fade had changed the little girl, the way it had changed the sheen of Sykes's Null drug.

"What will I play with if they don't come?" Natalie demanded.

What. Not *who.* And yet there was a tone in her voice when she looked at his siblings. . . .

"I'll get you new toys. Lots of them."

Natalie considered the Sensor's proposition, and her eyes glowed. "Are you rich?"

"No, but Natalie, I love you. You could be my little girl. I'd do everything—"

"Fine," Natalie said, sounding bored. "I want a hamburger." She smiled, looking too innocent, too sweet. "And then we can talk about the rest."

And just like that, Natalie and the Sensor left, leaving behind them four Nobodies.

"She saved your life," Claire murmured.

"She saved yours," Nix murmured back.

"She's just a little girl."

"She'll be fine."

Beside them, Nix's brother and sister whimpered, like puppies torn away from their litter.

"Natalie," the little boy said.

Nix knelt in front of them. "Natalie had to go away," he said. "But you're going to be okay. You're going to be perfect."

His brother.

His sister.

His.

All other worries, all other thoughts, paled in comparison.

"No one will ever hurt you again," Nix promised. "You're mine now. Ours. And we *will* live happily ever after."

Nix picked them up and settled one on each hip. Claire wrapped her arms around him, around the children. He leaned down to press his lips to hers, heat and power and overwhelming knowledge spreading from the kiss through his veins, to every inch of his being.

Warm.

Safe.

Home.

It wouldn't be easy. He had no idea where they'd go. What they'd do. How they'd survive, four Nobodies against the world. But at that exact moment, with his lips pressed against Claire's, with his flesh and blood in his arms and in hers, Nix didn't care.

They'd find a way to make it work. They would live happily ever after.

Nix believed it, and he put every ounce of that belief into the kiss he gave Claire. Fireworks exploded. Rivers roared. And one by one, the four Nobodies faded, a surge of light against an infinite expanse of darkness.

Forever.

Epilogue
Six months later . . .

Once upon a time, the little girl's name had been Nix, and she had lived in a small, small, small room with another Nix and the nicest, sweetest, most wonderful girl in the whole wide world. But now she wasn't Nix anymore, and the little room was gone. Now she lived in a big room, in a big old house that had been *onthemarket* for years and never ever sold until everybody forgot about it just like that. She and her brother and her other brother and Claire called it *home*, and the little girl who wasn't Nix anymore loved rounding her lips into that long *O* sound.

The other place, the bad place, got smaller and smaller in her mind each day, as new things pushed the old memories out.

New things like a big brother, who carried her around on his back.

And a Claire to read her stories.

And food and games and everything that a little girl could want and that four Nobodies could sneak out of a store.

Once upon a time, when she was Nix, the little girl couldn't breathe. Now she could. Now her name was Olivia because she loved the Olivia books, but Claire called her Livvie. And Livvie's brother's new name was Max, because he was a Wild Thing, and every night, Claire and the big Nix, the only Nix now, read to Max and Livvie, and they fell asleep and woke up in their very own beds in their very own home, where their very own family loved them best of all.

Livvie was happy.

And then one day, the four of them were out walking, running, blurring, shopping—when Livvie saw something. On a television, in a store. And it made her happy, too. It made her stop. And then Max stopped and Nix stopped and Claire stopped.

Livvie pointed at the screen, her memory rearranging itself, working its way through the haze. "Look!" she said. "It's the girl."

The sweetest, nicest, most wonderful person in the world. Livvie remembered her. She didn't remember the little room too well, but she remembered the girl.

"Natalie." Max remembered even better than she did. He was a wild thing.

Livvie tilted her head to the side, and she remembered

the small, small, small room and the blood and trying to breathe underwater.

"Natalie," she repeated.

"Vice presidential nominee Quentin Burrows, a long-time supporter of family values and child welfare, has put his money where his mouth was, with what appears to be an impromptu adoption. . . ."

Livvie looked up at Nix. Nobodies didn't ask questions but—Livvie did. "What's *adoption* mean?" she asked.

For a moment, Nix didn't say anything, and Livvie wondered why he looked like he'd swallowed a big ball of dirt. Claire—Livvie liked saying her name as two syllables, *Cuh-laire*, because one just wasn't enough—must have noticed that Nix looked funny, too, because she did that thing where she touched him, lightly on the arm and it was like she was talking to him, only without words.

"*Adoption* means that Natalie has a new family," Claire said carefully.

Livvie looked at the screen, and then at Max, and then back at Nix and Claire. "Like us?"

Nix picked her up. Nuzzled her face. Made her giggle.

"Like us," Max said, even though he didn't know what the word meant any better than she did.

Livvie squinted back at the screen and then nodded. Adoption was like a fairy tale. Like happily ever after.

It was good that Natalie had it, too.

Also by Jennifer Lynn Barnes

Cassie, Michael, Lia, Dean and Sloane are

THE NAT🕴RALS

A secret FBI programme for crime-solving teens

OUT NOW

www.jenniferlynnbarnes.com

Quercus